"The thing about childhood friendship is that it is part of the DNA of your formation, something all the Gunners, but especially the narrator, knows too well. *The Gunners* is one of the most moving portraits of friendship I've read, perhaps ever." *Refinery29*

"A vivid, layered novel … Endearing and intimate, Kauffman steers clear of veering into cliché, reviving a well-worn premise into something new and exciting." *Harper's Bazaar*

"Kauffman's prose is restrained in a way that causes it to actually vibrate in places, and her details are so richly observed they feel like gems, impossible things mined from deep under the earth. Funny, raw, and deeply elegant, *The Gunners* is ultimately a meditation on friendship, that least examined, most mysterious form of love, perhaps more sacred for its incompleteness, for the ways we can never fool ourselves completely into believing we truly know one another." Rufi Thorpe, author of *Dear Fang, with Love* and *The Girls from Corona del Mar*

"I inhaled *The Gunners* in a single sitting because I couldn't stand to be away from it once I started it. Rebecca Kauffman's brilliantly rendered story of six childhood friends tells the hard truth about human love—what it seems to be from far away, and what it really is up close—boldly, with compassion and warmth and humour." Kayla Rae Whitaker, author of *The Animators*

"A little bit like *The Big Chill*, Kauffman's quiet and deep second novel reconciles the responsibilities we carry and the secrets we keep with the outsize pleasure of being known and loved by a chosen family." *Booklist*

D0205546

REBECCA KAUFFMAN is originally from rural northeastern Ohio. She studied Classical Violin Performance at the Manhattan School of Music before receiving an MFA in Creative Writing from NYU. Her novel *Another Place You've Never Been* is published by Soft Skull Press. Rebecca has worked both in restaurants and as a teacher. She currently lives in Virginia.

"A moving novel ... Each character comes to terms with their dark past, and uncertain futures—like an intimate hangout session, dashed with suspense and few extra layers of emotional beauty. You'll find yourself thinking of *Freaks and Geeks*, *The Big Chill*, and maybe all those friends you've been meaning to text." *Entertainment Weekly*, The Must List

"A riveting portrayal of the joys and mysteries of growing up, and of friendship itself." *People*

"In the beautifully wrought *The Gunners*, life ends not with a whimper, but with a bang ... This engrossing book's suspense lies not just in what will happen, but in what already has ... Kauffman is interested in the muddiness of love—how it can be selfish and desperate, even cruel ... When it comes to love, Kauffman suggests, we're equal parts predator and prey." *Oprah Magazine*

"This story examines how the secrets held and harboured by friends, and the defining relationships of childhood and adolescence, never fully leave us." *Esquire*

"At the heart of this moving novel is the mystery of why a high-school girl suddenly turned away from her tight-knit group of friends ... While Kauffman doesn't tie everything up with a neat bow, that's hardly the point. What really matters is what's below the surface—a tale of friends who are driven together by circumstance and location but who become a family by choice." *The Daily Beast*

"Novels about friendships are the new fad but trust me when I tell you that this one is truly superlative. A gracefully endearing story which delves deeply into the nature of childhood friendship while also shining a light on chronic illness and LGTBQ rights." *Chicago Review of Books*

# THE
# GUNNERS
## REBECCA
## KAUFFMAN

This paperback edition published in 2019

First published in Great Britain in 2019 by Serpent's Tail,
an imprint of Profile Books Ltd
3 Holford Yard
Bevin Way
London
WC1X 9HD
*www.serpentstail.com*

First published in the USA in 2018 by Counterpoint Press, Berkeley, CA

1 3 5 7 9 10 8 6 4 2

Designed by Wah-Ming Chang

Printed and bound in Great Britain by CPI Group (UK) Ltd, Croydon CR0 4YY

A CIP record for this book can be obtained from the British Library.

ISBN: 978 1 78816 106 0
eISBN: 978 1 78283 470 0

For George

For we live with those retrievals from childhood that coalesce and echo throughout our lives, the way shattered pieces of glass in a kaleidoscope reappear in new forms and are songlike in their refrains and rhymes, making up a single monologue. We live permanently in the recurrence of our own stories, whatever story we tell.

MICHAEL ONDAATJE, *Divisadero*

# CHAPTER 1

Mikey Callahan discovered something about himself when he was six years old.

Students from his first-grade class were taken one at a time from the classroom and ushered to the gymnasium for standard medical tests. The woman who barked his name (although she called for Michael, instead of Mikey, as his classmates knew him) held his hand as she walked him down the hall, and her fingers were as dry and cool as a husk. In the gymnasium, there were rectangular tables, screens, clipboards, grown-ups dressed in white. A man with a rust-colored mustache put a cold rubber point into Mikey's ears, stared in at them, and led him through a series of easy tests: instructing Mikey to close his eyes and repeat words the man whispered, then listen to two recorded tones and tell him which was louder.

Mikey proceeded to the next station, where he was asked once again to close his eyes, and say "*Now*," when he detected that he had been touched, on his face or his arm, by the tip of a pen. Easy. Mikey liked this better than sitting in a classroom, and he enjoyed being touched in this way. Gentle, clinical.

At the final station, an easel at the far end of a long table displayed a white piece of paper with a pyramid of black letters on it.

A woman stood next to the paper and pointed at letters one at a time, and Mikey read the letters back to her. The letters got smaller as she moved down the page, and he struggled to read the final two rows. The woman made a note on her clipboard; then she handed him a black plastic spoon and asked him to cover his left eye with it. She replaced the set of letters with a fresh one and repeated the exercise, with similar results.

She said, "Cover your other eye now," and turned the page on her easel once again.

Mikey did not raise the spoon to his face. He felt the heat of dark blood spreading up into his cheeks. He said, "But that's my good one."

The lady said, "What now, hon?"

"I can't cover this one." He gestured toward his right eye, puzzled by her request. "It's the one that works."

The lady came and knelt before him. She looked at his face and said, "Oh, dear."

Mikey didn't understand.

She explained to him that both eyes were supposed to work; most people had two good eyes.

Mikey nodded slowly as he considered this. He had a compulsion to nod when faced with unpleasant information.

He said, "Please, let's not tell my dad."

When Mikey got home from school that day, his father stared at his left eye, the bad one, with a look of mild distaste; then he led Mikey through a series of his own tests, as though the school had exaggerated the condition. He made Mikey close his right eye and tell him how many fingers he was holding up. Mikey tried to answer correctly, fluttering his right eye open to peek. He begged his father not to make him wear a patch like a pirate, and his father said, "What in the hell would that accomplish?"

His father told him he must make the decision, right at that moment, whether the world would know about the left eye or whether it would be Mikey's secret, and he seemed relieved when Mikey quickly answered that it would be his secret. As though the condition, if known by others, would in some way reflect poorly upon both of them. They didn't speak of it again.

Mikey's father worked for the meatpacking facility in Eden, several towns over. He always smelled of blood and had red in the corners of his fingernails, carrying with him the insinuation of violence, brute force. His face was lumpy, as though it had been stuffed full, his eyes drooped. For Mikey's entire childhood, the two of them lived in the first floor of a townhouse on Ingram Street in Lackawanna, a depressed suburb of South Buffalo. Only half the homes on their block were occupied. The others had boards for windows, liquor bottles smashed into the front porches, stray cats shitting in overgrown lawns. The upstairs tenants in their townhouse wore slippers to the store and always smelled vaguely sulfuric, and they engaged in monthly screaming arguments with the landlord over late rent and threats of eviction. Mikey's father always paid rent on time, but sometimes he forgot about the utilities, and a man in navy would show up demanding a cash payment—saying that if they couldn't pay, he'd *pull the plug* on their house, and then how would they see at night? What would they eat?

Mikey's father ate four things: cereal, apples, white bread with cold cuts, and Chips Ahoy! cookies. Mikey was not introduced to other foods until he was offered them by his friends from their lunch boxes or by his friends' mothers in their homes.

Mikey did not have a mother of his own, and because his father refused to provide any information on this matter, Mikey took it upon himself to search their home for clues. He looked for things he had seen in the homes of his friends belonging to their mothers: a ball of panty hose or a shoe with a pointy heel, long lists written in cursive, a little plastic basket filled with nail polish or a box of Tampax beneath the sink, an apron with roosters or reindeer embroidered onto it. He recovered not one piece of hard evidence in his own home.

On one occasion, however, Mikey discovered a single item that didn't fit in his home; it wasn't quite right. It was a small suitcase located in the corner of his father's closet, beneath a stack of neatly folded sweaters in various shades of gray. The suitcase was tacky and bright—it was the only thing in their entire home that Mikey simply could not imagine his father purchasing. When Mikey opened the suitcase, the scent of the cobalt-blue lining inside tickled at a memory, as faint and faraway and indistinct as a single puff of smoke. Maybe a memory of a memory. Even so, Mikey began to wonder if he had not been born out of a lady's peeing-hole (like his friends), but had simply arrived in this suitcase, which was perfectly sized to hold a small child and vaguely womblike in its shape. Mikey had no proof that this suitcase had produced him, but as a young boy it was his most persistent theory, and he liked to open the thing and stroke its strange synthetic fur and imagine that life had begun in this soft, blue place.

Mikey's father was a man of dark and quiet emotions. Things were rarely horrible between Mikey and his father, at least not in the usual ways; things were not vicious or unbearable. But things were never easy. Mikey's father had bad knees and bad moods, a shadowy disposition. He drank too often (daily), but rarely too much in a single sitting—Mikey never once saw him stumble or slur or fall asleep upright in a chair. When Mikey was a child, his father's moods manifested in biting criticism over meaningless things and treacherous, silent evenings at home when, for no reason at all, he would refuse to let Mikey out to play with his neighborhood friends. On these nights, Mikey would put himself to bed early just to remove himself from his father's presence. He would close his bedroom window so that he would not be pained by the faraway voices of his friends.

Alice, Sally, Lynn, Jimmy, and Sam became Mikey's friends when they were neighbor kids, all living on the same block, all seeking playmates as well as an escape from their own homes. The children claimed one of the abandoned homes on Ingram Street as their official meeting place, and the rusted mailbox mounted to the front door of the house read THE GUNNERS in gold Mylar stickers. The house had been vacant for as long as any of them could recall, and they knew of no Gunners in the neighborhood, so they took the place over and assumed its name as their own. They furnished the main room of The Gunner House with items found on the side of the street: mildewed mattresses, throw pillows with cigarette stains, three-legged patio chairs, eyeless baby dolls, an artificial Christmas tree in such a tangle it took days to reassemble. They hung a flashlight from the center of the ceiling in this room, and it was in here that they invented jokes and games and secret languages, made plans, made trouble, bad-mouthed their parents, played cards, gambled, told stories, plotted against bullies, bickered, made up, luxuriated in boredom, and dreamed of the lives they would one day live, far from Lackawanna.

As children, The Gunners could not have imagined that by the time they were sixteen years old, one of them would turn her back on the others, and the group would be so fractured by the loss, the sudden and unexplained absence of this one, that within weeks the other friendships would also dissolve, leaving each of them in a dark and confounding solitude. Mikey Callahan became a sinkhole; everything inside sort of loosened and then just collapsed.

# CHAPTER 2

It was springtime, April, with one month left of her junior year of high school, when Sally Forrest cut herself off from the rest of The Gunners. She stopped speaking to them at school, never again set foot in The Gunner House, would not answer them when they called to her in the hallway or when they tried to approach her as she walked down Ingram Street. She would quicken her pace and lower her eyes and change her route. She would not answer phone calls to her house. The rest of them finally went directly to her home to seek her out, where Sally's mother, Corinne, said that Sally was unwell, and she would not allow the children to enter.

Sally did not replace the group with new friendships at school; she seemed altogether uninterested in the company of others, taking her lunch outside or to a classroom that was not in use. She never raised her hand in class. Her pale eyes went cool, and her posture was hard.

For several weeks, the others puzzled over the situation together, replaying recent conversations, devising theories, formulating vague and uncertain but genuine apologies. When they could not reach any single conclusion as to what might have caused Sally to turn on them, they began to turn on one another, with accusations and assumptions, resentment and suspicion. The Gunners found themselves behaving like strangers toward one another in the halls of school and the streets of Lackawanna for their remaining months of high school.

Mikey was one grade behind the others in school, and the only one, aside from Sally, who remained in the area.

Mikey moved out of his father's home after graduating high school, into a tiny ranch house twelve miles north, so that his commute to General Mills, where he worked on the maintenance crew, would be ten minutes instead of thirty. He rented the ranch home from an elderly woman named Louise who had just moved into a retirement center. Louise explained to Mikey that her daughters had both married weasels and she didn't have any plans of leaving the home to them, so Mikey should go ahead and do as he liked with the place, paint-wise, plant-wise, and pet-wise. Mikey brightened the dull gray-pink walls to a warm cream and planted a forsythia bush out front. He got a black kitten one Friday, and named the cat Friday.

After moving out of his father's home, Mikey made a habit of going to see his father every Sunday. His father would pour him a beer and they would stare tensely at the TV for a few hours, then his father would get up to take a piss and say, "Lock the door on your way out," and Mikey would feel a great sense of relief.

Mikey never left the area, or his job at General Mills, although he did receive two promotions over the course of a decade. He never left the ranch home either; he was shocked to find that Louise had actually left the house, and all that it contained, to him when she eventually passed. He hadn't realized she was so serious about those weasels.

Mikey took Louise's impressive accumulation of *Redbook* magazines, erotic novels, and cookbooks to the Salvation Army, except for *The Joy of Cooking*, which he kept for himself. He paged absently through this book, many of its pages stained with sauce or textured with crumbs, until one day it began to interest him. He learned to baste and blanch and caramelize, poach and macerate and emulsify, learned the quick mental math of dividing recipes into a portion for one. He pored over Louise's collection from the classical repertoire on cassette tapes, listening to this music while he cooked and late into the evening.

Friday became a dear and happy companion. He was a cat of the highest caliber. He purred when Mikey touched his head, while leaning and arching his back into Mikey's legs and walking figure eights through them as Mikey cooked, purred in the morning when he moved from the foot of the bed, where he slept every night, to Mikey's chest, happily and dutifully kneading at Mikey's neck with his little black paws, purring so rapturously that he gasped and wheezed fishy breath into Mikey's face. Mikey wondered what had brought him the great fortune of having such a merry and contented cat, who, unlike Mikey, never seemed to slip into dark, pensive, and ungenerous moods.

It was not long after Mikey left his father's home that his vision in his right eye began to grow worse. Faraway road signs, individual leaves on trees, and tiles on roofs were the first things to go. The change was so gradual that it wasn't until years later that he finally went to see an optometrist.

The optometrist performed tests and gave Mikey a prescription for his right eye. He inquired as to when Mikey had lost vision completely in the left.

"I never had it," Mikey said.

"I see." The optometrist stared back and forth between both of Mikey's eyes and shone a bright blue light into the right one.

Mikey picked out a pair of wire frames, and reiterated to the receptionist ordering the glasses that he would only need the proper prescription in the right lens.

Several months later, Mikey returned to the optometrist when he could tell his vision in his right eye had already grown worse. He was retested and given a stronger prescription.

A year later, he was back again, for the same reason.

This time, the doctor asked about blind spots. Mikey confessed that he had several and asked what this meant. The doctor explained that he was undergoing early-onset macular degeneration.

Mikey asked him directly, "Will I go blind?"

The doctor answered directly, "Probably."

"When?"

The doctor compared Mikey's new prescription with the previous one. "A few years most likely. Although you never know what might happen with technology between now and then."

Mikey felt an angry and fearful indignation shiver through the cold organs in his belly. He said, "Why is this happening?"

"Are you asking if it's hereditary?"

"I guess."

"Possibly," the doctor said.

Mikey was quiet for a bit. Then he said, "There was one time I looked directly at the sun when I was a kid."

The doctor smiled gently. "They warn you about that. But it's almost impossible to cause permanent damage that way. You didn't do this to yourself, I can assure you of that."

Mikey started to learn Braille. He started practicing to cook and clean and clothe himself with a piece of tape over his right eye. He also started to catalog images, colors, memories, and he created associations that would make sense to him when—if—he lost his sight. *The color red = the smell of cinnamon. Blue = fingers under running water. White = the taste of cream. A full moon is*

*Chopin's Nocturne, Opus 9, No. 2. The first snowfall looks exactly the*
*way sugar tastes. A tree-lined street with lampposts is Philip Glass's*
*"Metamorphosis One."*

Excluding Sally, the rest of The Gunners started up a group email thread within a year or two of graduating high school and going their separate ways. Any ill will among the rest of them caused by Sally's absence seemed to have been forgotten. Although this was never formally acknowledged between them, they reconnected easily over email, the ongoing thread coming to life every few months, and their contact was warm, often containing a happy childhood memory or an ancient inside joke. With all of them now around thirty, the past decade had seen a great deal of movement and change, all documented through these emails.

Jimmy had come into great wealth since moving to Los Angeles at age nineteen and making wise investments. Sam had been married at age twenty-one in a family-only ceremony, and was now deeply involved with the church he and his wife attended in Georgia. Lynn had attended a music conservatory in New York City, but now lived in a small town in Pennsylvania, where she and her boyfriend ran the local AA chapter. Alice had attended the University of Michigan, eloped with a graduate student who she referred to as "The Saint," been married to him for a year and then divorced him; she now dated women. She currently owned a small but successful marina on Lake Huron. Sometimes, Mikey felt embarrassed by how little his own life had changed since high school compared to the rest of them. In their emails, the others described marriage and travels and concerts. In Mikey's emails, he described renovations to their high school gym, a new recipe he had attempted, and minor updates to Friday's health.

On occasions when Mikey saw Sally Forrest out in Lackawanna, he had to fight his urge to report back to the others. As far as Mikey could tell, Sally remained in her mother's home after high school and he continued to see her out from time to time, standing in line at the CVS pharmacy, massaging peaches at Tops, or walking up Ingram with a cell phone at her ear, although Sally always seemed to be listening, never speaking into that phone. Mikey did not know if she worked. He did not know if she had new friends, or who spoke to her from the other end of that phone.

With high school behind them and the others far away, Mikey had initially been hopeful that he and Sally might be able to reconnect, that she might finally reveal to him what had caused her to abandon the group, and that he might have the opportunity to apologize if he'd had any part of it. But when they encountered each other in public, Sally continued to look past Mikey with the same cold disdain she had when they were still in school. As though she'd never known him, as though they'd shared nothing. When he saw Sally, Mikey was filled with a dense, aching emptiness, one that contained so much.

He longed to report to the others that their old friend Sally was still so, so thin, perhaps had even lost weight since the last time he'd seen her. She always wore sunglasses, so he could not see her eyes. She carried a canvas bag with a fruit basket embroidered on it, and there was a large, bright yellowish stain on the strap. He still missed her, wondered about her, wondered what had gone wrong, and whether the others did, too. But he always reasoned with himself that if the others cared, they would ask. No point picking at a sore and drawing fresh blood if everyone else was content to leave it be.

There was often talk of a reunion between the five of them, but plans never came together. Even so, with brief and infrequent face-to-face contact, and all these years later, Mikey still considered

Alice, Jimmy, Sam, and Lynn his dearest friends. He had trouble connecting with peers at work, and despised social events. He had not grown less shy over the years. He couldn't bring himself to start social media accounts because he hated all photographs of himself: left eye always a bit creamy and strange and faraway, right eye focused but never quite meeting the camera's lens, as though he feared its judgment. Cheeks always flaming, freckles overlaid with red. Cowlick always wild, as if it had an ax to grind.

Mikey therefore always read the emails from The Gunners with great interest, and felt deeply invested in their lives. He went on soaring Google Earth explorations through their towns, zooming around parks and downtowns and up and down residential streets. He made a habit of sending birthday cards—*actual* cards, via snail mail—to the others, who always expressed incredulous gratitude for the gesture.

Mikey did not tell his friends that he might be going blind and was mining childhood relics, yearbooks and journals and stacks of Polaroid photographs rubber-banded together, searching for pictures of his friends and meditating on them, knowing that these dear faces might one day elude him.

In early January, the city of Buffalo was fossilized beneath three feet of hard gray snow, the air bitterly cold and humid. People moved slowly, like cogs in an old machine, muscles hard, cold licking at their faces. Pipes had burst at General Mills, and Mikey was working twelve-hour days. Mikey's thirtieth birthday came and went, with a text from Alice and a generic card from HR in his work mailbox, the typeface meant to resemble actual handwriting, acknowledging him as a valued employee and wishing him a special day.

It was a week after Mikey's birthday that he received word of Sally's death.

The news came from a colleague, someone who had attended Mikey's high school but who was several years younger than Mikey. The colleague had not known Sally, but news of a former student's suicide had reached him through the local news. Her body was found in the Buffalo River, less than a quarter mile downstream from the Buffalo Skyway. Her car was parked just off the entrance to the Skyway, an elevated steel bridge that soared one hundred feet over the water beneath. Her mother had reported her missing late the night before. Although there was no note, it appeared to be a straightforward suicide. Her mother confirmed her struggle with depression. Video surveillance from the bridge showed that she acted alone, just after midnight. Mikey's colleague realized that Sally would have been about Mikey's age, and he asked Mikey about it at work, wondering if Mikey had heard the news about his classmate, wondering if Mikey had known or would even remember the girl. *Her name was Sally*, the guy said to Mikey. *Did you know a Sally?*

Funeral arrangements were announced—it would take place in two weeks at St. Mary's, the church nearest Sally's mother's home, just six blocks off Ingram.

Mikey was broken, muddled, distracted. He could think of nothing else, yet no matter how long and hard he thought on Sally, he could never reach her center. Furthermore, as he tried to recall memories of her, he realized he could never reach his *own* center—he could never reach something that felt entirely real, or true. He began to wonder if he had no center. A hollow man.

Mikey was in touch with Alice, Jimmy, Sam, and Lynn to make sure the news had reached them. They all planned to come to town for the service.

Knowing that he would see the four of them brought Mikey some measure of solace as well as nervous anticipation. Adulthood and years of living alone had taken a toll on his confidence. He wanted to believe that he would still be able to relate to his friends face-to-face, would still genuinely interest them, could offer comfort and share a laugh. But in pessimistic moments, he feared uneasiness between them brought on simply by the passage of time, too much life lived apart.

In the days leading up to Sally's funeral, Mikey got a haircut and shoveled snow and vacuumed up Friday's hair. He often found himself short of breath, even when he had barely stirred.

He avoided the Skyway, taking the long and indirect route north on Niagara Street instead.


Several days before the funeral, Mikey received a call from Jimmy inviting him to a catered dinner following the funeral service at the lakeside vacation home not far from Lackawanna that Jimmy had purchased years earlier for his family. Jimmy said he would be inviting Alice, Lynn, and Sam as well. Jimmy said there were enough beds for everyone, and all were welcome to spend the night.

Mikey thanked Jimmy for the invite and said, "Can I bring something?"

"Oh God, no." Jimmy laughed bleakly. "Zeppelli's catering the thing. There'll be enough for an army."

Mikey said, "How are you holding up, bud?"

Jimmy said, "I just can't believe she's gone. Again." It was quiet for a bit, then Jimmy said in a strange voice, "I can't stop wondering . . . Well, do you know anything, Mikey?"

Mikey's head felt way too heavy for his neck, not right at all. His heart was loud. He had the strangest sensation, as if he were being pulled at, as if he were in someone else's dream.

He stared out his window and saw that an enormous flock of grackles—there had to be a thousand of them, maybe ten thousand—had come to rest in the row of diseased-looking maple trees just on the other side of the street.

Mikey got up, phone still at his ear, walked to his door, opened it, and stepped out into the snow.

The air was thunderous, full and alive with the clamorous chatter and vibration of the birds. But moments later, when Mikey closed the door behind him, some of the birds nearest him were startled by the sound and took flight. Others followed. More. Mikey exhaled a white cloud, and his empty lungs tickled with cold. He coughed and watched the birds as they lifted off the trees in a magnificent ripple. It wasn't long at all until the entire flock had departed in a huge spinning black cone, leaving only a blank and depleted void in their wake. An *after* sound. A holy, yearning silence, like a prayer that was too sad and too deeply felt to be spoken aloud.

Mikey still held his phone at his ear, his lips now paralyzed by the cold, and Jimmy said, "Mikey? You there?"

Mikey finally said, "I don't know." As these words slid out of his mouth, they felt long and cool, like snakes.

# CHAPTER 3

When Mikey started kindergarten, he was a shy boy who sat by himself on the bus while other children hollered and clapped and traded jokes and insults and items from their lunch boxes. Mikey watched out the window in the morning as other children were picked up from his street, and in the afternoon as they were dropped off. The Italian kid with eyes the color of a swimming pool who hung out with the chubby, blond, pink-faced kid whose *r*'s came out like *w*'s, the two of them always talking football, drawing out plays with smelly black markers, *X*'s and swooping lines in a notebook. The tall, black-eyed girl with broad, high cheeks who ordered everyone else around, working in as many curse words and creative insults as possible. *Butt-slug! Ass-face-mouth-breather!* The freckled girl with the curly red hair who skipped recess to practice the piano in the music room. The slim, silver-haired girl who lived several doors up from Mikey. Usually, like him, she waited for the bus alone, but on rare occasion, her slim, silver-haired mother waited by her side. She typically sat by herself on the bus, too. Often, she sat in the seat directly behind Mikey, and sometimes he could hear her singing quietly to herself.

One morning, this girl sat down directly next to him.

As she sank into the seat, she said with low eyes, as though issuing an apology, "There are no more empty ones."

She smelled very clean. She wore a green headband. Up close, Mikey could see that her hair was not actually silver, but the whitest blond he had ever seen, so white that it took on the hue of other colors and lights around them. Her face was as pretty and delicate as lace. She arranged her backpack beneath her little legs.

Mikey said, "It's okay."

The girl sighed and touched the ends of her hair.

He said, "What's your name?"

"Sally."

"I'm Mikey."

"You're a kindergartner?"

He nodded. "What grade are you in?"

"First."

"Do you know how to read?"

"Mm-hm."

"I don't yet."

"That's okay," Sally said. "Is that your daddy who was soaping up the car?"

"What?"

"I saw a guy soaping up a car in your driveway the other day. A big old white car."

"Oh, yes," Mikey said. "That's him, and that's his car."

"Where's your mommy?"

Mikey said, "I don't have one."

"Is she dead?"

Mikey thought. "Maybe."

Sally was quiet for a moment. Then she said, "My mommy says my daddy's a deadbeat and some other things."

"Is that the same as dead?"

"I don't think so."

Mikey said, "Do you want a Jolly Rancher?"

"Yes."

Mikey offered her watermelon or grape or green apple. She took the green apple. She sucked on it silently, and her warm breath became sweet and strange.


The next day, Sally sat next to Mikey once again, even though there were empty seats available, and the day after that, too.

Usually, they didn't talk very much. The silence between them was easy, companionable. Sometimes, Sally placed her backpack on Mikey's lap, rested her head there, and slept. Mikey watched her sleeping face morph softly into and out of many expressions, and he tried to imagine what sort of dream produced each different one.


Alice Clancy formed the group, really made it official, the summer between her first- and second-grade year. School had been out for only a week, and already Alice was bored of TV and fights with her older brothers over who got the first or last or largest portion of things.

One afternoon, she wandered into the backyard of the green house just a few doors down the block from her own, after she heard voices and laughter lifting up from behind the house. She caught sight of a ball in the air.

She walked right to the center of things, between two boys wearing baseball gloves, and she stood there with her fists dug into her hips. She was six inches taller than either of them.

"You boys ride my bus," she said.

She looked back and forth between them. The chubby blond

kid punched his fist into his glove. He had round shoulders and a thick neck, and was the tiniest bit dim in the eyes. His nostrils and the thin, pale skin around his eye sockets was chafed pink, as though he cried a lot, or had lots of allergies. He didn't wear a shirt. His belly was fat but firm, accentuated by a disturbing little outtie.

Alice said, "What's your names?"

The black-haired, blue-eyed kid said, "Jimmy." His eyes were remarkable—as bright and interesting as tiny planets.

The blond kid said, "Sam. Why are you at my house?"

"I'm Alice and I live in the only brick house on the street, and we have that big black mutt named Jake." She paused and jerked her chin over her shoulder in the direction of her house. "Anyways, I have a club and I'm president," she said. "Looking for members. You guys in or out?"

Sam said, "Who's in it?"

Alice released an exasperated little noise and scowled at him. "None of your beeswax," she said, "if you're not members."

Sam shoved his thumb toward Alice's face. "Look at my blood blister," he said.

Alice said, "*Gross.*"

Jimmy said, "What do you do in your club?"

"Lots of secret stuff."

Sam tossed the baseball up and down to himself and said, "Me and Jimmy need to talk it over. We'll let you know tomorrow."

Alice returned the following afternoon. Sam reported that they had talked it over and decided that they would join her club if she would let them play with Jake, her big black mutt. Alice said, "Sure, but don't blame me if he snaps at you. He has some places he doesn't like when you touch."

Sam said, "So who else is in the club?"

Alice said, "I'm about to ask some other kids on this street. That little boy, the one who's a year younger and always sits with the white-haired girl on the bus, the two of them. And that red-haired girl who plays piano during recess."

Sam said, "Wait, so you don't *have* a club, you're *starting* one."

Jimmy added, "Like from scratch."

"What difference does that make?" Alice said, arms crossed, her tone both pushy and cavalier.

Sam was quiet for a bit. Then he said, "Can I be vice president?"

"What?"

"I want to be the vice president or we won't be in your club."

Alice considered this for a moment, then she said, "Fine, sure, whatever." She turned to Jimmy. "You wanna be something?"

Jimmy blinked. His eyelashes were black feathers framing those blue eyes. He said, "Maybe like treasurer? I'm good at money."

Alice said, "Okay. We'll have that piano girl be the secretary, and the other two can just be there unless they think up something special to be."

Alice, Sam, and Jimmy made their way up Ingram Street and successfully recruited Lynn, Sally, and Mikey. Alice had already scoped out The Gunner House as a potential gathering place, and they held their first official meeting later that afternoon. Alice brought her mutt, Jake, and a slotted spoon in case he pooped inside. "His bowels are rotten," she explained. Sam dragged in a taxidermied sheep's head that he had found on the curb just up the block. The place smelled strongly of mildew and cat piss, and dust hung thick and motionless in the hot, hot air above the children's sweating heads and their eager, happy voices.

# CHAPTER 4

hen Sally was eight years old, she and Mikey decided to walk all the way to Gasser Park. It was August. They were the only Gunners who weren't either enrolled in Bible School at St. Mary's Parish or away at summer camp in Ellicottville on this particular week.

Sally and Mikey had both been to the park before, but never without a parent. They knew that it was far to walk, but that they would reach the park if they took Ingram to Lakeshore, then followed that east for a long while. They filled a backpack with ham and mustard sandwiches, Fritos, Twizzlers, and a canteen of water. They had all day to make it there and back; Sally's mother would not be home from work until after five—much later than that if she went out drinking with one of her boyfriends—and Mikey's father would return around seven. Both Sally and Mikey were already capable at this very young age of letting themselves in and out of their homes using a key. At Mikey's home, this key lived under the doormat; at Sally's it was in a fake football-size rock that opened and closed on a hinge.

It took them an hour to reach the park.

Along the way, they talked about the upcoming school year. Sally told Mikey what he could expect from all the different teachers. She told him about the live crab that lived in Mrs. O'Casey's classroom and all the amazing facts about animals he would learn in her class. How ostriches can run faster than a horse, and that male ostriches roar like a lion. She told him about the strange and unpredictable migration of the snowy owl. She told him about the wood frog, which didn't hibernate like other animals but instead buried itself in the ground and allowed itself to freeze.

"It stops breathing," Sally said. "Its heart stops beating."

Mikey said, "But it's not dead?"

"Nope," said Sally. "In the springtime, or whenever it wants to come back into the world, it thaws with the ground and its heart beats again."

Mikey stopped when they passed a bed of clover along the side of the road, and he showed Sally how to pluck the tiny white-purple petals from the stem, how to bite on the inner tip, which was damp and sweet and edible. Sally loved spending time with Mikey. He never seemed to have a nasty opinion about anything. Like her, he seemed equally satisfied to talk or not talk, and he never asked hard questions. This suited Sally just fine. There were things she didn't want to talk about, things that Mikey would never think to ask.

It was quiet outside, and very hot.

When they finally reached the park, Sally felt grown-up and accomplished, and she gazed around the parking lot and picnic area, seeking some sort of acknowledgment for the thing they had just done. There was only one car in the lot, a dusty old powder-blue Crown Victoria, and no one else in sight.

The two of them stared at a large map of the park behind Plexiglas. They filled their canteen at the nearby fountain, then followed the trail leading to Turtle Pond, where they had decided to eat their lunch.

Turtle Pond was the size of a football field. The water was army green and the air smelled of burned grass and sewage. Dragonflies skirted through reeds and a black flip-flop was stuck upright in the muck. A charred Budweiser can floated aimlessly a little ways out. They stood at the edge of the pond for a minute, looking for turtles, then took a seat in the shade and ate their hot, damp, and deformed sandwiches and opened the chips.

Mikey ate a Frito, then inhaled sharply and pointed out at the water. "Turtle," he whispered. A little black head bobbed casually at the surface, six feet out from the edge of the pond. They rose to get a closer look.

"It's okay, fella," Mikey whispered. "You're so good, fella."

Sally could see down through the surface of the water that it was a box turtle, its shell no more than six inches in length. Its wary little half-closed eyes were sleepy and annoyed. Mikey inched a bit closer, Fritos in hand.

"I've got something for you, pal," he said, tossing a chip in the turtle's direction so that it landed at the water's surface just inches from its face. The turtle's head instantly dipped below the water, but a moment later, the chip disappeared, snatched from underneath. Mikey giggled. The sun was on his face, and his pale eyes were all iris, the color of honeydew melon.

Sally tossed another chip in, and the same thing happened. Mikey tossed in another one, this time a little bit closer in their direction, luring the turtle toward shore.

Mikey said, "I'm going to catch him if he comes close enough."

He took a very slow step into the silt at the water's edge, and his foot sank into it, a puddle quickly forming around his shoe. He took another step into the water, and then both feet were fully submerged. The turtle disappeared, and Mikey tossed five or six chips in a wide arc in that direction. He took another step in.

Sally said, "Don't you want to take your shoes off?"

Mikey said, "No, there might be a leech. Then we'd have to

burn it off before it sucked all my blood out. The water feels good anyhow, might keep my feet cool on the way back."

Mikey took another big step out into the water, so that it reached his calves. He laughed and made a face.

"It is *so* squishy!" he said.

He looked like he was having fun, and Sally liked his idea about keeping cool with wet shoes, so she decided to follow him in.

Soon the water reached her knees.

She said, "Maybe I'll get my shorts a little wet."

Mikey said, "Might as well."

Now when Sally took a step it was in slow motion, because the effort of lifting a foot out of the soft muck was so great. It felt weird, and exciting. Soon, the water was at her hip. The mud was above her ankles.

She suddenly noticed that Mikey was struggling. He was no longer laughing; his face had changed. He gripped the back of one knee with both hands as though to pry it up and out.

Sally said, "Are you okay?"

"I'm stuck," he said. "I can't move either of my feet . . . and I think I'm sort of *sinking*."

As soon as he said this word, Sally realized that she, too, was stuck, and nearly sinking.

"Okay," Sally said. "Here, let's . . ." and she tried the same move, pulling on her hamstring with both hands, but this did nothing.

Mikey said, "Here, why don't we . . ." and he struggled mightily, finally releasing one of his legs. He splashed backward into the water. With one foot out, he was soon able to finagle the other one out, too, and he paddled over to Sally. He reached into the water beneath her with his hands, trying to help. She held on to his head for balance. She felt him clawing at her legs, but before long, Mikey had gotten himself stuck again. The mud was crawling up Sally's legs like a snake coiling up a tree. The water suddenly looked as thick and black as ink.

Mikey said, "Don't worry."

But Sally could see that he was starting to panic, too. They held one another's arms for combined strength and balance, but the more they worked to free themselves, the faster they sank.

The water was past Sally's waist. They called for help, hollering back toward the lot, but their little voices were lost in humidity that was as thick as a pillow.

Then the water was at Sally's ribs. It smelled hot and raw and bad in her nostrils.

Sally said, "I don't want to die!" She sobbed into the crook of her elbow. She thought of her mother and the possibility that she could come rescue them, and realized her mother wouldn't even notice her absence until sundown, much later than that if she was out with a boyfriend. And even if her mother had been right there with them, it occurred to Sally, she had little faith that her mother would know what to do. Her mother was not the most sensible person. Then Sally thought of her father, way up in Canada. Even though she didn't know him much at all, had never even met him face-to-face, she was almost certain he'd know what to do. But he was so far away—sometimes her birthday cards from him arrived three weeks late, that's how far away he was. Given how difficult it seemed to get in touch with her father, Sally wondered now how long it would take someone to get ahold of him to deliver the news that his daughter had drowned in mud. She wondered if he would cry. For some reason, the thought of her father's tears sent a strong and fast pulse beating straight to the private place between her legs.

Mikey said, "I'm going under. I'm going to find my shoes with my hands, untie them, get my feet out."

He disappeared under the surface of the water.

Bubbles rose above him, and a bloated Frito drifted by.

Then Mikey burst upward, coughing, eyes round and wet-lashed, hair darkened and plastered to his head in spikes. He let out a sharp, barking cough. "I got out!" He emerged from the mud.

He dove down again, beneath Sally. She could feel him scratching at her left ankle, excavating, gripping her foot. She could tell it was going to work. She felt a sweet, glorious swell inside of her, an uncomplicated and unprecedented sense of reprieve. She was going to make it! Her mother would not have to come looking for her after all, would not have to pick out a funeral dress. Her father would not have to maybe cry.

Once they were out of the water, they panted and trembled and laughed in high, soft pitches. They rinsed the mud from their legs and hands. Sally pulled a small twig from Mikey's hair. They opened the Twizzlers. Sally's knees were starting to grow a little hair on them, and she noticed now how the fuzz shimmered in the sun.

They walked back up the trail, which was covered in acorn shells and stickery brambles, then walked up Lakeshore under a punishing sun, through ditches when the gravel on the shoulder of the road became too hot or too sharp.

By the time they reached Ingram Street, their feet were brown and bloodied and they were exhausted, weak, sunburned, out of water. They stopped in at Bakery Sczcepanski, which shared a parking lot with the Clean-Machine Laundromat, Benny's Liquor Store, and Gary's Grocery & Delicatessen. The woman who owned the bakery would give the children free baked goods that had expired that day if they caught her before closing time. They called her Babcia ("Grandma" in Polish). The skin of her face was as crisscrossed with lines as an old cutting board. Her bakery was decorated with framed photographs of dairy farms in Poland that had all faded to bluish gray.

On this day, Babcia provided Mikey and Sally with water and sesame cookies, and she scolded them for losing their shoes.

When they finally reached home, they drank grape sodas on Mikey's back porch, put Band-Aids on their feet, then sacked out on the couch. Mikey fell asleep five minutes into an episode of *ALF*. Sally looked around the room. Mikey's house was so clean and quiet it was like a tomb. Sally wondered if Mikey's dad ever brought girlfriends home. Mikey had said something very strange at one point on their walk home. He had fallen quiet for a long while, then said, "My dad might've been gladder if I didn't make it out of the mud."

Sally said, "What? Why?"

"I don't think he loves me very much," Mikey said, and Sally noticed that Mikey was nodding as he said this.

Sally stared at him. "He has to," she said. "It's a rule of being a mommy or daddy."

Sally didn't know how she knew this, but it seemed like a true thing.

Mikey said, "Okay," and he continued to nod.

Sally watched Mikey's sleeping face now and realized how many times over the years she had slept next to Mikey on the bus—because she slept more soundly on the bus than she did in her own home—how often Mikey had seen her sleeping face. Yet this was the first time she had ever seen his. His expression was as empty as the moon. The tiniest droplets of sweat decorated his nose, his cheeks were the color of bubble gum, and his dime-size cowlick, as always, invited a little clockwise swirl of the finger. It seemed inconceivable to Sally that this was the face of the person who had saved her life.

# CHAPTER 5

It was the third week of January, and the crust of yellowy-gray snow that had encased the city of Buffalo earlier that month had received a dusting overnight, an inch of fresh crystal powder. The air was clean and quiet and wondrous, the sky a pale bowl. It was Sunday. Mikey arrived at St. Mary's Cathedral thirty minutes before Sally's three o'clock service.

The lobby was dark and smelled like the inside of a sweaty old baseball cap. Mikey hung his coat and brushed snowflakes from his hair. There were a dozen people in the lobby, older folks, friends of Sally's mother, Mikey guessed. In the low light, grim and tucked within layers of black clothing, everyone there looked severe and vaguely bloodless. The priest was a flaccid-looking individual with a sad, high forehead, and he offered Mikey a nod that was both wary and polite. Mikey's hands were frigid because he hadn't worn gloves, and he stuffed them into his pockets, where they met his thighs and sent goose bumps to his groin.

Mikey considered whether he ought to make attempts at mingling or disappear to walk through quiet basement hallways and avoid speaking with anyone until his friends arrived. He was tempted by the thought of dark halls, dark classrooms, janitor's closets, drinking fountains mounted low on the wall. His low-grade anxiety was brought quickly to the surface by any sort of social interaction, much less one taking place in a church, and under this sort of circumstance. He felt anxious, shaky, hollow. He wore a dark gray suit from JCPenney and a poorly knotted blue tie. His armpits felt cold and stiff, suggesting wetness. In the mirror that morning, his pale eyes had looked wet and muddled, as if they were lost, had been placed inside the wrong head.

Mikey made his way across the lobby to a small coffee setup. He filled a Styrofoam cup with coffee that was not steaming, and he stirred in a packet of sugar. A chill nipped at him. Had he locked the door to his home? He had left extra food out for Friday, but was it enough? His fingernails were unclean. What would his friends think of him? Had he grown ugly and weird in the last decade? Had he grown old?

Mikey sipped his coffee, which was thin and cool, and tried to reach a relaxed pose as he gazed around the lobby. He drew his phone from his pocket and glanced at it for the time and notifications. Jimmy had called several hours earlier to say that his connecting flight was delayed and he was stranded in Denver. He had rebooked for later that day but would miss the funeral service. He said that the catering arrangements were already made at the lake house; Mikey and the others should head there without him.

Mikey's phone showed no update from Jimmy or any of the others. He slid it back into his pocket and breathed hot air into his fists since the coffee had not warmed his fingers. He was bothered by his cold hands. It seemed like the sort of thing a person would remember about another person, especially when there was little else to say about him. *The Man with Cold Hands.*

Mikey glanced over toward the door, where, mercifully, Lynn was entering. He adjusted his glasses to make sure it was her, and it was.

Lynn wore a puffy green coat that nearly grazed the floor, and her head was small and pale within an explosion of curly red hair. She was with a very tall and handsome man whose bald head gleamed with moisture. As the man helped Lynn remove her coat, she caught sight of Mikey across the room. Lynn straightened up in recognition, her face broke into delight, and she called, "It's you!"

She bounced on her toes and clapped her hands together fast and happy for a moment, then stopped, abruptly conscious of her display of joy in the somber room. Mikey made his way over to the two of them.

Lynn was very thin and her face was pocked with scars that Mikey did not remember, but her smile was generous and straightforward, her green eyes lively. For the first time in days, Mikey felt warm.

Lynn said, "Sorry to make a scene, but I don't care if it's a funeral! Mikey, you're a sight. This makes me happy. Can't believe how long it's been. This is my boyfriend, Issa." Her red curls were so tight it was as if each one had been formed around a pencil. Her nose was dusted with freckles.

Issa's voice was low and rich when he said, "Pleasure."

Mikey said, "You guys are in Pennsylvania, right? How long was the drive?"

Lynn said, "Jim Thorpe's the name of the town. Should be five hours, but the snow slowed us down. Left at"—she glanced down at her watch, then up at Issa—"five thirty this morning?"

Issa said, "Five. Couple stops along the way."

Mikey said, "Issa, have you been to the area before?"

Issa nodded. "Twice."

Mikey was glad he had rehearsed easy points of small talk: the drive, weather, traffic, location of restrooms, if needed. However, he hoped that in his efforts to be calm and composed he did not seem aloof.

Lynn explained, "We've been back here to visit my mom a couple times, but it's more often that she comes to us. She loses her mind over the Museum of Mason Jars in the next town over from us. You think I'm joking? She has to take the ninety-minute tour every time she visits. Last time she went, she picked up a job application for me."

Issa corroborated this with a nod. "And one for me, too," he said.

Mikey laughed. He said to Issa, "Lynn has told me, but I can't remember. Where are you from, before Pennsylvania?"

"New York before that, Addis Ababa before that."

"Is that Ethiopia?"

Issa nodded.

Mikey said, "How do you like the snowy Northeast?"

Issa said, "I don't. But Lynn's got this stuff in her blood." He turned to Lynn and brushed a little bit of snow from her hair, then placed a long arm around her. "Says she'd lose her mind without winter."

Lynn said, "True. It's the only good excuse to live the way I like."

Mikey said, "How do you mean?"

"Go to bed early," Lynn explained. "Spend all day in blankets. Watch *Law & Order* for ten hours straight. Eat soup from a can. All the things I love to do. But you act like that in the summertime, and everybody thinks you're off your meds."

Issa said, "She hibernates like a bear."

Mikey laughed. "Lynn, are you still playing piano?"

Lynn nodded. "Although . . ." She held out her left hand to display that she was missing her left ring finger. Completely gone, down to the fist, some puckered scar tissue gathered at the top of the metacarpus.

Mikey said, "I don't think I knew about that. Did you ever mention it in an email? When did it happen?"

"Long story," Lynn said. "I'll tell you later." She hesitated as she lowered her hands to her thighs. Pale skin stretched tight over her clavicles. She tucked hair behind her ears and said, "Did you see this coming?"

"What's that?"

Lynn nodded in toward the sanctuary. "Sally."

"No," Mikey said. "Did you?"

"Didn't *see* it coming," Lynn said. "But I felt it coming. Or *heard* it coming, I guess I should say."

"What do you mean?"

"I've been working on improv sets, practicing with old jazz trio recordings," Lynn explained. "The days leading up to her suicide, every time I sat down to play, the music that came out of me was . . . *wrong*. Ugly. Oppressive. I couldn't make sense of it until I got this news. It's like some part of me that *I* don't even know knew."

# CHAPTER 6

Lynn started taking piano lessons with her cousin Amy when she was four years old. Amy had taught Lynn her left from her right and the first seven letters of the alphabet before Lynn learned these things in school. One of Lynn's earliest memories was of Amy at her side on the padded piano bench, smelling of cigarettes and vanilla-mint perfume, and Lynn's own discovery that if she plunked down on enough keys at one time, using both full palms and strength from her upper arms, this noise was powerful enough to drown out the sound of her parents hurling insults at one another in the next room.

Lynn would practice for hours a day, composing her own songs after she had mastered the repertoire from her most recent lesson. Her parents did not push her in this direction, nor did they discourage it—it was entirely her own love of the instrument that inspired this level of discipline. They divorced when Lynn was seven, and her father moved to Pittsburgh to work for a sports broadcasting radio network.

By the time Lynn was eight, she had surpassed Amy's skill level, so she started taking lessons from the woman who played piano for their church's contemporary praise group. Lynn's mother had started attending church in the wake of the divorce, and brought

Lynn to services every Sunday and Wednesday. Her mother sang way too loudly in services, and raised her hands in worship at times when Lynn did not think it was necessary, or appropriate.

Lynn organized piano recitals for herself and invited The Gunners to her home. Her mother would pour red punch into wax-paper cups and serve store-bought cookies on a plastic silver tray. Lynn would wear the nicest dress she owned. The other five children would seat themselves on folding chairs Lynn had arranged in a semicircle around herself, and they would listen quietly as she played, then applaud when she had finished. Oftentimes, one of the other children would sit at Lynn's piano bench afterward and paw clumsily at the keys, trying to locate a tune. Lynn would laugh and try to teach them something simple: "Chopsticks," "Heart and Soul." At these times, Lynn felt that her friends were the best friends in the whole world. She dreamed that one day she would play on a huge stage, like Carnegie Hall, and be presented with an award and given the opportunity to speak, and she would thank each of The Gunners by name for their friendship and support.

When Lynn was thirteen, the teacher from church recommended her to a teacher at Buff State. She said Lynn was playing at an advanced level and would not find an adequate teacher outside of the university setting, so Lynn started taking weekly lessons with Brent, a tall, slim graduate student from Texas who wore wire-rimmed glasses and his long hair in a single braid down his back. He smelled a little bit like a horse on hot days, and he sucked on butterscotch candies.

When Lynn met Brent, she felt a painful, shivery yearning in her little body.

It wasn't that Lynn had no interest in her own peers; she was deeply invested in her friendships with The Gunners, but they were like siblings to her—there was nothing even resembling sexual attraction there. And outside of The Gunners, Lynn cared nothing for her classmates or other kids her age. She didn't need them, she barely even noticed them.

But what she felt instantly for Brent sent her careening after something entirely new, something *mega*: Lynn wanted sex things. At the age of thirteen, she wasn't even entirely clear on the logistics, but she knew that's what she wanted. She felt desire everywhere, most of all in the *zoom* between her legs, a vibration so fierce it panted and howled against the crotch of her pants.

Life in between her piano lessons became practically unbearable—Lynn could think of nothing else. Inwardly, she hurtled between euphoria and utter despair. She spent long sessions every evening contemplating her outfit for her upcoming lesson. She started to shave her legs. She started to massage her little boobies, having read in *Seventeen* magazine that this would make them grow faster. She tried to control her wild red curls with pins and a straightening tool and waxy pomade.

The Gunners were routinely swiping liquor from their parents, parents' guests, older siblings, and occasionally beer from the 7-Eleven when the sweaty, nearsighted guy was the only one working. Lynn took small canteens of her mother's gin to The Gunner House once or twice a month. More often than this, and more often than she liked to admit, Lynn was sipping from these canteens on her own. Sometimes to make a long day at school less tedious or to make the Christian network that her mother watched in the evenings straight-up hilarious. Sometimes for no reason at all except the simple fact that when she was sneaking sips of booze, she felt, quite frankly, the way a person was supposed to feel. It was like an *on* button.

Lynn started to sip before her lessons with Brent, too, realizing that it made her more clever and more confident. It made her playing less precise but more colorful.

They were about six months into their lessons when Brent announced to Lynn and her mother that he had been accepted into a PhD program in Cleveland and would be leaving town in May. It was April. Lynn was gutted. She asked her mother how far away Cleveland was.

At the first lesson after learning that Brent would be leaving, Lynn waited for her mother to leave the room. Then, instead of starting in to the passage that she was supposed to play, Lynn wiped her wet palms together and into her thighs. She opened her mouth to reveal herself to Brent. She had meticulously planned out her exact message, and imagined that she would reach the end and Brent would say, *Lynn*, wondrously, as though she were a mirage, his eyes shining; he would say, *Oh, Lynn, yes*. But now her message was a collection of words swimming aimlessly in her head, her whole script gone as loose and watery as old Jell-O: *too young, but . . . love . . . I know . . . I want . . . Cleveland . . . please . . .*

Brent stopped her after she had spoken only a single word, "I—" with a hand in the air between them. He adjusted his glasses and said, "Lynn, stop. I know you think you know what you want, but you don't."

"What?" Lynn's voice sounded to her own ears like a tiny toy. The wild heat between her legs instantly went cool and then dead.

"You think you want me," Brent said directly but not unkindly.

Then he lowered his voice and added, "And I can smell booze on your breath, young lady."

*Young lady!* Lynn threw her hands to her cheeks and began to cry immediately, mangled by shame. She shrieked insults at herself inside her head, as though there were two Lynns—one that was completely reasonable and knew all along that she was a child and of course Brent saw her that way, too. And another one that was so stupid it actually thought Brent might share her feelings, the attraction. She couldn't believe she had let the stupid one edge out the smart one. She couldn't believe the smart one had let this happen. *How could you be so stupid?* She screamed at both of them.

Brent retrieved a Kleenex and said, "You're going to get over this sooner than you think. I promise. But . . . take care of yourself. Okay? You're an *incredible* musician already. It'd be a shame if anything got in your way. If you got in your own way."

He helped Lynn compose herself before her mother returned. But when she did, Brent announced that there had been a change of plans and he would be leaving town earlier than anticipated—that today had been their last lesson.


Several weeks later, Lynn started taking lessons from another graduate student at Buff State, a female Brent had recommended.

Lynn forgot about her feelings for Brent soon after he left—he was right, she recovered from the humiliating incident quicker than she could have imagined—but she did not forget the feelings within herself that had been awakened. She began to explore her own body in private, especially after she'd had a few sips of gin, because alcohol heightened the electrifying sensation that when she touched between her legs she was powerless against her own power.

She began to wonder about the boys who were her friends, Jimmy and Sam and Mikey. She wondered if they had pubic hair yet and what their lips were like and if their penises got hard when they thought about her, or Alice, or Sally. And she even wondered about the girls; she wondered what Sally's slim body looked like without clothing, if those tiny breasts looked like breasts. She wondered what everyone around her was wondering.

# CHAPTER 7

Issa went to seek out a restroom before the service began, and Mikey observed Lynn as she reached up with her left hand to push red curls back from her face. Her belled sleeve fell loosely from wrist to elbow as she did this, exposing a little knot of waxy white scar tissue on her left inner forearm. Mikey tried to avert his eyes and suppress the pained twinge of deep discomfort, a vicarious instinct that always, for whatever reason, hailed from his groin.

Lynn had never gone into detail about her personal problems in her emails to the others over the years. Mikey recalled that an injury in Lynn's early twenties had prevented her from pursuing the piano competitively, and although she never fell completely out of touch, there were a few years when her emails were less frequent and less coherent, often containing some weirdly banal and clichéd message that she presented as deeply profound. *Dance like no one is watching. You have to look through rain to see the rainbow.* In recent years, Lynn was not bashful about her current role in leadership with AA, but it was clear that she hadn't wanted to provide the others with so much as a glimpse into her troubles until they had been sorted out.

Fortunately, Lynn's attention was elsewhere as Mikey's eyes

darted to and from her scarred forearm. She was gazing out over Mikey's shoulder, and cheerily announced, "Sam-Jam!"

Mikey followed Lynn to greet Sam at the coatrack.

Sam was ginormous. His blond hair had gone wispy at the crown. He wore a dark brown polyester suit, and a seam at his left shoulder had burst. His belly was a barrel. He looked puffy, kind, sad, and distracted. The pores on his nose were cavernous. His pink face cracked into a smile as he hugged his old friends. Sam's face had always worn emotion oversimplified, as plain as a puppet's.

Mikey felt tears blistering beneath his eyelids. Seeing the faces of both Lynn and Sam for the first time in over a decade filled him with longing and joy and some type of uncanny despair. It occurred to him, too, in that same moment and with nearly the same measure of despair, that he could not recall the last time he had been touched by another person.

Lynn said to Sam, "Did you drive all this way?"

Sam nodded. "Justine's sorry to miss it," he said. "She was gonna come but wasn't feeling up to it in the end."

Mikey said, "You drove all that way by yourself? You're south of Atlanta, aren't you?"

Sam said, "Got ten hours in yesterday, stayed in Ohio last night, only about five hours on the road this morning."

"Where'd you stay in Ohio?"

"Heck of a motel," Sam said. "Just outside Cincinnati. Place was decorated like a boat. The whole motel I mean, just like a big cruise ship from the outside, and the inside, the rooms all done up like a little cabin. Lifesaver things hung on the wall. The shower curtain a, like, what's the word? A *nautical* pattern, seashells on everything. Neat. You wouldn't believe the continental breakfast either. Waffle iron. You make your own." Sam clapped his hand over Mikey's shoulder. "How's life in Lackawannie?"

"It's good," Mikey said.

"Your pop still on Ingram?"

Mikey nodded. "Same house and everything."

Sam said, "You see much of him?"

"Every Sunday," Mikey said. "Not my favorite part of the week," he added.

Mikey knew that his childhood friends had always feared and disliked his father, who never raised a hand against any of them but who bristled noticeably at their presence in his home, spoke roughly to them. And there was always that vague smell of blood, blood beneath his father's fingernails, the suggestion of violence.

"How long are you in town?" Mikey asked Sam.

"I'll have to hit the road tomorrow morning. Got work Tuesday." Sam's lips were the same color of the flesh surrounding them.

Lynn said, "Us, too."

Sam said, "Awful nice of Jimmy, inviting us to the house for dinner and the night. Shame about his flight."

Mikey said, "Sounds like if they get him on the next one, he'll get in at Buffalo-Niagara around seven, out to the house by eight."

Lynn said, "Anybody know how Sally's mom is doing?"

Mikey shook his head. "Don't think I've seen her yet today . . . Not a hundred percent sure I'll know her if I do."

"What was her name?" Sam said softly. "Karen?"

"Corinne."

Alice had made a crack about Sally's mother once when they were young, pointing out to the others that Corinne "looked the way grapefruit juice tastes." She wasn't wrong, but Jimmy had jumped all over her for it, even though Sally wasn't present at the time. He said, "Don't do that. Sally's sensitive." Alice had snorted defiantly, but she hadn't brought it up again, at least not that Mikey could recall.

Lynn leaned forward. Her voice was a whisper, and it vibrated when she said, "Corinne mentioned depression in the obituary remarks, right?"

Mikey had finished his coffee, and he dug fingernail crescents into the lip of the Styrofoam cup. He said, "Seems that way."

Sam said, "No note, though."

Lynn said, "Sam, are you doing okay?"

Sam said, "Still reeling. But . . ."

An organ had begun to play inside the sanctuary, and Issa had rejoined them.

Lynn said, "Should we go in and grab a seat?"

The four of them filed into a pew.

Mikey felt his whole body go languid and loose as a wrung-out rag the moment he sank into a seated position. He had slept poorly the night before, fitfully, waking many times with a dry throat and racing heart and the sensation that he had been panting and running like hell through his dreams, but not sure if he had been running toward something or away from it. Next to him, Sam smelled of a hair too much cologne and stale sweat, presumably from a previous occasion when he had worn this same suit.

# CHAPTER 8

Sam introduced the others to Blackout when he was twelve. He had been taught the game by his weird older cousin, Marcus. Marcus spent several weeks at Sam's house every summer because he was a freak whose own parents couldn't stand him, or at least that's what Sam's mother always said before Marcus arrived and after he had left.

Marcus had left town that afternoon, and Sam pulled the mattress to the center of the floor in The Gunner House that evening, announcing that he was going to teach them Blackout.

"You make yourself pass out," Sam explained. "I've been doing it all week with my cousin. It's the biggest high. It's really scary."

Jimmy said, "How do you do it?"

"You get on your hands and knees like this . . ." Sam moved to the center of the mattress and crouched on it, his big bottom balanced on his ankles. "Then you hyperventilate a hundred times"—he demonstrated this now, whooshing breath in and out vigorously—"and then you do this—like, you bear down like you're taking a poo, go really tight in your head . . ." Sam did this for a moment, his face quickly going red. "Then you're out. You have like a crazy dream, like a super vivid, realistic dream, and wake up in a minute and have no clue where you're at for a little bit."

Alice said, "Sounds pretty friggin' stupid to me."

Alice was already out of sorts that night. Earlier in the day, Jake had pissed all over her collection of *New Mutants* comic books, so the pages were soft and smelled like pee and the colors were all bleeding together. She had spread them out all over the floor of The Gunner House in the hopes that they might be salvageable once dry.

Sam said, "Screw you, it's actually like . . . really cool, Alice. You just don't want to like it because it's my thing."

Mikey said, "It sounds scary. Does it make your brain go bad?"

Sam gave Mikey a condescending look. "Make your brain go bad? No, it doesn't make your brain go bad."

Jimmy offered, "Well, it probably kills a bunch of brain cells."

Alice smirked in Sam's direction. "That would explain a lot."

Sam struggled the most of all of them in school, barely passing classes and stuttering like a broken lawn mower when asked to read aloud. He said, "Screw you, Alice," and glanced around the room to see how others were responding to the dig.

Lynn said, "I'll try it." Although Lynn was usually fairly quiet, it was not uncharacteristic of her to be the first to try something. A year earlier, she had been the one to introduce alcohol to the group, filling a canteen with her mother's gin while her mother napped one afternoon and delivering it triumphantly to The Gunner House that evening.

Sam instructed Lynn once again, "Try to remember your dream."

The other children watched as Lynn crouched on the mattress and began to hyperventilate. She was wearing jeans and a tie-dyed tank top. Her forehead was drizzled with a trail of acne beneath the red curls. The sound of her labored breath began to disturb Mikey, and he tried to think of other things. Then Lynn sat upright and closed her eyes, her face and neck went tight, and several seconds later, everything went very soft. She fell back onto the mattress, wearing a blank and peaceful expression.

The others watched in silence.

After a bit, Sally said, "Should we wake her?"

Sam said, "She'll be up soon."

Mikey felt afraid. "Is she breathing?" he said.

"Yes, duh," Sam said, although he didn't seem entirely certain.

Soon enough, Lynn's eyes fluttered open. She rose and stared around the room. She blinked. She gave a quick smile and said, "Hm."

Sam said, "I told you guys so. I told you guys it was cool."

Alice said, "What was it like?"

Mikey said, "Was it like you were dead?"

"No . . ." Lynn said. She was quiet for a bit, then she said, "It was like I was alive then, and I'm dead now."

Sam said, "See, you guys? I told you."

Sally said, "What did you dream?"

Lynn said, "I dreamed I was playing a concert on a big stage and that guy from school who comes to fix the vending machine when your chips get caught . . . You guys know who I mean, right? He always smells like KFC? Anyway, he was my page-turner, sitting next to me on the piano bench, and in the dream, I think, he did not smell like KFC. But anyway, I was wearing a black velvet dress." Lynn's face was bright and animated as she recalled the dream. "I really . . . it was *so real*." She turned to Sam. "You're right . . . it was the realest dream I've ever had."

Sam said, "Who's going to go next?"

There was a brief and uncomfortable silence among the rest of them. Alice got up to check the progress on her comic books; then she returned.

Mikey said, "Are we having fun? Is this fun?"

Alice said, "Why do you always ask that?"

Sometimes Mikey felt like he was watching his friends through binoculars, even when they were right before him.

Sam said, "Alice, you always say my ideas are stupid. Why don't you actually try it, then? Unless you're too scared."

"Fine, I'll go, you turd, if it'll get you to shut up."

Alice took Lynn's place on the mattress. She was wearing overalls over a wifebeater, and a backward hat. Mikey wished he were wearing that, too. Instead, he was in denim cutoff shorts and a T-shirt with Garfield on the front and a plate of lasagna on the back.

Alice hyperventilated for many counts. Then she rose, clenched her muscles for a brief time, and wilted backward, just as Lynn had minutes earlier.

Silence. Thirty seconds. A minute.

Lynn finally said, "Was I out this long?"

Sally shook her head. "I don't think so."

Mikey said, "Do you think she's okay?"

Sam said, "You guys are such worrywarts."

It was quiet for a bit. Then Jimmy said, "It *has* been longer than Lynn, you guys."

Lynn said, "Is she breathing?"

Sam said, "She's totally fine."

Mikey stared at Alice's empty face. He said, "Are you sure?"

Jimmy said, "Yeah, are you sure?"

Sam leaned over Alice, briefly examined her face, and said sarcastically to the others, "Would you like me to see if she's breathing?"

Mikey was scared. He *did* want to know if she was breathing.

Sam said, "Well, okay, *fine*." He leaned down into Alice's face and put an ear to her mouth.

Alice immediately came to life with a blood-curdling shriek, directly into Sam's ear, and he was so startled he fell backward off the mattress, rolling lopsidedly onto the hardwood floor like an egg and panting. Alice sat up, boiling over with laughter.

The rest of them began to laugh, too. They laughed and laughed, relieved and jump-scared, tickled by Alice's trick.

Lynn said, "But it worked, right? You passed out first, right? Or were you just pretending the whole time?"

Alice said, "It did work. I just, when I woke up, I decided to pretend for a little bit to try and scare you guys."

Sally said, "What was your dream when you passed out? Can you remember?"

Alice said, "I did dream. Hang on, let me try to remember."

She closed her eyes, and shortly, something dark passed over her face. She said, "Oh," quietly. "Oh."

Lynn said, "Do you remember?"

Alice nodded.

"What was it?" Mikey said.

Alice didn't respond. Her eyes were still closed.

"What did you dream?" Sally said.

Alice opened her eyes. "I dreamed that something bad happened between us."

Sally stared at her. "Between you and *me*?"

"Between all of us. I dreamed that we weren't friends anymore."

It was very quiet for a bit as they all thought about this.

Then Jimmy said, "It was just a dream, Alice."

And she said, "But it felt so real."

# CHAPTER 9

Inside the sanctuary, it smelled of mildew, cologne, and spent matches. An elderly woman played the organ beautifully, and Mikey stared into his program, which did not contain a photograph of Sally, just the same words that had been offered in her public obituary, several lines of scripture, and the list of funeral service proceedings. Many flower arrangements were lined up across the front of the sanctuary. Massive tiger lilies, bundles of peach roses, pink hydrangeas, a wreath of snow-white roses and mini carnations and cushion poms and chrysanthemums, pale yellow freesia and alstroemeria.

Abruptly, Mikey felt a stiff pinch in his shoulder, near the base of his neck at a nerve, and he squirmed. He turned to see that Alice was settling herself into the pew behind him. He had to crane his neck around fully in order to accommodate the new blind spots in his right eye and get a good look. Alice imitated this gesture, his neck swivel, with added panache. Alice had always had a special talent for noticing the things about you that you most wished to hide from the world. How wonderful, Mikey thought, that this quality had carried over into adulthood.

She leaned forward to kiss Mikey's hair and ruffle it a bit, and she wrapped her arms around him in a warm hug. Her eyes were dark and bright, her broad, high cheeks flushed, her dark wavy hair pulled into a loose and messy braid. Mikey judged her to be at least six feet tall, which would mean she had grown another few inches after high school. She wore a black turtleneck sweater and navy fleece vest over her broad shoulders. Mikey was very conscious of cat hair on his own clothing—he had several lint rollers, including one in his car—so he could not help noticing now that Alice's dark clothing was covered with little white animal hairs, some of which transferred to his own shoulders when she hugged him.

Alice was accompanied by a stunning and younger-looking woman with platinum-blond hair and bright red lips. Alice waved hellos to the others in the bench; then she squeezed Mikey's neck affectionately a second time and said, "Hiya, pal."

He patted her hand. "Hi, pal," he said, and fought not to wince under her grip.

Moments later, Mikey heard Alice working some piece of gum or candy out of its wrapper behind him. She passed forward a little card with foil packets. "Gum?" she whispered. "My breath is always *the worst* in church. Like something deep in my gut just *died* when it realized where I was."

Mikey took the card and was about to help himself to a piece when he noticed that it was Nicorette.

He turned to pass the Nicorette back to Alice, and he saw Corinne, who was making her way up the center aisle. She was bent and tiny, a black shawl wrapped fully around her head, from crown to chin. Gray cheeks, a feathery pattern of wrinkles at her pale eyes, thin lips straight across and tight, a perfect hyphen, her posture oddly shaped and off-kilter, like an injured bird. She was closely followed by several more similar-looking older folks who Mikey guessed to be siblings or cousins.

Mikey's eyes fell to Alice as Corinne passed, and Alice's face was stretched open with grief, eyes dark, but she shed no tears. It suddenly occurred to Mikey that for all their many years of friendship, he had never once seen Alice Clancy cry.

The snowfall had grown heavier throughout Sally's service, and the sidewalk needed to be shoveled once again. A rosy-cheeked kid in a green knit cap and Carharrt overalls was clearing a path from the church to the parking lot.

Jimmy had provided everyone with directions to the lake house. He said that normally it would be a fifteen-minute drive from the church, but it might take about twice that if the forecast was as bad as it looked. He warned them about the steep descent from the road down to the parking area at the house.

Sam and Lynn said they were both going to make a quick stop in at their own parents' homes while they were in town but would be on time for dinner at six o'clock.

Alice and Mikey would go directly to the lake house.

Alice's girlfriend had ducked into the restroom right after the service, so Alice and Mikey walked out to his car together. Salt crunched beneath their feet, and the cold air tasted like metal.

When they reached Mikey's car, Alice took him by his shoulders and studied his face for a moment. "You haven't aged a day, you evil son of a bitch," she said. "I never noticed it before, but you look an awful lot like that actor. The younger brother. You know who I mean? The older brother's handsomer, no offense, and more famous. You know who I'm talking about?" She stomped her foot impatiently and stared at him with her mouth open, a warm red cave. "*Come on* . . . They both have woman problems . . . Older one screwed the nanny, and the younger one got himself in some kind of trouble, too. Slapped some girl's behind or something . . ."

Mikey shrugged with his eyebrows.

"Anyhow," Alice said. "You look exactly like that younger fella, except that you're blond and freckled-up. Otherwise you're a dead ringer." She paused to lick her thumb and smooth it over Mikey's cowlick. "And look at me!" she said. "Big fat old shitbag. I'm a beast. You know how I know I got fat?"

"You're not fat."

"Because of your face. Yes! That look right there. Picture paints a thousand words."

Mikey laughed. Alice reached for his glasses. He helped her release them from behind his ears.

"When'd you get these?" She put them over her own eyes, squinted, and grimaced. She opened one eye, then the other, and pointed at the right lens. "This one's like looking through the freakin' Hubble. How come you have perfect vision in your left eye and you're blind as a bat in the right?"

"Other way around. I'm blind in my left eye," Mikey said. "That's why there's no prescription. Only *partly* blind on the right."

Alice took off the glasses and stared at him. "So *that's* what's up with the snake-charmer dance." Alice once again imitated Mikey's neck swivel. "When did this happen?"

"It's always been."

She stared hard into his left eye. "How did I not know this when we were little?"

"So many people to mock, so little time, I imagine."

Alice laughed. "Don't be mad," she said. "It's my love language."

Alice handed his glasses back to him and gestured toward Mikey's car. "You safe behind the wheel, Mister One-Eye? And you all right in that little Civic? You don't even have tire chains put on. I can drive you to Jimmy's if you want."

"I've been driving this sort of car in this sort of weather for as long as I've been driving. And with only one eye, too."

Alice said, "I need to ask a favor." She reached for Mikey's hand, took his index finger, and guided it to a spot deep at the back of her jawbone where it met her neck.

"I've got a hair," she said. "One thick black one. Grows right out of here. Do you see it? Do you feel it?"

Mikey leaned closer. He said, "It's very short, though. I'm never going to be able to get it with my nails. I'd need tweezers."

"Damn!" Alice said. "Christine refuses to get it for me. I think she thinks it's the loving thing to do, pretend it doesn't exist. It makes me *crazy*. I'm like, 'Babe, I know it's there. Just pull it out!' Instead, I have to wait until it's long enough for me to do myself, and I'm telling you, thing grows like a weed. It'll be an inch long in a week, and half the time I forget about it altogether until it's like . . . a *disturbing* length. *Grrrrr.*"

Alice was quiet for a moment. Then abruptly she let out a single noise that sounded like a sob tucked within a cough.

Mikey said, "Are you okay?" He paused. "I could probably get that hair without a tweezers if I really tried."

Alice barked out a laugh. "I appreciate you," she said. She shook her head out violently and cough-sobbed again, a wild sort of noise. She said, "I can't believe Sally's gone. I don't know why it still has to feel so . . . Jimmy sounded so weird when he called me the other day. Like . . . *really* weird. It's all very . . . Anyway, I can't stop thinking . . ." Alice's voice tapered off to silence.

"Me, too," Mikey said.

It was quiet for a bit.

"I don't know what to say," Mikey said. "What should I say?"

Alice sniffed. "Yo-ho-ho," she said. She threw her braid over her shoulder. Mikey had always been impressed with Alice's ability to fly in and out of intense emotions without even touching ground.

A gust of wintry air hit Mikey's face like a slap. "It's good to be together now," he said.

Alice stared out over the white landscape for a moment. Smoke rose from the roof of the Chinese-owned laundry down the street. Snowflakes lifted and swirled and danced. The roof of the church was practically in shreds, lashed to pieces by lake-effect storms. Women in thick-heeled pumps and wool coats clutched at the black wrought-iron rail while making their way down the steps of the church entryway. People pressed against each other as they exited the church, as though they couldn't escape fast enough. It seemed there were twice as many people leaving the church now than had attended the service itself. And it occurred to Mikey that, outside of his friends, he hadn't seen anyone under the age of fifty at the service.

Mikey said, "It's good to be together now."

"You just said that," Alice said. "I heard you the first time."

"Did I?"

Alice nodded.

Mikey knew he had a habit of doing this, often unconsciously: repeating things he believed to be true. It made him feel safe. Sure-footed. Gave him a pleasing little jolt.

Alice's broad cheeks were flamed red with cold. No makeup surrounded her large black eyes beneath thick black eyebrows that were sharply arched, giving her the look of constant excitement.

Mikey said, "How tall are you anyway?"

"Six one. You wanna know how much I weigh, too?" Alice touched a small pimple on her chin and said, "I can't remember if I put my worms in the fridge."

"Excuse me?"

"I do my own worm-picking."

"*Worm-picking?* Like out of the ground?"

"No, out of my butt."

Mikey laughed. "Okay, but is this something I'm supposed to have heard of?"

"I guess you wouldn't've, not being in the biz. I pick my own worms 'cause the vendors'll gouge you," she explained.

"Ah, for your marina."

Alice nodded. She ran her finger over the roof of Mikey's car, collecting a fingerful of snow, and she put this in her mouth.

"What does this entail?"

"Two to four in the morning," Alice said. "Out in the woodlands, that's where you'll find the best colonies. Now, this time of year, traipsing around in the snow, that's a different story. I don't get out near as often. It's such an ordeal. But when it all thaws out, early spring, that's the best time."

"How much do you haul in?"

"In one morning? Ten pounds, fifteen pounds."

"That's *all worms*? Or some soil, too?"

"Half and half. You need a fair bit of soil so they don't kill themselves gettin' all wrapped up in each other. They'd do that, you know, all that meat and muscle. Clamping together till they squeeze the life right out of each other." Alice clasped her fingers together to demonstrate.

"I get it," Mikey said, gently slapping her fingers apart. "So you think you left them out and unattended?"

"I just can't remember's the thing," Alice said. "I think I may have left a coolerful back in storage, right next to the water heater. Maybe I'll call Kevin, have him check."

"Is he one of your employees?"

Alice nodded. "The one and only. Looks after everything when I'm gone, but he's uppity, though, is the thing. Likes to point out my mistakes. That's why part of me just wants to leave it, so he doesn't have the pleasure of fixing my problem. Know what I'm saying? I could really go for a big piece of cheese right now. I'm about famished. I just found out I'm lactose intolerant, though. Did I tell you that? It's terrible. I'd've rather found out I have diabetes. At least *they* get to eat cheese. Right? Do they get to eat cheese?"

Mikey said, "Listening to you talk is like . . . Have you ever tried to ride a bucking bronco? I haven't, but I imagine . . ."

"Bronco? No way. But I *have* tried to ride one of those fake bulls in a dive bar," Alice said. "They're not meant for people my size." Alice scooped more snow from the roof of Mikey's car and ate it.

Alice's girlfriend was walking out of the church, and Alice waved her over. The young woman smoothed her hair and breathed into her fists as she jogged their way, though the high heels on her black leather boots slowed her down considerably.

Alice said to Mikey, "This is Chris. Yes," she added with a wry grin, "believe it or not, *she* dates *me*."

Chris was wearing a fitted black leather coat and black leather gloves and a very expensive-looking green scarf. She extended her hand to Mikey. Her bright lipstick had worn off a bit and was faded unevenly. Her hair was like white silk, eyes a pale goldish hazel, teeth very straight and very white. She looked like a million bucks, but the sort of *pretty* that was so pretty it was disappointing. You wanted a raised mole, a gap in the teeth.

Mikey shook her hand.

Chris said, "And you must be . . ." Her voice was so unexpectedly shrill that Mikey had to conceal a grimace.

Alice cut in, "For crying out loud, Chris, this is Mikey, of course! I've told you about him a million times! He's always been my favorite. And I've always been his."

Mikey laughed.

Alice said, "All right, let's check on old Finny and hit the road."

"Finny?"

"Finn's my husky," Alice explained.

"That's right." Mikey remembered from the emails. "He's in your car?"

Alice nodded. "He's from the arctic, loves the cold. Does just fine in this. Got him a pile of wool blankets in the back, anyhow. He's a hundred years old, and I won't go anywhere without him. And, *yes*, I cleared it with Jimmy that I'm bringing my old-ass dog to his place. What, ya think I was raised in a friggin' barn? Look at me like that . . ."

Mikey said, "I wasn't looking at you any kind of way, Alice."

"Am I annoying you already?" she said.

"Yes."

Alice threw her head back and laughed in big *ha*'s that released thick puffing clouds into the air before her face, which she waved away with her hand as they evaporated. "This is making me want a cigarette," she said, releasing a tight, slow stream through her lips.

Chris gave her a stern look and whined, "*Baaaabe.*"

Mikey's earholes practically seized up. That voice! Alice and Chris had been dating for a good little while, so Alice must have made her peace with it, Mikey concluded, although he couldn't quite imagine how, and it would be unlike Alice to make peace with any sort of thing at all.

Alice turned to Mikey. "Chris says smoking takes seven years off the average life span." Alice made a distasteful face and spat something, or nothing, into the snow at her feet. "I say so does worrying about things like the average life span."

"I'll see you guys over there," Mikey said. "Don't get lost. Jimmy said the driveway's steep and hard to find—start watching for it soon after you cross the train tracks."

Alice said, "Yo-ho-ho."

Before Mikey got into his car, he glanced back up toward the church, where Corinne stood at the entrance. She was directing a young man who carried flower arrangements in brown paper grocery bags to her old teal Chevy Chevette. Above Corinne's car, a grackle perched on a telephone pole was chewing out the sky, really laying into it. *Raw-raw-raw! Wah-wah! Car-car! War-war-war!*

# CHAPTER 10

Mikey's father left for work at seven o'clock every morning, roughly twenty minutes before the bus came by for Mikey. He always woke Mikey before leaving and left a bowl and a box of cereal on the table. Mikey was expected to rinse his dishes and lock the door behind him. If he ever missed the bus, and this did happen on rare occasions, he was instructed to let himself back inside and call his father at work; his father would leave work to return and deliver Mikey to school. When this happened, Mikey knew it was better to sit silently on the drive over rather than offer any sort of apology or excuse.

It was on one of these mornings when Mikey was eleven years old that diarrhea had delayed him and he didn't make it out on time. He watched as the bus rounded the corner at the far end of Ingram, the morning sun fierce in his eyes, his bottom still burning and pursed unpleasantly from his session on the toilet.

He turned to go back inside to make the dreaded phone call to his father's workplace when a woman's voice from the sidewalk called, "Hey, you! Barney Rubble!"

Mikey turned. It was the slim, silver-haired woman, Sally's mother. Although he and Sally had been best friends for years, he had spoken with Sally's mother only a handful of times. Of all The

Gunners, Sally's was the only home where they never, ever played. Nevertheless, it surprised him that she didn't know his name.

"Barney Rubble!" she called out again, approaching with her hand in the air, a sloppy but unthreatening wave. She wore a sheer, pale blue garment beneath an unzipped Buffalo Bills hoodie, and purple flip-flops. Her silver hair was in some extravagant sort of updo.

Mikey waved back, and she approached the porch.

"It's Mikey," he said, "not Barney."

"I know *that*," she said. "Gimme a little credit! You never seen *The Flintstones*?"

Mikey shook his head.

"Well, that makes me sad," she said, although it didn't seem to make her sad at all. "Barney Rubble's a blondie like you," she explained, rumpling his hair with her spidery fingers. "And he wears a shirt that same shade."

Mikey's plain brown T-shirt was part of a ten-piece rainbow pack from Kmart.

"Ya miss the bus?" The woman shared Sally's delicate, pretty features, but her skin had an unhealthy sheen, and her teeth were a grayish hue. Within clotted mascara frames, both the iris and white of her eyes seemed too close to yellow. There were tiny threads of blood in the inner corners of her eyes.

Mikey nodded.

"I'm Corinne, Sally's mom," she said. "I know you know me."

"I do." Mikey nodded again. "I met you before," he said.

"I know," Corinne said. "You want a ride to school? I've gotta head that direction to hit the tanning bed anyway."

Mikey considered this. He had been instructed many times to never, ever get into a car with a stranger, but given his long friendship with Sally, surely this woman could not be considered a threat.

Corinne reached out to tug on his shoulder, and she said, "Come on. You can wait inside while I put on pants. Then we'll head on over. We'll probably beat the bus, anyhow. They've gotta make all those stops."

Mikey took a seat at the kitchen table in the Forrest household and gazed around the room while Corinne disappeared into another part of the house. Dishes were stacked high within the sink and on the counter, food drippings and splatters on every surface. Ant traps and roach traps sat out in plain view. Balled-up underwear. The house smelled of garbage and perfume. The TV blared the gleeful meows of a cat food commercial in the next room. There was a plastic bear full of honey on the table, a tiny golden bulb gleaming at its yellow tip.

Corinne returned from her bedroom in jeans and a white tank top, with the same purple flip-flops and hairdo. She held a photograph in her hand and gazed at it fondly for a moment before handing it over to Mikey, and she said, "Lookie."

As Mikey took the photograph, he heard movement and a man's phlegmy cough from elsewhere in the house.

Corinne said, "That's Billy. He's trouble." She laughed indelicately, her chin high in the air, then said, "He's harmless."

Corinne pointed back down to the photograph in Mikey's hands.

The photograph featured a young, silver-haired girl draped over a tire swing and straddling it. She gazed at the camera with pouting, model-like intensity. The girl looked so much like Sally that at first Mikey thought it must be her but then realized from the fading and softened corners of the photograph that it was an old photograph and therefore was not of Sally but of her mother.

"Is it you?" he said.

Corinne nodded. "Don't we look alike? Me and Sally?"

Mikey nodded. "A lot."

Corinne said, "We could easy be twins, don't you think? We look so much alike."

Mikey nodded again.

"People tell us that all the time," Corinne said.

A head poked briefly around the corner into the kitchen. Billy's big pale face was potato-like, slothful and indistinct, completely devoid of curiosity. He said, "Your AC's broke."

Corinne said, "So fix it."

Billy shuffled away, and Mikey heard steps in the bathroom, then a thick torrent of pee.

Corinne turned back to Mikey, took the photograph from him, and stared at it under the light with an expression that briefly became complicated. Then she looked back at Mikey and said, "Do you want to see more?"

Mikey glanced at the clock on the wall. They really needed to leave soon or he was going to be late. Then the school would call his father, and then he could *really* be in much more trouble than if he had just called his father right away. Corinne followed his eyes to the clock and said, "I guess I need to get you to school, don't I? Well, this has been just fine."

Corinne walked Mikey back out to the street, where her Cutlass Supreme was parked. She turned on the radio and headed up Ingram toward Ridge.

Mikey wondered what Billy was up to back at the house, if he might do some of those dishes or help take the garbage out. He wondered if Billy was responsible for the mess.

Corinne sang along with the Beach Boys, utilizing vibrato on sustained notes and harmonizing with the chorus. She glanced over at Mikey. "Sally has a great voice, too," she said, "although I don't imagine she ever sings for you."

Mikey said, "Sometimes really soft."

Corinne was quiet for a bit. Then she said, "She's your favorite, isn't she?"

Mikey glanced at Corinne. "She's what?"

"Your favorite. She's the prettiest. You love her. You like her the best."

"Oh . . ." Yes, Mikey supposed maybe he did love Sally, although not for the reason Corinne had suggested. Not for the way that Sally looked, nor for the fact that she and her mother were "practically like twins." If he loved Sally, it was because Sally had been his first friend.

Corinne lowered her window, pulled a pack of cigarettes from the center console, and lit up, briefly removing both hands from the steering wheel in order to do so.

When they reached the school, Mikey could see across the lot that his bus was just pulling in as well. He had made it on time! His father would not receive a phone call; he would not have to endure that silent ride, his father's seething silence. He thanked Corinne for the ride. She was right; this had been just fine.

Corinne cheerily lit another cigarette and waved to him through the window once he had gotten out of the car, and she said, "Make sure you tell your dad what a good driver I am! Toodle-oo!"

Later that day, Mikey mentioned all of this to Sally, how her mother had offered him a ride, how he'd been in their home, how her mother had shown him a photograph from her own childhood.

Sally looked as if this information might make her cry, so Mikey quickly said, "Your mom is very nice."

Sally blinked and stared at Mikey for a moment. Then she said, "I guess she is nice. Okay."

Mikey sensed that Sally did not wish to discuss any of this further, so he decided not to ask her about Billy, who he was, and why Sally's mother had said that he was trouble and that he was harmless.

That weekend, Mikey was outside helping his father wash the car when Corinne walked up the street carrying a bag from the 7-Eleven. She waved to Mikey and his father as she passed their home. It occurred to Mikey that their house was not on the way back from the 7-Eleven; Corinne had passed her own home up the block in order to reach theirs.

She called out, "Hey, John, your kid tell you what a good driver I am?" She delivered this question almost like a taunt, each word barbed.

Mikey felt his face immediately go hot with blood. He had not told his father about getting a ride with Corinne.

She stood grinning with the plastic bag hooked through her elbow and swinging against her waist. She wore what looked like a very large men's work shirt over pink pajama pants and sneakers.

Mikey's father didn't say anything, but he gazed briefly at Mikey, whose deep flush confirmed the story, then back toward Corinne, dipping his chin ever so slightly in lieu of a spoken *thank you*.

When Corinne had passed, Mikey's father spoke to Mikey in a voice that was low and dangerous, like an idling motor: "Tell me what happened."

Mikey told him everything, and at the end of his account, he added that Corinne had not once exceeded the speed limit on the drive over.

His father wrung out the sponge in his hands. Soapy water

plummeted to the paved driveway and landed with a singular and definitive splat.

His father said with lips curled and mean, "I don't want you going into that house again."

Mikey was hurt by the tone of his father's voice. He wanted to point out that Sally never invited him into her house, so he would have no reason to return anyway. He wanted to point out that it had all worked out just fine; he'd gotten to school on time without his father having to leave his workplace to drive him. And wasn't that a good thing? Couldn't they focus on that? He wanted to point out that Alice's big brother had driven Mikey to school several times, and *his* car smelled like what Alice said was a weed smell, like actual drugs, and *he* went fifty in a thirty-five.

Mikey blinked rapidly to prevent tears from spilling over onto his cheeks. He hated himself for being so easily hurt by things he didn't understand. What a wimp. As Mikey reached for the chamois to start drying the windows of his father's car, he felt resentment ripple up through him as black and dirty as tar. *Sally's mom is nicer than you,* he thought scornfully toward his father. *I like her better.* Mikey thought these words over and over, not just about his father but *at* him, lobbing the words through the space between them like darts and hoping that, even though he didn't dare speak these sentiments aloud, they would reach his father and hurt him bad.

# CHAPTER 11

It was rare that Mikey was truly angry at one of his friends but not rare at all for some conflict to be smoldering between two of the others, with the most frequent clashes occurring between Sam and Alice. Sometimes it escalated to raised voices and name-calling, a slap or shove with no real intent of injury, angry tears scooped up by a shirtsleeve. Sometimes it culminated with a dare. Alice was the only one to ever spend the night alone at The Gunner House, and it was because Sam provoked her.

They were all at the house together one evening, playing Hearts and passing a bottle of Popov around and around and around the circle. Alice was fourteen years old. It was summertime—they had no school in the morning, so their parents were happy to have them out of the house and seldom took notice of their activities unless they were out past nine or ten.

On this day, Babcia had offered the children half of a cheesecake, two poppy seed rolls, and a tray of spiced candies in tiny paper cups, which they had nearly finished. Their sugary fingers adhered to the playing cards. The windows were open, and there was a slight breeze that was not cool. A soupy dusk settled in, bathing the room in a soft, submarine light. Alice was quite drunk.

The subject of ghosts came up—Lynn had just watched *The*

*Shining* for the first time. They continued to play cards as they discussed this movie and others featuring paranormal experiences.

Alice announced that she didn't believe in ghosts and that horror movies bored her.

It was Sam's turn to play a card. His blond hair was darkened by sweat around his temples. He tossed a jack into the middle of the floor and said, "You know there's a ghost in this house, right?"

Alice reached for the plastic bottle of Popov and squeezed a small pinch into her mouth.

"I've seen it," Sam said. "A few times. So has Jimmy."

*"Pfft!"* Alice spat vodka from her lips and laughed. Several others laughed, too, and Jimmy did not confirm or deny that he had seen the ghost.

Sally said, "What does it look like?"

"Hard to say," Sam said. "It's always in the shadows."

The others paused the game to stare at Sam in a way that annoyed Alice. She disliked it when anyone else took control of the room.

"Funny, funny, funny," Alice said. She played her ace and collected the pile of cards.

Sally started a fresh hand with a six of spades. She picked up the final candy and said, "Where'd you see it?"

"Upstairs," Sam said. "I've seen it through the window before. That's where Jimmy saw it, too."

Sam was really pissing Alice off now. "You're an ass-butt," she said. She gripped the corner of her thumbnail between her teeth, ripped it off in a clean half-moon, tasted salt and something intensely bitter.

Mikey turned to Sam. "How many times have you seen it?"

"Oh, *come on*," Alice said. "He's just messing with you. Sam, quit messing with him."

Mikey said, "I'm just curious." He chewed his bottom lip for a moment then said softly, as though issuing an apology, "I think maybe I've seen it, too."

Alice tossed her head back, rolling her eyes. Since she felt the most protective of Mikey, it offended her the most when he defied her.

Sally received the bottle of Popov and sent it around to her left.

Jimmy grabbed the bottle by its neck and said, "It's true, you guys, the ghost is real. But I get the feeling it's scared of us." He took a sip of vodka.

Sally said, "What if ghosts think *they're* the real ones, and *we're* the dead ones? And that's why they're so scared of us?"

Lynn said, "I wonder if the ghost is the one that used my hairbrush. I left it here one night, and the next day it was sitting at the wrong end of the room."

Alice made a talking puppet with her hand. "Blah, blah, blah!" she said, her voice angrier and more percussive than she intended. "I suppose you've *all* seen the ghost, haven't you? Shared a beer with it, have you? Watched it take a shit?"

Sally giggled, and this pleased Alice.

Sam turned to Mikey and said, "Three times. That's how many times I've seen it. And I can always tell when it's here."

"Is it here now?" Lynn asked.

Sam closed his eyes and held up a hand, demanding silence.

Moments later, he opened his eyes and confirmed, "Yes. It is here."

Jimmy nodded in agreement.

Lynn made a small noise and captured her bottom lip under her teeth.

Alice had lost complete control of this situation and was now very angry. She said, "Shut up, all of you, would you please?"

It was unlike Jimmy to conspire against Alice with Sam this

way, even though Jimmy and Sam were best friends. It occurred to Alice that while Sam was clearly just trying to provoke her, Jimmy might actually believe the ghost was real.

Sam turned to Alice. "Why don't you spend the night here by yourself if you don't believe it, if you're so brave?"

Sam was the only one in the group who ever challenged Alice outright when she was already mad, and even that was rare enough that it still caught her off guard.

"No problemo," Alice said.

"When will you do it?" Sam said.

"I'll do it tonight if you're so worried about it."

A spider traversed the floor before Alice, and she flicked it with her index finger, really sent it soaring.

Jimmy said to Sam, "Cool your jets, man. She doesn't have to do it." Then Jimmy looked at Alice. "You don't have to do it."

Alice ignored him and turned to Sally. "I'll tell my mom I'm going to be at your house," she said, "if anybody asks."

Sally nodded. It was a safe bet and had worked before—Alice's mother disliked Sally's mother (all of their mothers disliked Sally's mother) and would never seek her out to confirm the story.

"I'll go home right now, tell my mom I'm going over to your place, pack my bag, and spend the night here," Alice said.

"How will we know?" Sam said.

"Know what?"

"How will we know you spent a whole night—that you didn't just go home later?"

Alice scowled at him. "Whoever doesn't believe me can show up, any time of the night. I'm gonna lock the door to keep the raccoons out, but you can peek right in the window, see for yourselves, or give a knock. I'll stay until dawn, so if you don't believe me, come on down and pay me a visit."

She sent a mean look around the circle. Sam was grinning. He was pleased with himself—he had gotten under her skin, and he knew it. Alice shoved her middle finger up into the air between them.

Then she screwed the cap back onto the bottle of Popov and rolled it over toward one of the mattresses at the side of the room. She would save the rest of the liquor for later that night, to put herself to sleep. The sound the plastic bottle made rolling gently across the hardwood floor was hollow and cool, like a conch to the ear.

Alice returned to The Gunner House an hour or two later. The others had all gone home for the night. In her backpack, she had a Buffalo Bills throw pillow, a sandwich, a flashlight, a Snickers bar, a disposable camera, a bottle of Coke, and the latest issue of *Time* magazine. She identified the least smelly mattress, which she would sleep on. She paged through the magazine, ate the sandwich, and swallowed Popov until she was nearly blind. Then she stumbled outside for a final pee.

Back inside, Alice locked the front door with the dead bolt. It provided the only access to the house—the back door was fully boarded over.

She lay down with the throw pillow at her cheek, her backpack on the ground next to her, and slept almost immediately.

Alice woke to soft yellow sunlight through the east window and sat up on the mattress. She rubbed her eyes. She was parched, and nauseous. She reached for the warm Coke and guzzled half the bottle. She stared around the room. *That was nothing,* she thought. *I could do it for a week!* That's what she would report to her chickenshit friends later. She threw the empty bottle of Popov across the room so it plunked off the far wall, and this sound activated a terrible headache. She ate the Snickers bar. She stuffed the pillow into her backpack and went home, eager to report the experience to her friends.

It was a success—they were all very impressed. Alice was the hero and the center of attention, and nobody said another word about that ghost.

Several months later, when Alice had filled up her disposable camera, she dropped it off at the neighborhood Rite Aid where Lynn's mom worked. The film was packed with summer adventures: long days at Woodlawn Beach, Lynn's piano recital, backyard fires, Jimmy's infected toe, a baby goat at the Erie County Fair, an impressive stash of empty liquor bottles at The Gunner House.

The next day, Alice paid for her developed photographs and took them home. She opened the pack in her room and leafed happily through the prints.

Two-thirds of the way through the pack, Alice reached a photo that immediately sent ice whooshing through her. She stared at the photo. It was of her, sleeping on the mattress at The Gunner House, backpack unzipped and on the ground next to her, Buffalo Bills throw pillow at her cheek, hands clasped at her chin, flash activated so that her white body shone.

Her chest tightened and went hot with the effort of not screaming. Her heart slammed out of her ears. She stared at the photo of her sleeping self and felt the urge to vomit, so she ran to the bathroom and was unable to empty herself, but she heaved and coughed until her throat roared with pain.

Sally's words about ghosts from months earlier sprang fresh to Alice's mind now. *What if ghosts think* they're *the real ones, and* we're *the dead ones?* Then she thought of something Lynn had said years ago, the first time they had played Blackout. Alice had never forgotten the moment when Lynn woke from her dream and said, *It was like I was alive then, and I'm dead now.* Alice's chin was still bobbing just above the toilet bowl as she thought about the way her pale body looked in that photo—wan, corpselike—and she considered the possibility that she was not alive and not real. She considered the possibility that somehow all of her friends had already discovered this; she was the last to know and the butt of the joke. The dead girl who still thought she was alive.

# CHAPTER 12

Jimmy was right about the driveway at the lake house—it was a steep and treacherous descent, and Mikey would have driven right past it had he not been advised to watch closely after crossing the train tracks. The house could not be seen from the road.

Once he had made his way back, Mikey could see that several vehicles were already parked and a clear path had been shoveled to the door.

The house was a massive and gorgeous timber A-frame. It looked magical and luminous, with tiny gold lights twinkling along the trim, smoke rising from the chimney, the frozen-over lake visible just beyond a large patio area that had already been cleared of snow. Mikey judged that the nearest houses were at least a quarter mile away in each direction—it was a sizable plot, and utterly enchanting.

He got out of his car as Alice was parking her Jeep next to him. He pulled a tray of croissants from his backseat—he had baked these that morning, for the group. For some reason, the croissants seemed stupid now. He decided to bring them in anyway, recalling Alice's hunger and not knowing if there would be anything to snack on before dinner.

Alice got out of her car, looking perturbed, her phone at her ear.

"You said a *lake cottage*, Jimmy," she said into the phone. "Not the freakin' Taj Mahal." She was quiet for a bit and rolled her eyes at Mikey. "If you say so," she said into the phone. "Safe flight . . . Right . . . I'm just saying . . . Yes, of course he's potty-trained, you dingus, but he's a dog, Jimmy. He's *got fur*, he's a *hundred years old*, he *has accidents* . . . Okay . . ."

Alice hung up her phone and said, "He's insisting we let Finn in even though this place is"—she lifted an arm and did a broad and grandiose gesture toward the house—"*this* kind of place."

Chris opened the door of the backseat, and she gently helped a large old husky out into the snow. Finn had one blue eye and one black eye, both of them watery and low-lidded, and a mottled tongue, long and limp as a noodle. He was mostly gray with a few black and caramel patches. His fur looked a few sizes too large for his frame, and he seemed uncertain on his thin legs in the deep snow. Mikey ran a knuckle over Finn's skull, and Finn leaned his head up at a sharper tilt. "Good old boy," Mikey said. "Good old boy."

"Not *that* old," Alice said. "Give the guy a complex."

Chris said, "My mom has a Chihuahua so old it has no teeth left, and she has to feed it through a squeezy tube, like Go-Gurt."

Mikey laughed, and Chris did not.

A distant train whistle sounded, howling mournfully over the snowy landscape.

Alice, Chris, Mikey, and Finn entered the home through a side door that opened directly to the kitchen, where they were greeted by several caterers who were scuttling between hot pans and cutting boards. It smelled magnificent—meat and rosemary and garlic and sweet balsamic.

One of the caterers introduced herself and pointed them toward the bar. "Jimmy said to help yourselves to everything," she said.

Mikey thanked her and hung his coat. Alice shook snow out of her dark hair and looked around the room and said, "Good God!"

Alice was wearing men's work boots, and she knelt now to unlace them. She took off her fleece vest and used it as a rag to remove snow and mud from Finn's paws. Chris's scarf was wrapped as elaborately as a turban, and she unfurled it, then unzipped and removed her stylish black coat and black boots. Under all that black leather, she wore an eggplant-colored sweater over skintight dark jeans.

They walked from the kitchen through the dining room, where a glass table was already elegantly set for seven, then out into the main room, which was massive and had floor-to-ceiling glass windows facing the lake. A gorgeous baby grand piano gleamed on the far side of the room, and several cream-colored leather couches surrounded a mahogany coffee table. Chris went to the piano and ran her finger over the keys, the whole way from bottom to top, then top to bottom, ending on a resonant bass note.

Alice went to the bar, grabbed a bottle of wine without reading its label, and used a corkscrew attached to her key chain to open it. She brought this and three glasses to the coffee table in the main room. Mikey set the croissants there as well.

Alice poured three generous glasses, then stared at the bottle. "French," she said. She spun the glass with faux expertise, then lowered her face deep into the glass to sniff the wine. "It's got a French stench," she said.

She picked up a croissant and bit into the corner. She chewed rapidly, and buttery flakes adhered to her lips and chin.

She gazed at Mikey for a moment, then said, "Please take off your tie."

"Why?"

"I've never seen you in a tie. It's making me nervous."

Mikey loosened and undid his tie. He draped it over the back of the couch.

Chris said, "Babe, I'm gonna go pick us out a bedroom, drop our bags off. Something on the lake side, maybe? Then I'm gonna hop in the shower. I could use a freshen-up." She took her wine with her as she went to select a room.

Alice settled in next to Mikey on the couch and took a large swallow of wine. She said, "That service just about did me in. What a mess. Sally, old Sally. I just can't believe it. I won't. The Skyway. Somebody a few years older than us offed themselves there, too, didn't they? Not long after we started high school. You remember that?"

Mikey nodded. "There have been plenty of others, too. They've been talking about installing netting for years."

"Well, why the hell don't they? How many people are gonna have to throw themselves off the damn thing before they do?"

Alice stared angrily out the window at the lake. She ate more of her croissant.

Mikey said, "How many suicides do you think you actually prevent with a thing like that?"

"I see your point," Alice said. "Person who wants to *stop living* is gonna find a way." She paused and shivered, gripping her own elbows. Then she said, "This'll turn me into a sad sack, starting out the night this way. Tell me about your life, Mikey, would you? What's new? You ever get that sourdough to turn out?"

Mikey was frankly shocked that Alice remembered this. He had mentioned his sourdough starter only once in an email several months earlier.

He said, "I did, actually. Trial and error, but I ended up with one perfect loaf."

"What'd you do with it?" Alice said.

"Ate it."

"How?"

"One slice at a time."

"*Ha-ha*, funny, asshole. I mean *with what*? And *with whom*?"

"I had some leftover pork shoulder. Open-faced sandwiches with raspberry-cinnamon jam. All by my lonesome."

"Sounds like a hell of a meal to eat all by your lonesome."

"My cat was around." Mikey sipped his wine. "So how long have you and Christine been together?"

"Six months," Alice said. She leaned a little bit closer. "Six looooong months," she whispered.

"Why's that?"

"She's a millennial, Mikey. Do you know any?"

"What are we?"

"We're Gen Xers."

"What's the difference?"

"Millennials take themselves very seriously."

"Oh?"

"She fancies herself an *artiste*," Alice said this with a flip of her wrist. "They all do."

"She's not?"

"Pfft! You're not on Instagram, Mikey. You wouldn't understand."

He laughed. "So why are you still together?"

Alice shrugged mildly. "We have some good fun. Dating a young hot person is good for my self-esteem. And I think she thinks I'm . . . novel."

"You are novel," Mikey said.

"Am I?" Alice sipped her wine.

Mikey nodded. "Charismatic. Disturbing."

Chris was at the stairs behind them, and she called, "Babe, I put us in the master. Up the stairs, second door on your left."

Alice gave an *A-OK* sign with her fingers, over her shoulder, without turning around.

Finn settled himself at Alice's feet in a slow and careful maneuver that looked painful. Alice nuzzled him with her toes. She said to Finn, "I love you, old man." She looked up to Mikey. "Did you ever talk to Sally over the years?"

Mikey shook his head. "We passed now and then on the street, in a store. She still . . . nothing ever changed."

Alice took another large swallow of wine and leaned back into the couch. "You know, I never wanted to bring Sally up with you or the others, because it was so . . ." She paused, fidgeting, and reached down to touch Finn's head again, an involuntary comfort measure she seemed to require. "I wanted to ask you a million times over the years if you ever saw her, how she seemed. But it never came up. I never stopped wondering, though, never stopped wanting to ask."

"I wouldn't have had any answers for you, anyhow." Mikey hesitated, then said, "Do you think there's a chance Lynn or Sam or Jimmy knows more than we do? Why she left us the first time?"

Alice cracked her neck. "Do you think Jimmy's flight was really delayed or he's avoiding us? Maybe it's all his fault. Everything is Jimmy's fault. That's my story, and I'm sticking to it. In fact, he probably lured us all here to kill us and eat us up."

Mikey laughed.

Alice said, "I'm just bitter because I'm jealous of the guy. I mean, look around." Alice gestured dramatically toward their surroundings: the immaculately furnished room, the spectacular view of the frozen lake before them. "Rich bastard."

# CHAPTER 13

In the fourth grade, while Jimmy's classmates were struggling through multiplication of fractions, he discovered he was able to complete in half a minute a worksheet that took everyone else the entire class period.

Jimmy's teacher, Mrs. Perry, took notice and kept him after class to discuss this. She asked if he was being tutored at home—he was not—and what his parents did for a living. (His mother worked as a line cook at Mulberry's, and his father drove trucks.) She then asked if Jimmy would be interested in moving ahead with new lessons once or twice a week, one-on-one with her, definitely in math and potentially other subjects, too, and if, down the line, he would consider joining the class that was a year or two ahead of his own. Jimmy said yes to the one-on-one lessons and no to skipping a grade. He didn't want to be separated from The Gunners in his class, and he *definitely* didn't want the attention associated with moving ahead of his classmates in school. Jimmy already stood out more than he would've liked as the only Italian on a street full of Polish and Irish kids.

Jimmy's parents were both first generation, and sometimes The Gunners liked to stand at the windows of Jimmy's house and listen to his parents rant and gossip and sing in Italian. Then they would imitate them later in great lilting melodies, and although Jimmy knew this was not mean-spirited, the attention embarrassed him. It made him conscious of the difference between his parents and the other parents. Jimmy kept his thick black hair buzzed to an eighth of an inch against his scalp. He pronounced his very Italian last name in the most American way possible, and although his first name was Vincenzo, he introduced himself to everyone as Jimmy.

The Gunners received news of Jimmy's math lessons surprisingly well. He kept it hidden as long as he could but eventually ran out of excuses for his after-school meetings with Mrs. Perry. He stared intently at his Adidas soccer shoes, a half size too small and very narrow in the toe, as he delivered the information to the others that he was . . . *sort of smart* . . . and Mrs. Perry was sort of trying to . . . *advance* him.

Sam was the first to respond. "Does this mean you'll do our homework for us? Say yes, say yes."

Lynn said, "Say yes, say yes!"

Alice chimed in, "How long does it take you to do one of them worksheets?"

"A minute or two," Jimmy confessed. "Sometimes less."

"Holy crow! That *is* really fast."

Jimmy took on homework duty for The Gunners. He would stand over their shoulders in the evenings when they brought their assignments to The Gunner House, and dictate answers for them to enter in their own handwriting. On top of this, Jimmy created an elaborate cheating scheme for classroom tests by devising a numerical version of Morse code that allowed him to communicate with others in his classroom by rapping his pen against his desk to signify answers. It was a complicated code, though, and Sally was the only one who took the time to learn it.

Jimmy devoured algebra with Mrs. Perry, and then moved into precalculus with a different teacher.

Mrs. Perry was always badgering Jimmy to set up a meeting with his parents, and she reached out to them directly a few times, but they both worked full-time and spoke poor English. His parents could never make the meetings at school or even carve out the time for a proper phone call. By the end of Jimmy's seventh-grade year, he was doing college-level math coursework.

One afternoon when Jimmy was thirteen, his after-school advanced theory class went long and he was late arriving at The Gunner House. Alice said, "So what are they teaching you in your fancy classes anyway? How to turn water into wine? How to make your shit not stink?"

Jimmy laughed. "We talked about paradoxes today."

"Para-what?"

"It's like a statement that's logical but contradicts itself in some way."

Sally was combing through her hair with her fingers. She said, "So it's both right and wrong at the same time?"

"Sort of."

Alice said, "Say one."

Jimmy said, "Okay. There's a crocodile who has taken a mom's kid. The crocodile tells the mom, *I'll give you back your kid if you correctly predict whether or not I give your kid back.* So, what happens if the mom says, *I predict you will not give my kid back*?"

Sam blinked at him. "Then the crocodile eats the kid, duh."

Alice said, "But the crocodile *just said* he'll give it back if she guesses right, you dummy."

"Okay," Sam frowned. "So then the crocodile gives the kid back."

Jimmy said, "But then he's violating his own terms, because the mom's prediction was wrong. See, there's no logical solution. That's what a paradox is."

Sam said, "I *hate* this."

Sally said, "Tell us another one."

Jimmy said, "Okay. The Abilene paradox has to do with group behavior. It's when everyone tries so hard to accommodate everyone else that no one ends up getting what they want."

Alice said, "Explain."

"You have this family sitting around. The dad says, *Should we go to Abilene for dinner?*"

"What's Abilene?"

"It's a city in Texas. But that's beside the point."

Alice said, "Why in God's name would anyone want to go to *Texas*? Bunch of dog-diddlers."

Mikey said, "What's that?"

"Somebody who diddles dogs," Alice said. "You know . . . like . . ." She screwed one finger into her other closed fist.

Lynn cried, "Gah-*ross!*"

"Hold up," Jimmy said. "So, the mom says, *Sure, that sounds like a nice idea, doesn't it?* And she looks at the son, who says, *Sure,* and the sister says, *Sure, that sounds nice.* So they go to Abilene for dinner. Then they get back home, and somebody says, *That wasn't fun. I would have preferred to stay home.* Then they look around and realize that all four of them would have preferred to stay home. So then they can't figure out why they went on a trip that no one wanted to go on."

"So why *did* they?" Sally said.

Sam said miserably, "I don't get this."

Lynn snapped, "What's the point of this?" Lynn's moods were confounding these days. At any given moment, she could go from grouchy and distracted to giddy and overly emotive to stormy and subdued with no warning and for no apparent reason.

Sally said, "I want to understand."

Jimmy explained, "The paradox is that because people want to do what the group wants to do, they might act against what they want individually. But if every single person is doing that, *no one* is getting what they want."

It was quiet for a bit.

Sally said, "Are we like this?"

Mikey asked her what she meant.

Sally said, "Do we ever do things we don't really want to do?"

Alice said, "Well, I know *I* don't. I make sure at least *one* of us is getting what she wants."

Sally laughed. "Tell us one more, Jimmy."

"The service recovery paradox," Jimmy said.

"What does it mean?"

"It means a customer is likely to have a higher opinion of a company after the company corrects a bad service than if there was no problem in the first place."

Lynn said, "You mean people think something's better if it's fixed than if there was never anything wrong?"

Jimmy nodded.

Sam whined, "Can we puh-*lease* play cards now? This isn't even *math*."

Lynn said, "Is there any of that Glen's left?"

"The vodka from the other night?" Alice said, "No, we finished that over the weekend. Don't you remember?"

Sam said, "My uncle Randy's coming tomorrow. He usually brings over like three cases of beer and a ham and these cleaning supplies he tries to sell to my mom, and he sticks around for about a week. I can probably snag a few of his beers."

Alice said, "My brother's dating some girl who's in college. She has those mutant kind of thumbs, and I don't like her. But I'll be real nice and ask her if she'll buy us something. We'll have to give her money, though."

Sally said, "What if the mom predicts that the crocodile will give her kid back?"

They all looked at her. "What?"

"If the mom predicts that he'll give the kid back, then the crocodile has to give the kid back, right?"

"No," Alice said, her face lighting up as she understood. "Remember? He only has to give it back if the mom guesses right. So if she says he's going to give it back, he can still eat the kid without breaking his promise. It works either way."

Jimmy nodded. He turned to Sally. "Do you get it?"

Sally nodded. "Okay."

As the deck of cards was retrieved and conversation strayed to other topics, Jimmy noticed that Sally seemed to linger on her thoughts. Jimmy knew Sally, and Sally's secrets, well enough to imagine what she was thinking about. He wanted to take Sally's hand, but he didn't dare offer this gesture in front of the group. What the two of them shared could not be made known to the others. Still, he was pleased that she liked his paradoxes. He would tell her more later that night, when it was just the two of them.

Since Sam struggled the most in school out of all of them, Jimmy was puzzled when, in early spring of their junior year of high school, Sam suddenly refused Jimmy's help. Sam stopped bringing his homework over to The Gunner House. He laughed less at Jimmy's jokes and wouldn't meet his eyes. There seemed to be a quiet anger, something just below the skin.

Jimmy felt rejected and confused. Sam was his first friend within the group, and for ten years, they had watched Buffalo Bills games together at Jimmy's house, in the wood-paneled den with green shag carpeting, a massive white ceramic cross on the wall, and a shelving unit full of Bibles and photo albums and tiny religious trinkets and figurines. During commercial breaks, Sam liked to look through the old photo albums from Jimmy's parents' childhoods in the old country. After a win, they would re-create plays in the backyard, diving around with Jimmy's Nerf football. Sam loved the sandwiches Jimmy's mother made, with oily meats and crusty bread, and he had learned to say *please* and *thank you* in Italian.

But now, in March of their junior year of high school, Sam wouldn't even look at Jimmy when Jimmy tried to discuss the recent trade of the Bills' second-string quarterback for a hotshot wide receiver from Dallas with well-documented legal troubles. Everyone in the city of Buffalo had their opinion on the trade, yet when Jimmy asked Sam about his, Sam murmured, "Don't know, don't care."

Jimmy didn't understand what had gone wrong. He speculated about the possibilities. Sam always liked to be at the center of things—making the loudest jokes, challenging Alice's authority, setting up competitions in areas where he knew he could win. Jimmy wondered if Sam suddenly felt ashamed that he required Jimmy's help with schoolwork. But what had caused the change? Jimmy tried to ask him indirectly, then directly, and Sam scoffed at him as though he had requested an unreasonable favor.

Even though Jimmy did not sense a change in anyone's feelings toward him outside of Sam, he was still afraid to talk about it with any of the others, even Sally, with whom he shared almost everything. He worried that if whatever was bothering Sam were to be aired publicly, the others might come down on Sam's side of things.

Jimmy tried to console himself with the idea that the overall group dynamic was becoming more complicated as they grew older, that change was unavoidable. Now there were pimples and breasts and untimely boners. There were Lynn's erratic moods. There were secrets. There was a new intensity to all of them. Life felt shifty. But this was all just part of growing up, Jimmy reasoned with himself; perhaps he was reading too much into Sam's behavior toward him.

Besides, Jimmy had other concerns outside of his friendship with Sam. Namely, his own penis. He had a love-hate relationship with the thing. He *loved* its appearance when hard: the pleasing, uniform pinkness of it, the handsome little ring of curled black hair that surrounded its base, the stately stiff ridge, its overall symmetry and its size. It was the right size, a *great* size quite frankly. He loved the victory of ejaculation, that staggering, psychedelic moment. Ohhhh, but he *hated* its appearance when soft. A shriveled white acorn. He *hated* when it betrayed him, stiffening at the wrong times, disobeying strict orders to cease and desist. And for the ultimate betrayal, Jimmy's worst and darkest secret, his penis was entirely to blame.

# CHAPTER 14

am had been in love with Sally all along. When they were little, and before they really even knew each other, he loved and admired her silver hair and her sweet smells. When they grew a bit older, he loved her teeth, the tiny, even spaces between them, her pale eyes, a little pink top she wore. By the time they were twelve, he had come to love her legs, as flawless as cream, the earliest suggestion of breasts that rose beneath her shirt, and he loved to make her laugh.

Sam had a large rotation of jokes and tricks and funny faces that he employed to entertain Sally. He could make her laugh and laugh, until she had to clap a hand over her mouth and wave for air. He loved to make her laugh because as soon as she stopped laughing, her eyes became grave. Sam was convinced that he was the only one who could save Sally from the mysterious sadness that seemed to so easily overtake her. He loved her. He would have traded all the rest of them for her, even Jimmy, his best friend since they were five years old. He would have traded his own siblings for her. His own mother.

Sam felt certain that Sally loved him, too, but he worried that she would reject him if she thought a romantic union might isolate the two of them from the other Gunners. Sally had a mild and agreeable personality—she always wanted everyone to get along, everything to be fair.

So, for Sally's sake, Sam waited.

He watched her go from a little girl to a young woman, and his desire for her intensified.

Sam started saving money to buy Sally a ring to give to her for her sixteenth birthday. He knew she wouldn't marry him at this young age, but he was ready to express his love to her. They were hurtling through adolescence, juniors in high school now, and he had watched serious and lasting romances form between classmates at school. He knew that if he waited too long, he would lose Sally to someone else. He had convinced himself that the rest of The Gunners would understand, maybe they would even be happy for the two of them.

Sam pruned his grandmother's shrubs and collected recyclables from street trash, which were worth five cents apiece if he took them to the center. He had his eye on a little gold ring with an emerald heart that he had seen at JCPenney's—green was Sally's favorite color. Sam worked and saved and worked and saved, and finally earned the fifty-eight dollars needed to purchase the ring. It came in a beautiful red velvet box that was as soft and warm as a baby animal.

During the days leading up to Sally's birthday, Sam made plans to meet up with her on the evening of her birthday, after dinnertime. He'd had almost no contact with Sally's mother over the years; it seemed almost like an unspoken rule, but approaching Sally at her home was the only way he could avoid encountering any of the other Gunners who might interfere with the plan. The plan was this: He would go to Sally's home and ask if he could take her on a walk. He would say he'd gotten something for her birthday. They would go to the park on James Street. The park wasn't much to see—splintered fencing covered in graffiti, a tilted merry-go-round, sun-faded swings on a squealing iron frame—but it was the nicest outdoor location he could think of. He would tell her of his great love. She would be stunned, but overjoyed. She would put the ring on. The two of them would make a plan to tell the rest of The Gunners so that they wouldn't have to hide their relationship. He would maybe and probably even kiss her.

The evening of Sally's birthday finally arrived.

Sam combed his hair and stuffed himself into his slimmest pants.

He admired the ring, put the box in his pocket, and at eight o'clock, he left his home and walked up Ingram, his pulse beating against his skull.

At Sally's home, Sam rang the doorbell, but there was no answer. He rang it a second time, then a third.

He knocked on the door, thinking that perhaps the bell was broken.

Was no one home? Earlier in the day when he had casually asked Sally if she had plans for her birthday, she had said that she did not and would probably just be "around."

Sam turned back toward the street, and noticed now that Sally's mother's Cutlass Supreme was not parked out front. Perhaps she had taken Sally out for dinner. But the lights were on . . . Corinne was probably working late or with a boyfriend, Sam thought, and Sally was probably in there alone, wishing she had someone to spend her birthday evening with.

Although he'd never once set foot inside the home, Sam knew

which side of the home Sally's bedroom was on. He decided to make his way around to that side, to see if perhaps she was listening to music or watching TV, which had prevented her from hearing the doorbell. Sam felt a little squirrelly about sneaking around their property and snooping on her bedroom this way, but if Sally was in there by herself . . . Well, it could be perfect, and romantic, couldn't it? Like a movie, the one with the guy holding the handwritten sign professing his love outside the girl's house, although now Sam couldn't remember how things had turned out for that guy and his handwritten sign.

Sam made his way around the home, and the light in Sally's room was off. He was about to head back to his own home and formulate a new plan for tomorrow when a bit of movement from inside the bedroom caught his eye. Sam returned to the window. And it was dark in there, but he could see now that there was someone inside. There was . . . There were . . . He could see the back of Sally's head, and the rest of her was beneath the covers. And *what*? There were two bodies. Sally was on top. There were hands on Sally's head, behind her neck, and beneath the covers. There were rhythms. *No.* Sam felt like his knees were bending the wrong way. He felt like time did not exist.

Sam's impulse to continue watching, to find out *who*, and to break into the house and strangle whoever had taken this from him, was overtaken by a swell of nausea and the impulse to get as far from this scene as he could. He ran back to the street and made his way up Ingram unevenly, loping up the street like an injured animal, face wet with tears and twisted with rage. Not back to his home, where he might encounter his mother and have to explain himself, but instead to The Gunner House.

It was dark and empty, and when Sam entered, he didn't turn on the light but pulled the door shut behind him. He drew the ring from his pocket and threw the little red velvet box across the room and let out a painful scream. The room smelled exactly the same way it always smelled, and Sam wept.

*Who?* He lay back on the mattress and closed his eyes.

It had to be one of them. Sam had been watching Sally long enough to know that she didn't have friends outside of The Gunners. She didn't talk to any other boys. She didn't even give them looks.

It had to be one of them. But which one? Sam's stomach lurched and soured at either possibility.

Sally and Mikey had been best friends before the group came together. The two of them sat together on the bus and shared an early bond, both trapped in a home with a sad-sack single parent. But Mikey was so small, so shy. He was a year younger—still just a sophomore, he was so . . . *innocent.* Under the covers with Sally that way? Holding her head and her neck that way?

But Jimmy was Sam's *best friend.* Jimmy! How could he? Sam had never spoken of his feelings for Sally, not even to Jimmy, but how could Jimmy not know? How could Jimmy sneak in and . . . Oh, it made so much sense, of course. Those turquoise eyes. Sam knew how girls looked at Jimmy. The whiz kid. That stupid tapping code Jimmy had developed that only Sally understood . . . Jimmy could have been saying *anything* to her, and no one else would have ever known.

Sam's thoughts turned to the morning several months earlier when he had gotten up at 6:00 a.m. to take the family dog out. The sun wasn't even fully up yet, and Sam wore boots and a winter coat over his pajamas. He was groggy as he opened the door and trudged up the block with the dog, who always required a brief expedition to locate the perfect pee spot. As Sam passed Jimmy's house, where all the lights were still off, something down by the basement storm window caught his eye. Something had appeared for a split second, as though it were about to emerge from the storm window, but then it had disappeared just as quickly back inside. Sam stared at the storm window. It was a flash of white, something that had been scared off by Sam's presence. And now it was gone, whatever, or whoever, it was. Sam yawned and continued up the street with the dog. It could have been nothing just as easily as it could have been something.

Now, as Sam thought back to that morning, he knew with great certainty that the white flash had been Sally's hair. Sally had spent the night with Jimmy and had been about to sneak out before Jimmy's parents woke, but she had caught sight of Sam a split second before he'd fully caught sight of her. *It had to be.* And as Sam thought about it more, it was *so* obvious now that Jimmy had been hiding something for a long time. Little things. Moments when Sam could tell that Jimmy had moderated an impulse before speaking. Withdrawn silences, expressions of guilt. Finally, Sam understood.

Who knew how many nights Jimmy and Sally had already spent together? Sam couldn't even begin to imagine how long this might have been going on, how many loving and agile sex-things had been done in Jimmy's basement and Sally's bedroom.

Sam wanted to strangle something with his bare hands, and so he forced himself to stay there in The Gunner House, knowing that if he left he would do some violence. He would ruin his life if he did the things he wanted to do. He counted breaths. He spoke a mantra to himself: *You fat, hopeless loser, what did you expect? You fat, hopeless loser, you don't deserve love. You fat, hopeless loser . . .* And although these words did not make Sam feel any better, they transferred some of the anger toward Jimmy onto himself so that his murderous rage gradually began to subside. He rose from the mattress, punched the wall until his knuckles were mangled and flaked, did push-ups, returned to the mattress. *You fat, hopeless loser . . .*

An hour later, Sam was startled by someone entering the front door of The Gunner House. He lurched upright as the figure stood in the doorway, lit from behind by the streetlight.

Alice seemed equally spooked by Sam's presence in the dark room. She said, "Who's there? Scared the crap outta me!"

Sam said, "It's me."

Alice entered the room and reached up to turn on the light. She was so tall, especially from Sam's seated position. Her dark hair was tied sloppily on top of her head. She wore men's jeans that only reached her ankles, a Buffalo Sabres T-shirt, a pair of lime-green Chinese mesh slippers with sequins across the toes.

Sam blinked. His face felt as if it were covered in clay. "What are you doing here?" he said.

"What are *you* doing here?" Alice said. She pointed toward the far corner of the room. "*I* left my bio book here last night, and that paper's due Monday." She examined Sam's face and said, "Dude, you look like you just fought a war. What is *up*?"

Sam's fingers went to his face. He felt wrecked, and wronged. His heart, it actually hurt. And while he hated the idea of displaying vulnerability in front of Alice, who at times over the years he had hated more intensely than he'd hated all of the rest of them *combined*, he also trusted Alice and longed to confide in someone.

Sam said, "Sally's with somebody."

Alice frowned. "What?"

"She's . . . *with* somebody."

"*With* somebody?" Alice said. "What? Who? How do you

mean?" She studied Sam's face for a moment with her black eyes and then said, "You're in love with her."

"*No*," Sam snapped.

Alice sat down next to Sam on the mattress. "Why do you think she's with somebody?"

"I went over there earlier. Just to see how her birthday was. I saw through her window. She was in her bed, and there was someone else in there, too."

Alice said, "Who?"

Sam shook his head. "I couldn't see. But it's gotta be one of them. It's gotta be Mikey or Jimmy."

When she didn't respond, Sam turned to face her straight on. "Alice," he said, "it's got to be Jimmy."

Alice was quiet for a little while.

Surprised that Alice didn't seem to share his indignation, and deeply irritated by this, Sam said, "Can you believe it? This *sneaking around*? These are supposed to be our *friends!*"

Sam watched Alice's face. Her expression remained calm but flickered through a small series of thoughts that he couldn't follow.

Finally, Alice said, "We're in high school now. Things are changing. We're not kids anymore. Things are gonna happen. If Sally and whoever she was with don't want to share anything about their relationship, that's their business. So you should probably get used to it, because if we're all going to stay friends, we just need to accept that things are going to change."

Sam stared at her. "You aren't pissed?"

Alice said, "It was only a matter of time."

The two of them sat in silence for a while longer.

Sam gazed around the dark room, taking in all of its details. Then he lost himself to memories of it, of times when things were not hard and not complicated, when there weren't lies and secrets, when you couldn't stay mad. Laughter. Sweat. Grass-stained knees. All the hours the six children had shared here, where they were protected by one another and this space from their parents and the outside world. Alice was right—things had changed. This place was no longer safe and happy. These people could no longer be trusted. Sam felt a dark creature coming to life, sniffing the air, inside himself.

Finally, Alice said, "I need to get some work done on that paper. You coming home or staying here awhile?"

Sam left with Alice, and the two of them walked up Ingram together. The moon was pale and pinkish, and the March air, depending on the exact moment, was both warm and cool.

At eleven that same night, the phone rang at the Forrest house, and Sally answered.

"Sam knows you're with someone," Alice said. "He came to your house tonight and looked in your window. He saw you in bed with someone."

"How much does he know?" Sally said.

"Just that you were with someone . . . He doesn't know who."

Sally was quiet for a bit. "Does this mean we have to stop?"

"No," Alice said, "we just need to be more careful."

# CHAPTER 15

Alice turned to Mikey. "You think I can eat an entire croissant in one bite?"

Before he could answer, she had snatched another one off the coffee table and methodically balled it up between her palms until it was the size of an apricot. She shoved it into her mouth, cheeks puffing wide as she chewed. Down the hatch. She slapped her hands together victoriously, crumbs flew.

Mikey said, "Wonders never cease."

Alice nodded out toward the wall of windows and said, "Have you heard the one about the lawyer from Toronto?"

"A joke, you mean?"

"Not exactly. True story. Fancy-pants rich lawyer works on like the thirtieth floor of a firm in Toronto. He's got a room full of colleagues, decides to run into the floor-to-ceiling glass on the other side of the room to prove that it's unbreakable. Apparently, he'd done it a bunch of times before. But this time . . ." Alice paused to sip her wine, and she slapped her hand violently through the air. "He busted through. Kaput. In his defense, the glass didn't actually break; the whole window just popped out. But I'm just saying, please do not try this at home. Or at Jimmy's home."

"He died?"

"Dead, dead, dead. Sorry to be grim," Alice said. "But while we're on the topic, my dad got cancer in his colon."

"How bad?"

Alice sucked air in through one side of her mouth. "Bad. Probably got a year or two at most. Just found out last month."

"How're you doing? How are they doing?"

"I'm thinking of moving back down here to help out."

"Really?"

Alice nodded. "I could sell the marina up there—already got someone who's interested—move down and open one up around here . . . I was looking at some property online. Up near the harbor in Lewiston, there's a rinky-dink old boathouse I could turn around."

"I'd love to see more of you, Alice," Mikey said, and he felt a hope spike through him. "I'd love it if you moved back here."

Alice said, "I'm sure you'd get your fill of me after a week or two. Then we'd have a big fight and hit each other in the face and never talk again."

Mikey laughed.

"Don't say anything. I haven't talked it over with Chris yet." Alice finished her wine in a single swallow.

Mikey said, "Have you heard from The Saint recently?"

Alice and her husband had gotten together when she was a junior in college. He was the TA in her marine biology class. They'd been divorced now for eight years. More recently, Alice liked to report to the others when The Saint had sent her a Christmas card that included a braggy letter. Alice had never provided details on their breakup. She would mock The Saint until she was blue in the face, but the actual explanation of their divorce was the one thing Mikey had ever known Alice to be reluctant to speak on.

Alice nodded. "Just the usual Christmas card. Speaking of The

Saint, there was a guy in a bar the other day who reminded me a little bit of him. You know what this guy in the bar said to me? The weirdest insult I've ever received."

"What did he say?"

"He cuts right in front of me at the bar, before the bartender's got my order, and I call him on it, tell him to learn some manners. You know what this guy says? He spins around and goes, *Oh, yeah? Oh, yeah? I bet you think you're pretty freakin' tall, don't you?*"

"How tall was *he*?"

"Your height, probably. What are you, five ten?"

Mikey nodded.

Alice said, "I was so taken aback I didn't have anything to say, not a word. Imagine that. Anyway, I'm still hungry. I think I require something with sugar in it next."

She rose to go to the kitchen and returned a few minutes later with another bottle of wine, a jar of fig jam, a jar of strawberry preserves, mustard, and a knife. She spread these items on the coffee table before them; then she sat back down and leaned forward to touch the stained rim of her glass to Mikey's.

She sighed heavily after sipping from her wine and licking a purple drip that slowly made its way down the outside of her glass. "Mikey, I'm going to tell you something before the others get here."

"Okay."

"I never wanted to betray Sally's trust. And I was afraid that the rest of you would blame me if you knew, so I didn't say anything. But it was because of me."

"What was?"

"Sally leaving our group." Alice reached down to touch Finn's head again, running a single index finger knuckle between his eyes, and he blinked slowly and groaned happily. "Don't hate me."

"What?" Mikey stared at her.

Alice sat back in the couch and fiddled with a loose thread in her sock before releasing another heavy sigh and finally stating plainly, "Sally and I were involved."

Mikey felt his eyes double in size. "Involved with each other?"

Alice nodded. "It started when we were fourteen or fifteen. It started, like, experimental. Purely physical."

Mikey couldn't help the awkward laugh that escaped him. He apologized immediately. "Sorry, I don't mean to make light, I just . . . We were so young! I had no idea."

"I know," Alice said. "We kept it totally secret. Sam almost found out once, and it tore him up. He didn't know it was with me, but just knowing that Sally was involved with someone . . . Sam was in love with her, too."

"*Really?*" Mikey said.

Alice nodded. "That's another reason I haven't wanted to say anything. He nearly caught us. I lied to cover it up."

Mikey said, "Did something in particular happen between you, leading up to the time when she cut herself off from all of us? A fight?"

Alice clicked her tongue against the roof of her mouth. "That's what's always been weird," she said. "Nothing out of the ordinary. I was falling in love with her, but I couldn't tell if she had real feelings for me. It was hot and cold. We never had a proper conversation about the status of our relationship, and I wasn't going to force that. I was too scared, too proud."

"So things ended between the two of you when they ended with all the rest of us?"

Alice nodded. "I had no more warning than any of the rest of you."

Mikey said again, "I had no idea."

Alice pulled the rubber band from the end of her braid, redid the bottom few inches of braid, tightening it, twisted the rubber band back on, and tossed the braid over her shoulder.

Mikey said, "So you think she cut herself off from all of us because she felt awkward about ending things with you?"

"I think so, yes," Alice said. "Maybe she felt shame. Didn't want to be gay. Realized she wasn't gay. But . . . well, not to get into it too much, but when things started, she was very much the initiator."

"*Really*," Mikey said.

Alice nodded. "At that point, I didn't know what I was, gay or straight or something in between. Sally and I were walking home together late one night. She invited me in to her place, her mother wasn't home, said she had something to show me, and . . . well . . . It was my first kiss, first everything."

Mikey said, "Did she seem experienced?"

Alice said, "I don't know if it was experience, but she definitely wasn't timid."

"Sure." Mikey stretched out his neck, wildly uncomfortable with this information. He brushed absently at the colorless hair on his forearms.

"From right when it started," Alice said, "I just sort of had the sense . . . I was afraid she was going to go through me."

"You mean, use you? Then go on to someone new?"

Alice considered this. "*Use me* isn't quite right . . . Too simple. Crude. I actually mean I had this sense that she was going to pass through me, like a ghost, then go on to somewhere unknown. *Poof.* Leave me shaking."

Across the room, the fire spat.

"And I guess I wasn't wrong," Alice said. She was quiet for a bit. Then she said, "Sally was *beautiful*, wasn't she? Something magnetic about her. Hard to explain. Anyway, least that's how I remember her." Alice paused and cocked her head vaguely sideways, looking at Mikey. "Were you in love with Sally, too? You knew her before the rest of us."

Mikey said, "Sally was my first friend."

These words brought an unexpected swell of emotion, and Mikey had to swallow several times to disperse the warm, hard lump that rose in his throat. Then he said, "I don't recall ever feeling anything romantic toward her, though. I don't think I did."

Alice said, "I think we were all sort of in love with each other at different times. Isn't that just what happens when friends grow up together?"

Mikey said, "I don't know about that."

Alice said, "Oh, come on, Mikey. Are you saying you were never in love with me?"

This made Mikey laugh. "No," he said. "Sorry."

"Who were you in love with?"

"I don't think I was . . ." Mikey said.

"Was *what*?"

"Capable of it."

Alice sipped her wine. "Well, aren't you the heartbreaker? *The boy who couldn't love.*" Alice laughed.

Mikey laughed, too, but the beating in his chest suddenly felt like sobs.

They sat in silence for a few moments.

Mikey's nose was running, so he went to the bathroom, blew his nose into a square of toilet paper, and looked at himself in the mirror.

When he returned to the main room, Alice had grown impatient and was hollering for him, "*Hey!* Get back in here and continue bonding with me!"

Already the sky was growing dark over the lake, which appeared to be frozen over as far as Mikey could see. The snow that had accumulated over the frozen lake had a slightly different look than the snow on land. A blue-gray hue, striations and veinlike patterns, as if it belonged on a different but similar planet.

"Been strange, hasn't it?" Alice remarked. "Seeing where all of us ended up. How all of us changed."

Mikey nodded. "It has been strange. Interesting. Although ... I don't know that I believe people ever change," he added. To Mikey, things just sort of happened to you, rolled over you like a tumbleweed, then went bouncing along.

"Really?" This seemed to surprise Alice. "You don't think so? Well . . . I guess you've worked the same job, lived in the same house for the past ten years. And I don't mean any offense by that. But . . . Jimmy? Going from a shy math nerd to this wealthy LA hotshot? And Sam, big old tough guy that he was when we were young, everything *Fuck this, screw that.* Now he's this churchy guy, *God bless* at the end of all his emails? Well, and Sally, of course. She went from so *close* to us, to . . . whatever she was at the end. You don't think that's a person changing?"

Mikey thought on this for a bit. He was briefly tempted to press Alice on the topic of her divorce—what, or who, had changed there—but he decided against it.

He said, "I think at various times in life we're either more or less true to who we really are. But that essence, that *who we are . . .* I don't know that that ever changes."

"So who are you?"

Once again, the word *hollow* made its way to the surface of Mikey's thoughts.

But before he had a chance to respond to Alice, she said, "Quite frankly, I disagree with the whole premise. I think it's a pile of crap."

"How's that?"

"I think that deciding you have some unchangeable essence is just an excuse."

"For what?"

"For *not changing*, dummy."

"Fine, wonderful," Mikey said. He was tiring of Alice's opinions and eager now for the others to arrive.

"Don't get testy. I can agree with you on one point: that there is a fundamental difference between us. You and me."

"Just one?"

Alice said, "You're serious unless you're instructed not to be. I'm not serious unless I'm told that I *have* to be. Try not to be offended."

"Or you could try to not be offensive. Either way."

"Oh, come on." Alice reached over to shake at his shoulder. "Do you need to go try to move your bowels or something before the others get here? Work yourself into a better mood?"

Mikey said, "I will give you one dollar for every minute you can manage to not speak, starting now, until somebody else gets here." He pointed at his watch.

Alice completely ignored this and said, "Have you ever read that book . . . oh, wait, now what's it called? *How to Make and Keep Friends*? It's something like that."

"Do you mean *How to Win Friends and Influence People*?"

"That's the one. Anyway, you should probably get yourself a copy."

Alice got up and did a sun salutation in the middle of the room.

# CHAPTER 16

Sally's science teacher started talking about the upcoming solar eclipse in October of Sally's third-grade year, a full month before it was actually set to happen.

Sally mentioned it to Mikey on the bus one morning.

"What is it?" Mikey said.

"It's a time when the moon goes in front of the sun," Sally explained. "It's only happened like a few times ever in the history of the world. Your teacher hasn't said anything about it yet?"

Mikey shook his head.

"I'm sure she will," Sally said. "We're all learning about it, because it's going to happen while we're at school. We're all going to see it together."

"What will it look like?" Mikey said.

"A big beautiful shining thing, I imagine," Sally said.

"Okay," Mikey said.

It was quiet for a little bit.

"It might be the most beautiful thing we'll ever see in our whole lives," Sally added.

In the row behind them, Alice was figuring out how to turn on the Supersonic Boombox cassette player she had finally managed to steal from her older brother.

Sally looked back over her shoulder, just as Alice pressed play. The introduction to The Emotions' "Best of My Love" blared out from the dimpled silver speakers, jazzy descending bass beat, horns accenting the percussion.

Alice shared a seat with Lynn, and in the seat across from them, Sam and Jimmy looked up from their football play-making notebook when Alice's music came on. Jimmy snapped along with the music while Sam did a funny, seductive little dance in his seat, something he'd learned from MTV no doubt, chubby little hips grooving, lips pushed out.

Alice turned the music up louder when the vocals kicked in. *Doesn't take much to make me happy, and make me smile with glee* . . . Lynn nodded along with the music, lips murmuring the lyrics in synchrony with the recording. *Never never will I feel discouraged, 'cause our love's no mystery* . . .

Jimmy and Sam joined hands and bumped roughly against each other in their seat. *I like the way you make me feel about you, baby, want the whole wide world to see* . . .

Alice got up out of her seat when the chorus came on. She turned the volume even louder, heaved the boombox up above her head, and strutted back the aisle of the bus as though it were a runway. She sang very loudly and slightly off-key. *Whoa, whoa, you've got the best of my love! Whoa, whoa, you've got the best of my love!* Other students on the bus were taking notice. They watched Alice, pointed, giggled.

From the front of the bus, the driver glared into his broad mirror and hollered, "*Clancy!*"

Alice ignored him. She continued to dance and sing, up and down the aisle, stumbling but recovering quickly when the bus took a turn. She wore a men's white V-neck T-shirt that was way too big for her and pants that were way too short. Beat-up Reebok sneakers. A plain black baseball cap backward over a long, thick dark ponytail that swung back and forth like rope as she danced.

Other students began to sing along.

Alice turned the music up all the way, to full volume. *Oh oh-oh-oh, you've got the best of my love! Oh oh-oh-oh, you've got the best of my love!*

The bus driver bellowed, "Clancy, sit your ass *down!*"

Alice wouldn't stop. Up and down the aisle she went, singing and dancing, the boombox high above her head. *Oh oh-oh-oh, you've got the best of my love! Oh oh-oh-oh, you've got the best of my love!* Other students had gotten out of their seats to dance along, the chorus reaching a fever pitch, thirty voices, shrieking joy, madness, Alice leading the charge.

Sally leaned over and whispered to Mikey, "She's something else."

When Alice drew close to Sally and Mikey's seat, she leaned down and said, "What are you waiting for? Get up and dance!" Her breath smelled of strawberry gum; her face was sweating, her dark eyes dangerous.

Mikey said, "I don't know how." His father never, ever played music in their home.

Alice said, "Just watch me and do what I tell you."

# CHAPTER 17

Once Lynn, Issa, and Sam had arrived at the lake house, they all took a seat at the dining room table, with one empty chair remaining for Jimmy, who had yet to provide an update on his arrival time. The room was warmly lit by a rustic cascade chandelier made from real deer antlers and faux white candles. A shelving unit on the modern wood-paneled wall held a large framed photograph of Jimmy's family from his childhood, a Bible, several potted cacti, a ship in a bottle, and a tiny snow globe featuring the Buffalo skyline.

The caterers produced several large dishes and carried each platter around the table to serve everyone individually. French green beans sautéed with lemon and garlic and white pepper. Pomegranate salad with mint and feta and orange zest. Rolls with butter and honey. Roast lamb with rosemary and arugula pesto.

Sam buttered a roll, bit into it, and said, "What is it with rich people and unsalted butter?"

Wine was served to Mikey, Alice, and Chris, but Lynn, Issa, and Sam all said they'd stick with water.

Alice said, "Sam are you teetotalin' these days, too?" She turned briefly to Lynn and Issa. "No offense."

Sam smoothed wispy blond hair back over his brow, a gesture

that would have been glamorous had his hairline been intact, and took a sip of his water. "Sort of."

Mikey had also been surprised moments earlier when Sam declined a drink, but his desire for peace between Sam and Alice surpassed his curiosity. He sensed now that Sam didn't particularly want to answer the question, and quickly interjected, "I'd be teetotallin', too, if I knew what was best for me."

Alice ignored this and turned back to Sam. "Empty calories? Trying to lose a few?"

Sam didn't respond.

Mikey muttered, "For crying out loud, Alice."

Alice glared at Mikey and tossed her thick black braid over her shoulder. "Oh, excuse me. Are you offended by my poor manners? *Obviously* I could stand to lose a few myself. And you could stand to get down from your high horse."

She turned to address the rest of the table, as though they should all join in conspiracy against Mikey. "Can I not ask a man, if he doesn't drink, why he doesn't drink? We're all friends here." She dipped her chin toward Chris to her left. "Well, except you."

Issa lifted his finger and said, "And me."

Lynn said, "I obviously don't mind talking about why I don't drink. I say it to a room of thirty people every week. But some people don't like talking about it . . . Maybe Sam's just not in the mood to talk, or maybe there's nothing to talk about." Lynn flipped her wrist casually. Her shoulders were small nubs under her oversize black shirt. "Or maybe he doesn't like Pinot Noir. Maybe he prefers Shiraz."

Mikey said, "Or maybe he doesn't like being interrogated two seconds after sitting down to dinner."

Sam was stirring the ice around his water with his butter knife. He seemed preoccupied.

"We're *friends*," Alice said again. "Just because we haven't sat in the same room together in fifteen years doesn't mean we have to tiptoe around like the friggin' pope is at the table. I didn't drive ten hours to be bored. I'm allowed to ask a friend a question, and he's allowed to say he doesn't want to answer if he doesn't want to answer." She turned to Sam. "It surprises me to see that you're not having a drink. Would you care to say why, or would you care for me to shut the hell up?"

Mikey said, "Let's take a vote around the table."

Alice said, "All right, all right, all right. But it was just an honest question. I don't see what's so wrong about that."

Issa said, "Do you want to know what my mom used to say about honest questions?"

"What's that?"

"They can be like farts. It feels good to let them out, but once you do, sometimes they just make the whole room stink."

Everyone laughed, including Sam.

Sam said, "Alice, I don't mind you asking. It's not that I have a *problem* with alcohol, and, yes, I'm always trying to lose a few, but that's not why either." He paused and pursed his lips for a moment before a noisy sigh shot out of him. He ran one hand down from his throat to the buttons stretched tight over his belly and smoothed the napkin over his lap. "Beyond that," he said, "I don't want to talk about it anymore right now, please and thank you." He offered a minimal smile.

Alice said, "Are you pregnant?"

Before anyone could respond, she threw her white napkin in the air, a sign of peace, then waved both arms around as though deflecting invisible weapons, and cried, "I'm kidding, I'm done, I'm done!"

Now everyone had a full plate before them, and Alice said,

"Let's do a toast. Here we all are. So let's drink to that. It's really very nice and very cool being together again. Too nice for this to be entirely depressing, even given the circumstances. So, to being here."

"To being here."

"Being together."

"To being here, together."

"Being together."

They raised glasses, and as the others began to eat, Sam bowed his head briefly in prayer.

When he opened his eyes, seeming restored, he announced that he'd never had lamb before.

"Ever?" Chris said.

Lynn said, "Mikey, you're big into cooking these days. Have you made lamb?"

Mikey nodded. "I did a braised shank when I first got my Crock-Pot," he said.

Alice said, "The last thing I did in my Crock-Pot was a shoe."

"Did you say a shoe?"

Chris laughed. "She's not lying, you guys!"

Mikey said, "Why on earth—"

Lynn said, "Did you eat your shoe?"

Sam said, "Alice, you are *so weird*." He had not yet taken a bite of his meal, but he was still staring at the setup before him. He leaned toward Issa and said, "Which fork am I supposed to use?"

Issa said, "Beats me. I'm just using the little one 'cause she is." He nodded toward Lynn.

Lynn said, "I think you do salads with the little one, meat with the big one. But I don't know about the beans. We really need Jimmy here to teach us how the rich live. Also, is there salt in that Mason jar? Weird. Can you pass me that?"

Alice said, "Correction, it wasn't a shoe. It was a boot."

Sam said, "Explain."

Alice said, "A few months ago, time came to retire the pair of boots I'd had for years. I worked up a big salty beef roast, then took the meat out, stuck my boot in and slow-cooked it in that fatty broth for six hours."

"How'd it turn out?" Sam said.

"Finn loved it," Chris said. She had already finished her glass of wine and now was reaching to take a sip from Alice's glass. "He ate the whole stinkin' boot!"

Alice gave a proud glance around the table, then took her glass back and set it on the far side of her plate, out of Chris's reach.

Chris said, "Alice loves Finn more than me. She's never once cooked a meal for me in the whole time we've been together. *Boo-hoo-hoo.*"

Mikey tried not to stare. Genuinely, genuinely disturbed by the voice. It felt like a betrayal.

Alice swallowed the food in her mouth and said neutrally, "Don't take it too hard, hon. I love Finn more than me, too. Mikey, how's your cat?"

Mikey said, "Happy and handsome."

"No more cancer?"

"No more cancer."

When Friday was four years old, a bad cancer had grown in his shoulder, and it cost Mikey three paychecks to have it removed, along with Friday's front left paw, where the cancer had spread.

Alice said, "Did you save his paw? The one they removed?"

Mikey snorted. "Yes. I put it on a string and use it like a toy for him to chase around."

Alice stared at him. "Are you serious?"

"*No!* Are you nuts?"

"Sorry," Alice said. "I didn't realize you had developed such a daring sense of humor." She sipped from her wine. "But you didn't want to wear it around your neck or keep it in your pocket, like a rabbit's foot? I mean, what is there, a special recycling bin at the vet's office for tumors and paws? If you care about your pet, you should care what happens to their paw."

Mikey made a face. "Must you have such a strong opinion about everything?"

"Yes. *Especially* irrelevant things that I know nothing about." Alice stated this with great bravado, a finger in the air.

Issa laughed very loudly. "You know what? I actually agree."

Alice said, "You and I are going to be such good friends!" She poured more wine for herself and sent the bottle around the table. She rose to retrieve another from the cabinet, flinging a triumphant smile back over her shoulder.

When she returned, Sam was poking at the medium-rare center of his lamb with his fork and whispered, "Do you think they'd cook this up a little bit for me? I don't wanna offend the cook, but I'm not too big on blood."

Alice sliced off the medium-well edges of her cut, and she sent it down the table to Sam. "I'll trade you," she said. "Send me your bloody scraps."

Sam said, "Do you remember when those neighborhood bullies, Pete and what's-his-name, smeared raw meat on the front porch of The Gunner House?"

Lynn said, "That's right! After we stole the chains off their bikes. Damn, those guys were tough and scary. One of them had a ponytail and—"

"The other one had a *mus*tache!" Sam said.

Alice said, "Whatever happened to those guys anyway? Pete and . . . Jackson, was it? You know what became of 'em, Mikey?

They stay in the area? I think they both dropped out of school around their sophomore year, didn't they?"

Mikey nodded. "I heard Pete's in the clink. Stabbed his grandma."

"Oh, no!" Lynn said. "Really?"

Mikey nodded. "Something about milk. He was living with her at the time. She got one percent instead of two. Or the other way around."

Sam said, "Oh, no!"

"Sheezus!" Alice said. She turned to Mikey. "And you thought *I* had strong opinions . . ."

Lynn asked Sam about his work.

Sam said, "I got employee of the month twice now. Company of three hundred. It's just 'cause I kiss my boss's behind, but it's all right. They've given me some neat things. Branded fleece, the right size and everything, had it made special for me. And when you get employee of the month, they give you fifty bucks and your own parking spot. I get to park next to the handicaps."

Mikey said, "And all's well with your church?"

Sam's emails often focused on church activities: hayrides and ice cream socials, a new kid they were sponsoring in Venezuela, food drives for the community, visiting missionaries from the Sudan.

Alice emitted a small groan.

Sam turned to her. "What's that now?"

"What?"

"You made a sound."

"Did I? It was involuntary," Alice said. "I was just preparing myself to feign interest in church."

"Oh," Sam responded, appearing unfazed. He chewed intensely for several seconds, then deposited a small fatty bit of lamb into his napkin. "Well," he said again, wiping his lips, which were shiny with grease, "this may actually interest you, believe it or not. Pastor who's been there for ten years got the boot about a year ago. Messy business."

Alice said, "Oh, *delicious*! What'd he do? Seduce everybody's wives?"

Sam said, "Just a few of them."

"*Really?*" Alice said, her expression wide with delight. "Say more."

"Messy business," Sam said again. "Went for all the women who were involved in the AA program the church runs. He'd wait for the session to end, then offer *private prayer sessions* for anyone who wanted them."

"Oh, what a *dog*!" Lynn cried.

Alice said, "What a smoothie-boy white knight! Commie bastard!"

Mikey hadn't a clue what, specifically, Alice meant by this. Her insults were often obscure, which conveniently rendered them indisputable.

Sam cut into his lamb. "Sure. Everyone was pretty darn shocked. The board met, ousted the guy before the next Sunday."

"So what's he doing now?" Mikey said.

"You guys are gonna love this," Sam said. He took a sip of water, breathing heavily from the effort of sawing the rest of his meat into bite-size pieces, then said, "Nowadays, he's writing historical romance novels, all of them about famous ladies' men and their lovers. Gets 'em self-published. Me and Justine looked him up on Amazon. Titles like *Ben Franklin Leaves No Trace*."

There was an outbreak of laughter around the table.

"Amazing!" Alice exclaimed. She held a small bone at her lips and chewed the last bit of meat from it. "Do you guys remember when we tried to write a book about ourselves when we were little? We all six had a special power."

Lynn said, "That's right! We picked our own power. Mine was mind reading."

Alice said, "Mine was something stupid and boring like flying." She paused, then turned to Mikey. "What was yours?"

"I can't remember," Mikey said.

Lynn shook her head. "Me either."

Sam said, "Mikey, I think you wanted to be invisible."

Mikey said, "Really? I thought that was Sally's."

"No, Sam's right," said Alice. "That was yours."

It was quiet for a bit. Mikey ran his fork over his plate. *Invisibility*. It had maintained its appeal over all these years. How he would enjoy evaporating himself at will. And it seemed oddly noble at this stage of life.

Sam said, "Anyhow, that's all the church gossip I've got."

Issa said, "Have you always been religious?"

Sam shook his head. "It was around the time . . . well . . . around the end of high school." He took a very large bite of lamb, seemingly hopeful that he might evade further questions on this topic.

Sam had left Lackawanna to work at a Bible camp in Georgia as soon as he had graduated high school, and it occurred to Mikey now that he never knew exactly when, or why, Sam had become religious. There seemed to be a certain level of discomfort surrounding this subject, some element that Sam never wished to disclose.

Chris turned to Mikey. "What do you do for work?"

"Maintenance at General Mills," Mikey said.

"Fixing up the machinery and stuff?"

Mikey nodded.

"You get free cereal?"

"Dozen boxes at the end of the quarter if sales were good."

Seemingly restless at not being at the center of the conversation for even a moment, Alice said, "I love cereal, but I'm lactose intolerant. Sometimes I get a box and just eat it dry by the handful."

Issa said, "You don't like the fake milk? The soy kind?"

Alice shook her head. "Can't stand the stuff. It tastes like an unscented candle."

"It does, doesn't it!" Lynn said. She sipped her water. "Alice, are you still doing those events with the women's rights drives?"

Alice nodded. "Helped them raise eight grand last year alone. Which *reminds* me, you guys, freakin' make sure you're writing your governors, okay? Wankers are always trying to take us back to the 1950s. State of Texas? Some women have to drive four hundred miles to terminate a pregnancy." She looked at Sam. "It's almost that bad in parts of Georgia, too."

Sam cut into his lamb and didn't respond.

Alice stared at him, her nostrils flaring. "Do *not* tell me you're one of them, Sam. Do you know how many women a year die from complications attempting to abort on their own? Because they're denied adequate care?"

Sam blinked slowly and finished chewing his lamb. He said, "No, Alice. And I don't particularly care to know that statistic."

Alice dropped her steak knife onto her plate with a noisy clatter. Her eyes were black fire, jaw jutting forward. "You're probably one of the ones voting to keep Deal the Heel around, aren't you?"

Sam said, "Who's that?"

Alice threw her hands into the air, face open wide, incredulous. "Nathan Deal? The governor of Georgia? Sam, you know, *the state where you live*?"

Mikey said, "Sam, you are not obligated to tell her who you vote for."

Sam said, "If it makes you feel better, Alice, I don't vote. Period."

Lynn laughed into her fist. Mikey stared at his lamb and tried not to smile.

"That's even worse!" Alice shrieked. "Do you know how many—"

Lynn was still laughing as she cut Alice off. "Relax, Al, would you please?" Lynn said. "For the record, I agree with you. But can you leave it be? He's allowed to have his opinions."

Alice cracked her neck, then looked around the table. "Oh, *what*?" she said. "We consider women's reproductive rights another *unsavory* topic for dinner conversation, do we? Am I being tacky? Am I a downgrade from you all's typical Sunday evening company? Is it time for me to take a time-out?"

Lynn said, "I don't think that's necessary. Maybe just a cooldown. Your company is, as always, very . . . exhilarating."

"Fair," Alice said. She pushed at strands of dark hair that had sprung loose from her braid. "But am I exigent? My brother called me that recently. I had to look it up, and when I did it really hurt my feelings." Alice released a noisy sigh before anyone could respond, and she turned directly to Sam. "You know I love you, right?"

Sam said, "We're good, Alice."

It was quiet for a bit.

Alice's dark eyes were shining with emotion, and several glasses of wine. "I'm serious. You're my friend since we're six years old, and I love you even if you don't drink and you don't vote. You know that, right? Hell, I don't exercise and I don't floss. You know what else I don't do? Put money in the Salvation Army bucket. Not even at Christmastime. I'm a monster. I'm the Grinch."

"We're good, Alice," Sam said again.

# CHAPTER 18

**A**lice turned to Lynn. "When'd your finger go missing, by the way?"

"Let's see," Lynn said. "I must've misplaced it about . . . nine, ten years ago. Even after I retraced all my steps."

Issa patted his breast pocket and said, "I've got Lynn's finger right here, Alice. Take it with me everywhere, like a rabbit's foot."

Alice roared. "You're gonna give me a hemorrhage! Is that what you get from laughing too hard?" She turned back to Lynn. "You were saying?"

Lynn looked around the table. "I didn't tell any of you guys?"

Mikey said, "I remember you saying you had an injury and that's why you dropped out of school."

Lynn nodded. "Right. It would've been my second year of school that my teacher started me training for the senior concerto competition. Winning pianist gets a big grant, performance at Carnegie Hall, yada yada. So I was practicing for that, nine or ten hours a day, often late into the night, sometimes until dawn."

Lynn paused and took a sip of water. Under the light of the chandelier, her hair glimmered red and orange and gold and yellow, and shot out dramatically from her small, pale face. Her pupils were practically nonexistent.

"One night in the practice room," Lynn continued, "I left for a quick bathroom break. When I came back, I sat down to play. Third movement of the concerto opens with a huge crashing octave in the left hand." She demonstrated a long stretch from pinky to thumb with her left hand. "And when I brought my hand down, it met a needle that was stuck between the keys."

"A needle was stuck in between the piano keys?!" Alice cried. "Oh, *no!*" She shuddered dramatically, her tongue sticking out one side of her mouth. "That makes my vagina contract and disappear inside itself."

Sam said, "Mine, too!"

Mikey said, "Someone put the needle there? To sabotage you?"

Issa said, "You can't know how crazy these conservatory kids are unless you've been one."

Sam said, "Were you a student there, too?"

Issa nodded. "Jazz department. Lynn and I didn't know each other at the time."

Alice said, "Did they find out who it was? I'll kill him. You *know* it was a guy. A girl would've just started a rumor that you were screwing your teacher. Am I wrong?"

Lynn said, "This was before they had surveillance cameras on every hall. Could have been anyone. The students there . . . the competition . . . It wasn't a friendly place. They never did find out who it was."

"So, and your hand?"

"It wasn't bad at first," Lynn said. "It hurt because the needle pierced the skin, but mostly it just freaked me out. I ran back to my dorm room, locked myself in there, didn't practice for a day or two. Called campus security and my teacher. Tried to get my head on straight. At first it seemed like my hand was going to heal up fine, but a few days later, it got worse. Red. Painful. Turned purple, then almost to black. Numb right at the knuckle. That's when I went to a doctor."

Alice said, "Infection?"

Mikey said, "Was there something in the needle? Or on it?"

Lynn nodded. "I bolted from the room that night, and by the time campus security got there to check it out, the needle was gone."

"What'd the doctor say?"

Lynn said, "He did all sorts of tests, trying to figure out the source of the infection. It was clear that it wasn't *just a needle* . . . I would have recovered from a pinprick in two days. There was something on it. Someone knew what they were doing, but they never found out who, or what it was."

"And that's when you had your finger removed?"

Lynn said, "The doctor recommended surgery to remove the finger right away. He said that if he didn't amputate, there was a very high likelihood that the infection would grow worse, spread quickly. My whole body could go into sepsis. I could die."

"So you had it done then?"

"Nope." Lynn shook her head. "I walked out of the hospital, went home to my dorm. Decided to wait and see what would happen."

Alice stared at her. "At the risk of *dying?*"

Lynn nodded. "My thinking at the time was that if I lost a finger, I'd no longer be a pianist, at least not a serious one. Death seemed . . . I know that sounds outrageous. But I didn't feel like I'd have enough to live for."

"Wow," Alice breathed. "It's that important to have all ten fingers?"

"Classical repertoire, yes," Lynn said. "All the stuff that would win me any awards, get me any big jobs."

Alice said, "Damn, that sounds like discrimination. I smell a lawsuit!"

Lynn laughed. "My doctor thought I was a complete lunatic. He pled with me. Told me it was fifty-fifty that I would live another *month* if I didn't take the operation."

"So . . . what happened?"

"In a couple days' time, it was getting worse, and *fast*. Spreading. I got a fever."

"And he was able to change your mind then? Convinced you to get the surgery?"

Lynn said, "*He* didn't change my mind."

"So what did?"

Lynn said, "I guess I realized I didn't want to go just yet." She sipped her water.

Alice said, "And was it worth it?"

"What do you mean?"

"Was life worth living? Worth sticking around for?"

Lynn said, "There were a few years there where I wasn't sure."

Alice said, "There are times I'm not sure myself. I mean, do the pros *really* outweigh the cons? Life can be such a patronizing fucker."

Sam frowned. "I don't like to hear you talk like that," he said.

"Oh, don't worry," Alice said, waving her hand. "I'm not gonna off myself. Especially not right after Sally. I don't want my funeral to be sloppy seconds." She paused. "I'm *joking*, you guys."

Sam said, "I never know when you're serious. It's very annoying." He turned to Lynn. "So when you got the surgery, you were, what, twenty? Twenty-one? Alone in the city?"

Lynn nodded. "After the surgery they got me on a bunch of hydrocodone for the recovery, and it wasn't long at all until I was totally hooked. I'd go to doctors all over the city, get them to prescribe me painkillers."

"Were you working?"

"Office temping. I couldn't hold anything for more than a few weeks. I moved out to Queens when I dropped out of school because I had to leave the dorm and couldn't afford Manhattan anymore. Eventually . . . well, it didn't make sense to take the subway forty-five minutes into Manhattan to try and finagle one more scrip out of one more doctor when I could buy smack on the block where I lived for a fraction of the cost. Eventually, I was selling, too, because I couldn't hold down a job and had no other way to get my fix and scrape enough together for rent."

"Jeez," Mikey said softly. "I had no idea things were so bad, Lynn."

"But you still managed to keep in touch with us," Alice said. "That's something."

Lynn offered a weary, desiccated little smile. "I didn't have a computer, but I'd go to the public library, an hour-long walk from my apartment. That's where I'd go to check my email. And managing to crank out a coherent response to you guys . . . Well, it was all a rather painful and extravagant charade."

"So when did the two of you meet?" Sam nodded in Issa's direction.

"We met in AA in Queens," Issa said. "I had my own set of problems. Like Lynn, I made it into the conservatory on full scholarship and couldn't relate to the classmates, most of them rich kids from private schools. I didn't fit. I graduated but barely, drinking a fifth of rum a day. Eventually moved out to Queens and got a job doing music at a Pentecostal church. Started AA. My second meeting, this one shows up, and I'm like, *I know you, but I don't know why* . . . We put it together then: we would've crossed paths at the conservatory a hundred times, just hadn't properly met. Then I found out she was *that* girl, with the finger. Everyone at school had heard the story. We were all examining pianos top to bottom every time we sat down at a practice room, looking for needles and broken glass and razor blades . . . Even still, I sort of thought it was urban legend, didn't know it had actually happened. Then she shows me her hand. I tried to get her to come out for coffee with me. Took a good little while to convince her."

Lynn said, "They tell you not to start dating someone you meet at AA, and I was trying to follow all the rules."

Alice said, "So you guys have been together now, what, eight years?"

Issa said, "Don't even bother saying it, Alice, it's no use . . . I've been trying to get Lynn to marry me since our first date."

Lynn protested, "Not true."

"It absolutely is true," Issa said to the others.

Lynn held up her left hand, cheerily wiggling the fingers around the missing one. "Where would you propose putting a ring, anyway?"

Issa gently pushed a few red curls back from Lynn's face and leaned over to kiss her cheek. He said, "That's her favorite excuse."

Alice turned to Lynn. "So what's the problem? What're you scared of? What's the *worst thing* that could happen? You get divorced?" She paused to drink more wine. "Speaking from experience, I can assure you that getting divorced hurts about as much as a beesting."

Lynn laughed.

Sam said, "You guys run the local AA in Jim Thorpe, right?"

Lynn nodded. "Even in a small town, last place you'd expect, you've got loads of people in need of help." She was quiet for a bit. Then she said, "You guys wouldn't know this, but I was already using in high school. Before, even. Twelve or thirteen."

"We were all drinking by then," Alice pointed out.

"Sure," Lynn said. "But it was different for me. I wanted it more than you guys. I could just tell it was different for me. The pathology. It wasn't long till I *needed* it and started looking for harder stuff, too."

"Were you using pills when we were in school?" Alice said.

Lynn nodded. "I was buying from those older guys on the street. You know, the nutter who apparently stabbed his grandma, and the other one. They were actually in with some *really* bad-news guys. Townies. Junkies. Dropouts. They always had stuff on them. I started buying whatever they had, as much as I could afford."

"I had no clue," Mikey said.

"I know," Lynn said. She paused to eat a bite of lamb. Then she said, "Sally knew."

Sam's head jerked upright. "Sally knew?"

Lynn said, "I wasn't planning on bringing this up, you guys. I know it's already a sad occasion. But it's been on my mind . . ." Lynn paused and ran her napkin over her lips. She sighed and pushed red curls back behind her ears. The corners of her mouth drooped. "I think it was my fault, you guys."

Sam said, "What was your fault?"

"Sally leaving us."

Alice said, "What do you mean?"

Lynn said, "I never wanted to tell you guys this because I felt so ghastly about the whole thing."

"What happened?" Sam said.

"A few weeks before Sally left us, she caught me."

"Using something?"

"Buying something. Outside the 7-Eleven. Sally walked out and saw me mid-handover. It had to be obvious. She walked on by in that moment but brought it up with me later that night. She was worried. She knew I wasn't up to any good, and she knew I was lying when I said it was just cigarettes. Being caught in a lie made me so defensive, scared of getting found out, the rest of you turning on me if you knew . . . I felt cornered. It made me mean." Lynn shook her head. Her posture had gone so low she sagged in her chair like damp laundry. "I can't believe I brought her mom into it."

Sam said, "What about her mom?"

"Did you say something about her mom?" Alice asked.

Lynn nodded. "Something like, *You act so naïve, but your own mother's an alcoholic, you know. You've lived with one your whole life. So don't act like I'm some degenerate. Like I'm some kind of shock to you.*" Lynn fanned briskly at her deeply flushed face with all her fingers, as though to cool it. When she spoke again, her voice was thin and watery. "And then I made her promise to keep all of this secret from the rest of you guys. Made her swear. I was mean. Seriously nasty to her. She was scared."

Alice said, "You can't beat yourself up like this, Lynn. We were kids, for crying out loud."

Sam nodded, "That is true."

Alice added, "And Corinne *was* messed up. *Sheeeeeeez*us. Not trying to pile on, but did you guys see her today? That poor woman looks like something the cat threw up."

Mikey said, "Don't be mean."

"I know," Alice said, hand in the air, conceding to this. She turned to Lynn. "You didn't say anything about Sally's mom that wasn't true; that's all I meant to say."

Lynn said, "Sally never, ever spoke ill of her mother, did she? Very protective of her."

Sam said, "She never said much about her, period."

Mikey could recall a single occasion when Sally had spoken somewhat disparagingly of her mother, but it was such a mild, fleeting observation that he wasn't even sure it could count as "speaking ill." Sally was eleven or twelve at the time, and Mikey was helping her memorize a vocabulary list on the bus on the way to school.

Sally said the word *delusional*, spelled it, and offered the definition. She stared out the window in silence for a moment, then she said, "I think my mom does this sometimes."

"Does what?" Mikey had said.

"When she tells stories about other people, like when my aunt Rhonda comes to visit, or Grammy, or when we visit them, or when my mom's boyfriends are over . . . Anyhow, whenever my mom remembers things, she always remembers it wrong. Like that people were mean to her when they were actually nice." Sally thought on this for a moment, then added, "Or that people were nice to her when actually they were mean."

Sally fell silent again, and these would be the last words Mikey ever heard her speak of her mother.

Alice turned back to Lynn. "Did you and Sally make amends before she cut us all off?"

Lynn nodded. "I apologized. Things still felt a little chilly between us, but I got the impression it was going to be okay. But then it wasn't even a full month after that happened that she cut off all of us. I couldn't help feeling that was why."

Alice said, "Lynn, you're a sweet sap."

Lynn said, "It's one of those memories that still lives hot in me. Do you know what I mean? Still comes at nighttime in pieces and waves." She looked around to meet the eyes of the others. "The other thing I've wondered . . . Do you guys think there's any chance Sally started using something? I hadn't thought about it all that much, but then with the suicide . . . And with Corinne, obviously it would run in the family. Anyway, there were times when I was really in the thick of it, my own addiction I mean . . . I was right at the edge." Lynn's voice had grown faraway and indistinct, and Mikey thought of the scar he had seen on her forearm earlier that afternoon.

Alice said, "What do you mean?"

"Self-obliteration," Lynn said. "If I'd had the wherewithal to get myself to the edge of a bridge, I probably would've jumped off it. I just wonder about Sally's state of mind. What took her there."

Sam turned to Mikey. "Did Sally look healthy more recently when you saw her out?"

Mikey said, "I never got very close, but . . . I wouldn't say she looked *un*healthy."

Sam said, "How *did* Sally look?" His broad pink face was wrinkled with emotion. He tapped his fork silently against his lip.

Mikey said, "She never stopped looking . . . exactly like herself."

Mikey's hands, resting in his lap, suddenly looked dead and felt dead.

Alice said, "You can't blame yourself for any of this, Lynn. You got scared and lashed out a bit. I've probably done worse in the past twenty-four hours. I gave three different people the finger just on the drive over here! You'd probably fall out of your chair, go running for the hills, if you knew half the bad shit I've done."

Mikey wondered where Alice was going with this but was relieved at the prospect of a new topic of conversation. "Like what?" he said.

"Yes," Lynn said, brightening. "Like what?"

Alice said, "Stole one piece of a thousand-piece puzzle at the library."

Mikey said, "Do better than that."

Sam said, "Tell about the chicken thing. Remember? Sixth grade?"

Alice looked at him. "The chicken thing?" She looked puzzled for a moment. Then she grimaced. "*Oh*," she said. Alice pushed wild black hair back from her face. "That's nowhere near the worst thing I've done, but . . ."

"What's the chicken thing?" Issa said.

"You must not think bad of me," Alice said, straightening up in her chair, holding up her right palm as though speaking under oath. "I was young. And these hoodlums"—she looked around the table, indicting the rest of them—"put me up to it."

"Did we?" Mikey said.

Alice took a swallow of wine and continued. "My aunt who lived out in Springville had a pool. Sometimes my mom would drive the whole lot of us out to swim in the summer. She was out in the boondocks. Had chickens. One afternoon, we got McDonald's on the way, and I didn't finish my nuggets."

Lynn said, "That's right. I remember now."

Alice said, "I tossed my leftover nuggets into the coop when my aunt wasn't watching."

Issa said, "Oh? Ohhhhhhh. They ate them?"

Alice winced and nodded.

Mikey said, "They devoured them."

Issa said, "Diabolical."

Lynn laughed. "Oh, come on, Alice. That's not that bad. You know those nuggets barely even have any real chicken in them, anyway."

"Well," Alice said, "I felt so bad that the next day, I killed a man and ate him so I'd know what it was like."

Mikey was laughing and laughing.

Alice looked at him. "All right, Funny Pants, what's the worst thing you've ever done?"

Mikey cleared his throat. "Hm." He was quiet for a bit. *The worst thing I've ever done?*

Alice said, "Well?"

"I'm thinking," Mikey said. He could quickly recall plenty of shitty little things he'd done: petty grudges, nasty insults under his breath, moments of quiet rage, terrible thoughts toward people.

But Mikey had never acted out on them; his anger had always been suppressed at the critical moment. Right? The *worst thing* he'd ever done? Was there anything truly unforgivable?

Mikey's thoughts turned, and the question was reversed in his head. What was the *best* thing he'd ever done? The birthday cards to his friends? Fresh baked goods now and then to his father, who probably still preferred his Chips Ahoy! when it came right down to it? Offering to work Thanksgiving and Christmas so a colleague could spend it with their family, when for Mikey it was a great relief not to spend an obligatory holiday with his father? These were small niceties, and they required so little of him . . . Was there a best thing? Even a great or truly good thing? Mikey was suddenly disheartened by all these manufactured little courtesies he performed, disheartened by the idea that his *very best things* amounted to jack shit. He quickly tried to put this out of his mind. His thoughts returned to the question at hand, *the worst thing,* and there was abruptly a nagging pull on his brain, almost physically painful, a sharp tug in an uncertain direction. He just hadn't quite landed on it, couldn't quite find the words.

Alice said, "Let me guess . . . One time . . . you . . . cut the tag off your mattress."

Mikey laughed and took a sip of wine. He finally said, "I'll have to get back to you on that."

Alice said, "Mikey, you really are a disappointment to me." She took a sip of her wine then asked, "Too many *worst things* to choose from or not enough?"

"I'm not sure," Mikey said.

Alice said, "Maybe your worst thing is still yet to come. Look out!"

The caterers cleared their plates and began to set out silverware for dessert.

Lynn said, "I'm stuffed. Can we take a break, take some Tums and stretch out our tummies before dessert? Lie around in the other room for a bit? I'll brew coffee."

Alice said, "I'm going to eat more lamb in that case."

Mikey said, "Let's send the caterers on their way—snow's really coming down out there."

Alice filled another plate with lamb and poured two glasses of bourbon over ice. She handed one glass to Mikey.

He said, "I don't know if I need—"

"Be a friend," Alice said. "I hate drinking alone. I'll do it, but I hate it."

Lynn brought a pot of coffee and mugs and a bowl of sugar into the main room.

Mikey checked his phone, where he had a voice mail. He reported to the others, "Jimmy's flight got pushed back again. Set to land at nine. He may not make it out here tonight—depending on the weather, he may just grab a hotel near the airport and try to catch us in the morning."

Alice said, "He *is* avoiding us! I knew it!"

Sam said, "Maybe one of you musicians would want to play us some tunes?"

Lynn said, "That is one serious piano."

Chris, appearing quite drunk and vaguely ghoulish with wine-stained teeth, said, "I'm more comfortable on vocals."

Alice said, "Babe, why don't you take a knee on that?"

Chris shot her a nasty look and said, "Then I'm going to go check my phone for a while." She wobbled a bit as she went up the stairs to the master bedroom.

Alice gave them all a weary look and said, "Trust me, you do not want to be subjected to her vocals."

Mikey sipped his coffee and said, "Is her singing voice quite similar to her speaking voice?"

Sam snorted into his fist.

Lynn said, "She's very beautiful, Alice, and she seems very nice."

"She is," Alice agreed, "and she is. I know I'm too hard on her. I'm just too hard." She took a sip of her bourbon and threw her braid over her shoulder.

Issa took a seat at the piano and began to play a melody that was soft and warm and slightly sad.

Sam said to Lynn, "What's he playing?"

Lynn said, "Thelonious Monk . . . ''Round Midnight.'"

Issa swayed gently over and back the keys, up and down between registers. His head rolled smoothly over his neck, fingers lifted and grazed and caressed the keys, a slow and beautiful dance.

Mikey glanced over at Alice when a low vibration emerged from her lips.

"Are you *purring*?" he said.

"I'm relishing the moment."

Alice, Lynn, Mikey, and Sam listened to the music and didn't speak for a few minutes. It was completely dark outside now, and darkish in the room, which was lit by only a few hanging lamps that gave off a soft, golden light. Fresh snowfall was illuminated against the wall of windows. The fire on the far side of the room crackled and hissed.

When Mikey glanced at Sam's face, he was surprised to see that Sam's broad pink cheeks shone with tears. Mikey reached over and patted Sam's knee. "You all right?"

"Oh," Sam wiped his eyes. "It's the reason Justine's not here."

"Uh-huh," Mikey said.

Alice said, "Yeah?"

"She miscarried," Sam said in a broken and uncontrolled voice, and then he wept loudly, wetly.

Alice leapt up from her seat to go next to Sam, and she threw her arms around his neck. Sam leaned his head against Alice's and sobbed harshly for a moment, then hiccupped. "We've been trying for years. She was nine weeks along. Size of a lima bean, they said. Justine was already sure it was a girl. We called her Bunny."

Alice rubbed his back.

Sam hiccupped once more. "We were going to announce it to you guys in person . . ." He sniffed and wiped his eyes. "Anyhow, Alice, that's why it's hard to hear about . . . It's not that I don't agree with your cause, it's just hard . . ."

Alice said, "I get it."

Sam wiped his eyes with the back of his wrists, and moved Alice's black hair out of his face, handling it like a dirty Kleenex, something he didn't particularly want to touch. "When we were having a hard time getting pregnant," he said, "Justine got it in her head that if I stopped drinking, it'd be better. Some doctor told her that having a cleaner system can help with the sperm count."

"So that's why you're not drinking."

Sam nodded. "I stuck with it once she got pregnant, too, thinking that'd make it easier on her. It obviously doesn't matter now. I don't think she'll be up for trying anytime soon, but it still seems like the right thing to do to stick with it. I should've just explained earlier."

Alice nodded. "I get it. Sorry I gave you so much grief." She grabbed Sam's hand and kissed the back of it five times fast.

Sam said, "I wasn't gonna come here after all, but Justine encouraged me. She's staying with her sister."

Mikey said, "I'm so sorry, Sam."

"Better days ahead," Sam said with a heavy sigh.

Lynn nodded. "Always."

Alice said, "Is there anything we can do?"

Sam shook his head. "It'll happen for us when it's supposed to happen for us."

Lynn said, "You will make a great dad when it happens."

Alice kissed his hand again, then held it in her own lap, and he rested his head on her shoulder.

They listened to Issa's music without speaking for a few minutes.

Mikey's thoughts turned unexpectedly to his own father. Mikey still had no clue about his mother's identity, or even if she was still alive, and could not help wondering now how it had all gone down thirty-one years ago. Mikey tried to imagine how a mother might have announced to his father that she was expecting and what his father's reaction might have been. Mikey had never once seen his father display joy. He could not imagine his father ever having the same sort of emotion toward him that Sam already had for the lima-bean-size Bunny—the depth of the joy, the grief over the loss. Mikey thought it was very possible that his father never wanted to be a father. Or perhaps, Mikey thought, his father had once been like Sam, completely in love with the lima-bean-size dream of Mikey, but the love had disappeared along with Mikey's mother. Or perhaps the love had drained from him over the years, a slow leak. Either way, the result was a father who now seemed to have no more feelings toward his grown son than he had toward the weatherman. Had there ever been more between them? Mikey almost wished there was a break he could clearly identify. It seemed things might be easier if he could trace their trouble back to one particular event, one ultimate fight, a precise and abominable deed, or some official diagnosis of alcoholism, depression, or neglect, but the exact source had no name.

Alice had gotten out of her seat and was doing a downward-facing dog in the middle of the room.

Sam's voice interrupted Mikey's thoughts. "There is something else I wanted to talk to you guys about," he said.

Mikey watched as Sam's features drew together, reaching a dark and troubled expression.

"I was gonna wait till Jimmy was here, but . . ." Sam scratched his chin, tilting his head up, and he swallowed, his Adam's apple leaping and bulging. He pushed his blond hair back from his brow.

Alice completed her stretch and sat back down on the couch, breathing heavily, rubbing the heel of her hands into her long, firm thighs.

Sam said, "Lynn, what you said about your own incident with Sally just a few weeks before she left us . . . That might've been a factor, but I'm afraid mine is much worse. I'm afraid that mine . . . Well . . . sometimes I'm afraid that Justine's miscarriage, and before that, our trouble getting pregnant . . . Sometimes I'm afraid these things are my punishment."

Mikey stared at him.

Alice said, "What on earth for?"

Sam said, "Alice, you were asking Mikey earlier about the worst thing he ever did? Well . . ." Sam released a hot sigh that smelled bad, as though these next words had been stewing around in a sour belly for far too long. "The worst thing I ever did was to Sally," he said. "She left the group because of me."

# CHAPTER 19

"I was in love with Sally all along," Sam explained. "From the time I was six to the time I was sixteen. And eventually . . ." Sam paused, shaking his head slowly. "Eventually, I thought, after all those years loving her, I had it in my head that loving her so long and so hard meant that I *deserved* her," Sam said, wincing at this word.

Sam cracked his knuckles over his large belly before continuing. "On the night of her sixteenth birthday, I had a gift for her and was going to go to her house to tell her that I loved her. I had it all planned out."

Mikey glanced at Alice. She ran her fingers through the tip of her dark braid, swirling that black tail around a single bony knuckle.

Sam continued, "But I got there and saw through her bedroom window that she was there with someone. Someone else was in her bed." He turned to Alice. "You probably remember, I was at The Gunner House later that night. You came and found me there. I told you what had happened. I was *burning up* with jealousy, turning inside out." Sam turned to Mikey. "I thought for a minute that it could be you . . . Then I realized it *had* to be Jimmy."

Lynn said, "Jimmy and Sally were together?"

Sam nodded. "There had been other things over the years . . . a time I caught her spending the night at his place, in his basement . . . Anyway. I always tried to ignore it, convince myself otherwise, but that night when I saw her in bed with someone confirmed it. I caught up with Sally the next day on the way home from school. Cornered her as she went to her house. I told her I knew what was going on with Jimmy, I had seen. At first I tried to conceal the fact that I was in love with her, tried to make it like I was just angry because they were being secretive, but my emotions got the best of me, and that came out, too. I told her that I loved her and she had hurt me worse than anyone had ever hurt me before."

"What did Sally say?"

"She was crying. She begged me to calm down. She said, *I never knew. I never meant to hurt you.* She said she would do anything to make things okay, that she didn't want anyone to know what I had seen because she didn't want our group to be busted up." Sam rubbed his temples before continuing. "We were at her house. Her mother wasn't home. I cornered her, pushed her against the wall."

Sam's voice vibrated as he continued, and his eyes were crammed shut, as though he were in a car and the brakes had just gone out. Awaiting the collision. "I grabbed her by her shoulders," he said. "We . . . I . . . I told her to kiss me."

Mikey suddenly felt hot blood flashing through him.

Sam continued in a voice that had thickened with emotion, "And I touched her breasts. Outside her shirt. But . . ."

Mikey had to look away from Sam, and when he looked back, Sam's face was drenched with slime, and Mikey felt ill.

"When our lips met," Sam continued, "all I could taste was the salt of her tears. I let go immediately, backed away. I knew I'd been wrong—I *never* deserved her, and she didn't owe me anything, not even a kiss. I begged her to forgive me and told her if she wanted to be with Jimmy, she should be with Jimmy. I told her I would never talk to her again." Sam paused, and he stared down into his lap. "I can't look at you guys," he said quietly, and a few tears dropped to his belly, darkening his white shirt like oil spots. His whole body was curled into itself like a pill bug, and he made hollow sounds.

Lynn said, "Sam, it's okay. You held back, right? That was it?"

Sam nodded. He sniffed long and hard, ground the heel of his hand into his temple. "And right away, she said she forgave me. I didn't deserve it, but she said it was okay and that I didn't have to stop talking to her. She said she didn't want anyone else to know any of this because she didn't want things to change." Sam sniffed again, a wheeze and a rattle.

Lynn said, "It's okay, Sam."

Alice said, "Yes, it's okay," in a comforting tone.

Mikey felt that he should reassure Sam, too, so he did, as a courtesy, but his heart was not in it.

Sam pushed his wrists in his eye sockets, as though to scrub them clean.

Lynn said, "Is this why you became religious?"

"I wasn't really running toward anything in particular, religion or otherwise, as much as I was running from Lackawanna. From home, and you guys. I responded to an ad for a room-and-board-included camp counselor position in Georgia. It was just the first thing I found."

Lynn said, "And did you find what you were looking for there?"

"Nothing took away the shame. No amount of scripture or sermons that tell me I'm forgiven, or even Sally saying so herself. It still makes my insides squinch up every time I think about it, wakes me up at night. Still makes me feel like a hopeless loser. I still feel like I'm being punished. Like I said, I think about, sometimes, our difficulty getting pregnant . . . the miscarriage . . ." Sam's voice trailed off to a murmur.

Mikey was trying to reconcile in his mind the image of Sam at age sixteen forcing his large mouth onto Sally's small mouth, his large hands onto her small breasts, with Sam at age nine, putting underwear over his head for laughs, so pitiful and needy for the validation of the others that he would stop at nothing to entertain them, and Sam now at age thirty-one, still wrecked by the memory, still convinced he was a hopeless loser, still certain he was being punished and was deserving of this. Mikey wasn't ready to speak words of comfort to Sam, nor any of condemnation. He hoped this information would not forever contaminate their friendship, but he still did not find himself eager to extend generous words.

Sam turned solemnly to Mikey and said, "You knew about this, didn't you? What happened between Sally and me."

Mikey looked up at him sharply. "What? No. This is the first I'm hearing any of this."

"Really?" Sam gazed at him with one brow arched. "I could've sworn . . . Well, I guess my eyes deceived me."

"What?" Mikey frowned at Sam, awaiting explanation.

"A few days after that happened between Sally and me," Sam said, "I saw her coming out of your house in the evening. Hunched over, like she didn't want to be seen. The expression on her face was like she had been crying. I figured she had confided in you about what happened between me and her. The two of you were always close. I couldn't imagine any other reason she'd be at your house . . ."

Mikey said, "Sally hadn't been in my house for years, not since we were little. Once we hit middle school, before even, we always just hung out at The Gunner House. My dad didn't like when other people were over." Mikey closed his eyes to briefly search the recesses of his mind, allowing for the possibility that something had escaped. "No," he said definitively, eyes snapping open. "She wasn't there. You must have been mistaken."

Sam wiped sweat from his face. "I really thought for *all these years* you knew what happened but just had the good grace to let me back into your life in spite of it."

"No." Mikey was shaking his head. "I didn't." He cut himself off a split second before adding *I wouldn't.*

Mikey was angered by Sam's assumption that he had just somehow privately made his peace with Sam, without any sort of reckoning. He quickly drank more of his bourbon and stared at the far wall to avoid eye contact with any of the others. His jaw was tight, his teeth bearing down as if they had been adhered top to bottom with cement. He felt pissed off, indignant, unsympathetic, and ultimately ill-equipped for an actual fight with his friend.

With a cough, Lynn broke a lengthy and uncomfortable silence to ask Sam something else about church.

Sam answered, "It's helped me in a lot of ways. My temper. Outlook. Being a better person and partner than I would be otherwise." Sam paused. "I know you guys think it's a weird way to be, this church stuff. And trust me, I do not think it makes me any kind of saint."

Alice said, "You know what my gram said right before she died? Her last words?"

"What's that?"

"She had a chaplain in there with her, and the guy starts reading scripture. Gram seems all annoyed. She looks around the room, asks who this guy is and why he's reading to her. My dad explains to Gram that the chaplain is there to bring her peace, to help her, just in case she's scared. You know what my gram said? She goes, *Sure, death's a little scary, but* life *is the real bitch.* Then she closed her eyes and croaked."

Lynn laughed. "Those were really her last words?"

Alice nodded. "And the chaplain was quiet for a minute; then he looked around the room and said, *You know what? I completely agree with her.* What I'm trying to say is that I think there are some things we can all agree on."

Alice took a sip of her bourbon. She pulled a throw blanket from the top of the couch and spread it over her legs. "Listen, I told Mikey this earlier and wasn't going to bring it up tonight—I didn't know how much we'd really feel like getting into all this business—but, Sam, you ought to know that I was the one in Sally's bed that night."

Lynn said, "You mean you were sleeping over?"

"*Hah!*" Alice let out a bark of a laugh. "Sorry. No, guys, Sally and I were involved. Sexually."

Lynn and Sam stared at her.

Sam's mouth flopped open. "Sally was gay?"

Alice said, "We were involved for over a year before that night when you saw us together at her house."

Sam said, "But you were at The Gunner House that night . . . We talked . . ."

Alice nodded. "I didn't want anyone to know."

Sam blinked. "Did Sally say something to *you* about what happened with me the next day? The kiss? The other stuff?"

Alice shook her head. "Not a word. I knew you thought it was Jimmy and Sally who were together, but when nothing happened over the next few days, I just assumed you had decided to leave things be. I had no idea you confronted her. She didn't tell me that."

Sam was rubbing his chin, still wearing an awed expression. "So . . . *wow* . . . how did things end between you and Sally?"

Lynn said, "And when?"

Alice said, "She never officially ended things with me before ending things with all of us. We all lost her at the same time."

It was quiet for a bit. Alice picked at a loose thread in the throw blanket.

Mikey said, "It sounds like there was a lot that Sally knew about us that we didn't know about each other."

Sam nodded. "I guess maybe she thought she could protect us from each other."

"Or ourselves."

Lynn said, "I wonder how Jimmy's doing."

Alice turned to Mikey. "So what's *your* deep, dark secret?"

Mikey was quiet for a bit, and Alice revised her question. She said, "What did Sally know about you that no one else did?"

Mikey said, "I can't think."

"No secrets?"

"Mm."

"That's a pity." Alice poured another bourbon for herself and Mikey. "You disappoint me yet again."

Sam said, "I have one more secret."

Alice said, "*Please*, no more secrets from you. Good God. What's next? You litter? You steal flowers from graves and give them to your wife? I knew it! I knew it!"

Sam laughed. "This is a good secret," he said. "When Justine made me quit drinkin' . . . a buddy of mine . . . well . . . anyhow, the point is I have myself a smoke from time to time, and I've got a joint all rolled up and ready out in my glove compartment. Would anyone care to partake?" He glanced at Lynn. "As long as it wouldn't bother you."

"Not even remotely," Lynn said. "Weed is the one thing that never got me into trouble. You guys go right ahead."

Sam went out to his car, Alice went up to the master bedroom to check on Chris, and Lynn joined Issa, sitting next to him on the piano bench. He scooted over to make room for her. She rested her head on his biceps, and he leaned over and kissed the crown of her head. Issa moved his current melody down two octaves, and Lynn softly began to improvise above him with her right hand.

Alice returned, and she now had a small spot of thick white cream on her chin.

Mikey said, "You've got somethin' . . ."

Alice said, "It's benzoyl peroxide, duh!" She stared at him for a second. "You know . . . *for acne*?"

Mikey said, "Ah."

Alice said, "I'm re-upping on bourbon. You are, too. You want ice?"

Mikey nodded and gazed down into his empty mug. The coffee pot was still half full and steaming on the coffee table. He filled his mug with coffee and said, "Can you grab me a splash of milk, too?"

Alice said, "And a splash of milk for the Little Prince."

She returned from the kitchen with a tray of ice in one hand and the bottle of bourbon in the other, and she set these items on the coffee table.

Mikey said, "My milk?"

Alice leaned over Mikey's coffee so that her chin was mere inches above the lip of the steaming mug. She opened her mouth, and a small quantity of milk plopped out of her mouth and straight into his coffee. She grinned with white lips.

Mikey stared at her. "You are sick," he said. "Sick."

Milk was still dripping from her chin. "I don't have three arms!" she cackled. "What was I supposed to do?"

Mikey scooted the mug away from him.

Alice wiped milk from her lips and chin with her sleeve, and continued to giggle gleefully as she jogged back to the kitchen, then returned with the carton of milk and a fresh mug.

She said, "Don't be mad. I'm just trying to lighten the mood, Grumpy Grouchman."

Alice placed ice in both tumbler glasses and poured a fresh inch of bourbon over them. "I enjoy you," she said, and Mikey wasn't sure if she was addressing him or the bourbon, so he didn't respond.

Sam returned to the room with snow in his hair, the joint and a lighter in hand. His cheeks were bright pink, and he smelled cold.

Sam took a seat next to Alice, lit the joint, started it off with a good pull, the end glowing orange, and released a thick, thick cloud. He passed it to Alice, who took a hit, then passed it to Mikey. Mikey hadn't smoked since high school and pulled harder than he'd intended. A cough sputtered from him, and he felt very hot and unpleasant for one moment. He passed the joint to Sam and sank back into the couch.

Soon, Mikey noticed something new in the texture of his lungs, and the fact that it was taking twice as long as usual to empty them. A warm sensation filled his eye sockets. He stared at the floor-to-ceiling windows across the room, the black sky and frozen lake beyond—something about their colors forced a giggle from him. His muscles felt long and warm. Someone had turned up the brightness of this world, and turned down the pace. He giggled again and stared at Alice, who now held the joint. All of her angles and edges were highlighted by shining rainbow thread. He couldn't take his eyes off her.

Alice passed the joint his way, and Mikey said, in the slowest, thickest voice he had ever heard come forth from himself, "No, no, no."

Alice laughed, and it sounded like a symphony.

Mikey smiled and watched as Alice and Sam continued to pass

146    REBECCA KAUFFMAN

the joint back and forth. His sullen grievance toward Sam was diminishing. If Lynn and Alice could forgive Sam's transgressions against Sally, Mikey decided, he could try to do the same.

He gazed at Alice, who was chewing on ice from her own glass of bourbon, and she winked at him. He winked back. Next to Alice, Sam was now hunched lopsidedly into a seam of the leather couch, eyes closed, wearing a peaceful smile. Lynn and Issa continued to play softly together, Lynn's head resting against Issa's shoulder. Mikey closed his eyes and listened to the music, feeling a deep thrum of warmth for all of his friends. The music was the most kind, good, and gorgeous thing he had ever heard. He felt as if he had stepped into someone else's beautiful dream—one so good he didn't deserve to have any part of it.

# CHAPTER 20

Sam eventually stirred, his eyes opening one at a time, and he licked his lips. "That was a doozy," he said. He blinked slowly, his hair disheveled.

Alice crossed her eyes. "This stuff ain't like it used to be. No, sir. Catatonic."

Mikey reached for his bourbon, and the coldness and sharpness of the drink clarified his awareness. He felt slightly less profoundly stoned.

Sam said, "Where's Issa?"

"He went to bed a few minutes ago," Mikey said.

Lynn was still at the piano, where she continued to improvise by herself.

"Time is it, anyway?" Sam said.

Mikey looked at his watch. "Ten thirty," he said.

Sam said, "I'ma take a piece of pie to my bedroom. Wake me up if Jimmy gets here."

Alice went to the kitchen with Sam, and after he had gone upstairs, Alice returned to the main room with an apple pie, a carton of vanilla ice cream, plates, and silverware. Lynn joined Alice and Mikey on the couch, and the three of them ate together.

"Any word from Jimmy?" Lynn said.

Alice and Mikey both double-checked their phones and shook their heads.

"*Damn*," Lynn said. "I hope he'll come by early tomorrow. I'd hate to miss him altogether."

Now that Mikey was less high, his mind was once again cycling unpleasantly over the information he now knew about Sam and Sally, the scene taking on new horror and specificity in his imagination. He felt goodwill leaching out of himself.

He turned to Alice and said, "I don't mean to beat a dead horse, but what are you guys actually thinking about what Sam told us? Are you still thinking about it? Are you . . . okay with it?"

Alice grunted. "*Okay* with it? Hell no. Hell no, no, no. But . . ." She was quiet for a bit. "What are we gonna do? Excommunicate the guy?"

Mikey said, "You just seemed quick to offer him . . ." His voice dropped off. He wasn't sure what he meant. He didn't want to seem ungenerous.

Lynn suggested, "Comfort?"

Mikey said, "Not that he doesn't deserve it. That just wasn't my instinct in the moment."

Alice said, "A lot of people have been more generous with me than I've deserved over the years. I know how I can be. So I guess I feel like it's in my best karmic interests to offer other people generosity when I can. Comfort. The guy's obviously suffering."

Mikey nodded.

Lynn said, "It just seemed like the right thing to give him in that moment. It's obvious he's sorry. Still hurting. Mortified. That being said . . . and I really hate the phrase *forgiven not forgotten*, but . . ." Lynn chewed over her words for a moment. "It's also just not the sort of thing you can completely dissociate from a person once you know it. You guys know what I'm saying? I don't mean to sound harsh."

Alice nodded. "It's true. Frightening how several seconds of your life can impact someone else's opinion of your entire person-hood. You know what I mean? How quickly your mind changes in some cases, and how impossible it is to change it in other cases once it's been made up."

Alice seemed to speak with a deep personal knowledge of this, and Mikey's thoughts flickered once again to her first husband. He wondered if Alice's opinion of The Saint had changed on a dime and what sort of circumstance had brought that about.

Lynn said, "That happened to me once. Long time ago, but it still . . . disconcerts me to think about. Exactly what you're saying, Alice."

"What happened?"

"Before my injury, would have been early in my sophomore year," Lynn said. "I'd been dating a guy for quite a while. We were out for cheap Chinese food with friends, and I was sitting next to him. The bill comes at the end and they haven't split it up, so he suggests we send it around the table, let everybody estimate what they owe. He says he'll count up the cash once everybody's tossed in. So, and I swear I wasn't even paying *attention* to this, but it just caught me, snagged my attention, that my boyfriend didn't add anything to the cash pile."

Alice said, "He didn't contribute any cash of his own?"

"Nuh-uh," Lynn said, shaking her head. "He counts it all up, and sure enough, of course we're short. So a couple people, myself included, reluctantly throw in a little bit more."

"You didn't say anything?"

"I wish I had," Lynn said. "But I didn't want to embarrass him in front of the whole group if I was right about what had happened, and also a tiny part of me wasn't sure. I second-guessed myself in the moment, like maybe he had thrown in and I had just missed it."

Mikey said, "Or maybe it was an honest mistake? He thought he'd put his money in, just misremembered his own actions?"

"Sure. And that's what really gets me about all of this," Lynn said. "It was entirely possible that either my perception was wrong or it had been an honest mistake . . . Even so, it was like you were saying, Alice. My entire opinion of him just turned on a *dime*. My whole idea of *who he was* flipped in a single moment."

Alice said, "Did you break up with him?"

"Well, that's the happyish ending. I didn't break up with him right away. We never discussed it; I was too nonconfrontational. For a while, I just tried my hardest to rationalize it or redo it in my head . . . Ultimately, though, I just couldn't rid myself of the idea that he was a person who wouldn't pay his fair share if he could get away with it. That he was, fundamentally, shitty."

"Well, yeah," Mikey agreed. "I'd say that is a fundamentally shitty thing to do."

Alice said, "So where's the happyish ending?"

"Oh, right," Lynn said. "I made up some other wimpy excuse to break up with him a few weeks later. Said I needed to prioritize my music, make more time to practice or something like that. And then I found out not long after that he'd been cheating on me anyway. With a vocalist, no less. A *soprano*, matter of fact, to add insult to injury. So."

Mikey laughed. "Is that the ultimate insult?"

Lynn nodded, and her curls bounced like springs.

Alice said, "You dodged a bullet, my friend."

Lynn said, "I dodged a cheater. But to this day I don't know if I was even right about what happened at the Chinese restaurant.

Cheating aside, it could still be the case that I was wrong about the one tiny moment that changed my entire opinion of the guy. Night and day. Good to bad."

"But . . . he was a cheater, so who cares?" Alice said.

"It scares me, that's all," Lynn said. "And it *really* makes me shudder to think how many things I've done over the years that might've caused someone to believe, or decide, that I'm *bad*. In a heartbeat. Jeez, how the hell did we get onto this anyway?" She returned to her bowl of pie, stirred the melted ice cream a bit, and took a bite. "I *am* bad, of course," she said. "But you guys know that already."

Mikey laughed. "You are not bad!"

Lynn said, "You're my friend, you have to say that. That's what friends are for, isn't it? To tell you you're good even if you're bad? *Now* I remember how we got onto this. Sam."

Mikey said, "But I imagine it happens the other way, too."

"How's that?"

"A person can go from *bad* to *good* just as quick. I used to hate this guy I work with. He's *constantly* complaining about how much harder he works than everybody else and how little money he makes. He's just a melodramatic pain in the ass. Then once I saw him at Walmart. I was behind him in line, he didn't see me there, and I notice what he's buying: a box of ramen noodles and a bag of the nicest dog treats you can find. Organic. Real chicken in 'em. That's all he's buying, just those two things. And he's counting out change, using his last dime to make the purchase. Spent twice as much on his dog's treats as his own food. Made me . . . well, like you said, just changed the way I saw him from then on."

Alice said, "You're right, that's a good man." She took a sip of her bourbon and tapped her fingertips rhythmically along the glass for a moment, then said to Lynn, "I've got a bone to pick with you."

"Oh?" Lynn said, her mouth white, full of ice cream.

Alice said, "You've been with Issa for eight years. Why won't you marry that good man who wants to marry you, you bad girl?"

"Oh." Lynn laughed and swallowed.

Alice said, "What're you waitin' on? Grrrrrr."

Lynn pushed red curls from her face and said, "Since when did you become some sort of champion for marriage?"

Alice said, "I'm not." She swung her bourbon in a slow circle so the ice tinkled around the glass. "Just yours."

"Why?" Lynn said again.

Alice said, "Because I like weddings!"

Lynn laughed.

Mikey said, "Always lookin' out for number one," and he tipped his glass toward Alice.

Lynn was quiet for a moment. "I guess part of me has always felt unsettled. Not with Issa, certainly not with our life together, but just unsettled with *before*." She sighed. "I don't have the healthiest relationship with my past," she explained.

"Nor do I," Alice said.

"Me either," Mikey said.

"But what's that got to do with getting married?" Alice said.

Lynn ate a bite of pie before continuing. "Maybe this is just a cop-out," she said, "but I think a lot of the problems I've had as an adult came from losing Sally. If I really go back to the sort of *center* of the problems I've had, I think something had already changed inside me before I went to school and had the injury, and before the addiction became . . . consuming. I had already darkened. Much earlier." Lynn wiped her lips with a napkin. "When we lost Sally, something inside of me changed, is what I'm trying to say."

Mikey nodded. "Me, too."

Alice said, "Me, too."

Lynn continued, "Sally taught me something about people that I never wanted to know."

Alice said, "What was that?"

"That people can disappear," Lynn said. "Right before your eyes. That you'll never understand it and there won't be a thing you can do about it."

Alice placed her hand over Lynn's knee. "You're afraid of the people you love disappearing."

Lynn nodded.

It was quiet for a bit.

Alice turned to Mikey. "Are you?"

"What?"

"Afraid of disappearing?"

"Not particularly," Mikey said. "Although I'd want someone to feed my cat."

Lynn laughed.

"I meant of *other* people disappearing," Alice corrected herself. "The people you love."

"Sure," Mikey said, and his mind tickled at something unpleasant.

He picked up the crust of his pie and ate it with his fingers.

Alice said, "Could be worse, Lynn. At least you didn't marry a Saint because of Sally."

"How's that?"

"I was still brokenhearted," Alice said, "even after I'd been away from home at college for years. So when someone came along who thought I was a little smart, laughed at my stupid jokes . . . I mean I just lapped that up like a sad, dehydrated little puppy. It was the first romantic relationship I'd been in since Sally, and I was starved for affection. Validation." She shook her head with disgust at the thought of this.

Mikey said, "So you were never in love with him? Is that why it ended so quickly?"

Alice shot him a look of annoyance. "That's a story for another time, Inspector Clouseau," she said.

Lynn yawned. "I'm gonna head to bed, you guys. Wake me up if Jimmy gets here tonight?"

Finn was stirring around in front of the fireplace across the room. Alice turned to Mikey. "Finn's gotta be overdue for a pee. You up for a walk?"

Alice grabbed the bottle of bourbon, and the two of them suited up. Alice pulled Chris's gloves from her black leather coat and offered them to Mikey since he didn't have gloves of his own. They were very snug, but he managed to get them on over his fingers. He put on his coat. Alice pulled her vest over her sweater and zipped it. She withdrew mittens from the pockets in her vest and put them on.

Alice said, "All I got's this vest. You think Sam would mind?" She nodded toward Sam's large, puffy blue coat.

Mikey said, "Nah."

Alice pulled Sam's coat on and said, "Good God, it's a perfect fit. How depressing. Let's go."

She retrieved a little baggie of bone-shaped biscuits from her purse. Then they walked out the side door, and Alice briefly surveyed their surroundings. Thick woodlands to the south, a few faraway lights to the north, the frozen lake out to the west. She nodded in this direction. "Wanna head down toward the beach?"

"Sure."

Finn moved slowly, happily snuffling the snow with a lopsided grin, his blue eye bright.

Alice and Mikey trudged together through the thick snow. She unscrewed the cap of the bourbon, took a swig, and handed it Mikey's way. He took a swig as well, felt the heat of it like a shock.

Alice said, "So's there a special lady in your life? You never say so in your emails, but I always assume you're just being coy."

Mikey laughed. "No . . ." he said, and he tried to come up with some sort of joke to steer the conversation in a different direction, but nothing came to mind, so he just said "No" again. His glasses were covered in fog, so he took them off and wiped them clean with his fingertip.

Alice said, "What's the matter with you? Are you on drugs?"

"Excuse me?"

Alice stopped walking for a moment, then moved into Mikey's path so that he could not proceed without her. She looked him directly in the eye, through his glasses, which had already partially fogged up again. "Mikey, you're like . . . I don't say this lightly . . . You are *actually* the best person I know. You are actually my favorite."

"Thank you. And you were about to tell me what's the matter with me?"

"Why aren't you in a relationship? Do you date?"

"I have," Mikey said. "It's just, nothing quite took."

Alice took a step back. She stared out over the frozen lake before them for a bit. The moon was fat and gray overhead. In addition to the pleasant heat and tickle of the bourbon, Mikey felt the lingering effects of the marijuana—the world was still a bit strange and slow. Falling snowflakes were big and lazy and funny, the white mist billowing from his nostrils with each exhale a wonder. The sky was packed with stars. A distant train's horn sounded.

Alice said, "Are you a virgin? I'm not going to make fun."

"Leave me alone, Alice."

"Wait . . . Really?"

"Please shut up."

"I'm not making fun. It's just . . . *Really?*"

"Thank you," Mikey said. "Your empathy is truly admirable."

Alice stepped toward Mikey, very close to him, set the bourbon on the ground beneath her feet, stuck it straight into the snow. Then she rose and took Mikey's right hand in both of hers. She tugged Chris's glove off his hand and tossed it into a bank of snow. She held his bare hand.

She said, "Now close your eyes and pretend I'm not me."

Mikey closed his eyes, but he found himself unable to imagine anyone other than Alice standing before him.

Alice took Mikey's hand, and she didn't unzip Sam's coat or her vest but felt her way up under these layers of clothing, guiding Mikey's hand first to her soft belly, then up underneath her bra, to her left breast. Mikey suddenly felt his own heart flashing. Alice's breast was full yet light, warm, textured with goose bumps. Then Mikey felt Alice's mouth on his own. Her tongue gently pushed into his mouth and around it, tasting of bourbon, tasting raw and scary and good. Then Alice's hand was on his crotch, rubbing him through his zipper. He felt pressure everywhere, blood squeezing tight through every passage.

Alice's lips moved to his ear, tugged it gently, her breath warm and ticklish, then back to his mouth. Lust was zipping through Mikey, a fist squeezing his chest. *This is so unlike me*, Mikey thought. *This is so unlike me.*

He abruptly pulled away from her and opened his eyes. "Alice," he said.

"Why not?"

"I'm not in love with you."

"What does that matter? You love me, don't you? And you know I love you."

Mikey paused. "I'm not sure what I think about love."

Alice frowned. "I hope you're not thinking about Christine.

That's not it, is it? We're in what they call an *open relationship*, Mikey. All the kids are doing it."

Mikey laughed and said, "Okay," but when Alice leaned in to kiss him a second time, he backed away again.

Alice bent to grab the bottle of bourbon from the snow beneath her feet, rose, took a long swig from it, grimaced and coughed. "Are you not attracted to me?" she said. Her finger went to her chin. "Is it the zit cream?"

Mikey laughed. "No," he said. "You're very beautiful."

Alice threw a hand in the air with exasperation. "Now you're just telling lies, like I'm some kid you have to console. Like I'm not tall enough to ride the ride but you still want me to feel like I'm having fun. I'm not in love with you either, but, well . . . it's so cold out here. I just wanted to warm up with you. I wanted to have some fun."

Alice did a fast, funny little dance in the snow.

Mikey laughed. "It *is* cold out here," he agreed. He tried to find the right words to explain himself. He said, "I don't do things I haven't thought about for a while first. That's just not me." He paused, then said again, "I don't do things like that."

Alice leaned her ear closer to his mouth. "Who?"

Mikey thought maybe she'd misheard. "*Me*," he said. "*I* don't."

"Well." Alice's chin jerked into her neck, a look of irritation curled across her face. "I'm glad you know you so well," she said.

She paused and took another sip of bourbon before passing the bottle to Mikey.

"Anyhow," she said, "don't make it weird, okay? Between us. I couldn't handle that. Let me explain myself."

"You really don't have to—"

"I wanted to have an experience with you. Share something special. Anyhow, I don't know what I'm saying."

Mikey said, "We *do* share something special, don't we?"

Alice said, "Blah blah blah." She stared out across the frozen lake. "I don't like what you said earlier though."

"Which part?"

"You said you don't know what you think about love."

"Oh . . ." Mikey said. "Well, I don't. Why, do you?"

"Not entirely," Alice said, "But I've probably told fifty people that I love them, and I've meant it every time." She paused. "Of course, I've probably told that many people that I hated them and meant *that* every time, too."

Mikey laughed.

Alice said, "This is a serious question. Have you ever in your life told someone that you love them?"

Mikey's whole chest suddenly seized, as if he'd had the air knocked out of him.

Alice stared at him. "Mikey." She took him by his shoulders and looked straight at his eyes. Her eyes were black and intense, like she could have been in great pain, or ecstasy. "Mikey," she said again, "has anyone other than me, five minutes ago, ever told you that they love you?"

Mikey thought of Alice's question from earlier, at the dinner table. *The worst thing I've ever done.* Suddenly, the words were right there, bubbling up like lava from a dark place.

"No," Mikey said. "And I don't think I love him either."

Alice stared at him. "You mean your father," she said.

Mikey nodded, still feeling these words deep and black in his chest. He said, "It's not simple."

"I don't imagine it is," Alice said.

"What I mean is, he hasn't given me any good reason not to love him," Mikey said. "And it's not that I haven't tried."

Alice was quiet for a bit. Then she said, "Then why don't you just decide that whatever you feel toward him is love?"

Mikey cocked his head sideways and looked at her broad, handsome face. "You can't just change the definition of things to suit yourself."

"Why not?"

"Because that's straight-up delusional."

"Maybe so," Alice said, "but you'd never have to know it. And at least then you wouldn't have to act like you're completely at the mercy of yourself."

"Aren't I? Aren't we all?"

"Good God!" Alice said. "That's the worst thing I've ever heard! Good God. That's horrific." She breathed into one fist, then the other and asked, "How are you so sure that what you feel for him isn't love?"

Mikey considered this. "Because it doesn't feel like it."

Alice said, "You have a hopelessness that I've really come to cherish."

The callus of bitter resentment was so thick it had overtaken Mikey's heart like a tumor, and the range of emotion he could now access toward his own father felt practically microscopic. Long ago, Mikey had accepted that they would never have the relationship that he wanted, and he had lost his desire to change his father, understand him, or connect with him; Mikey only wanted to be as inoffensive to his father as possible. Nowadays, every word he spoke was an attempt to neutralize a situation or dynamic between them. His ultimate goal was that nothing of any substance or emotional value be revealed or exchanged—that nothing upset the balance. A net zero. Mikey had become so skillful at concealing his true self in his father's presence, it was as if he had sewn himself in under his own skin. He only wanted to be agreeable. Flat. Nothing. *Hollow.*

Alice said, "Do you feel like you love *me*?"

Mikey looked away from her. He didn't know what he felt. Numb? Weary?

He said, "I don't know what I feel."

Alice said, "*Why?*"

Mikey stared out over the white lake, then up into the thick splatter of white stars. How would he remember this black sky, positively stuffed with stars, when he no longer had sight? He couldn't—there was no way. It would be lost. At one point, he had decided that a clear, starry night sky like this was Liszt's *Waldes-rauschen* for piano, but realized now that the piece didn't quite capture it. It wasn't right.

Mikey heard a dog howling far away, and the shriek of a predatory bird. His hands were fists. He felt tears on his cheeks, and they were cold and weird.

Alice said, "Mikey, you're hurting me."

He said, "I know."

# CHAPTER 21

Finn had been circling a tree up the path, and now he returned to them, nosing his old gray face up toward Alice's crotch. Alice laughed and leaned down to kiss his head. She drank more bourbon, then passed the bottle to Mikey, who did the same. He drank so much his throat turned to fire. He shivered.

Alice reached down to retrieve Chris's glove from the snow where she had thrown it moments earlier. She shook off the glove and was helping Mikey maneuver his stiff and swollen fingers back into it, when the moment was interrupted by a snowball that smacked directly into Mikey's back.

Mikey spun around.

A thin, athletic figure was running down the path from which they had come, sprinting at top speed, kicking up little snowstorms in his wake.

Alice said, "*What the . . .*" And she stared at the approaching figure for a moment before shrieking, "Jimmy!"

Jimmy hurtled toward the two of them, then performed an elegant slide right at Alice's feet. He rose and brushed snow off himself. He laughed and threw his arms around both of them. In the soft light of the moon, with flushed cheeks and bright eyes, Jimmy looked healthy and radiant, sporting a neat black beard, his dark hair long and wavy.

"What are you guys doing out here in this snow?" Jimmy said.

"My dog had to piss, and I decided to try to seduce Mikey," Alice said. "Thought it'd be like taking candy from a baby. I was wrong."

Jimmy laughed heartily, then clapped Mikey over the back. "It's been way too long!"

Alice said, "How'd you know we were out here?"

"Just pulled in five minutes ago," Jimmy said. He clapped his hands together and danced up and down for warmth. "On my way into the house, I saw footprints out the side door. Couldn't tell who they belonged to, but figured I'd come find out and check."

"Yo-ho-ho," Alice said. "Well, I'm just about frozen now, and Finn's had more than enough time to pee. Let's head in and warm up. We've just about killed this bottle of bourbon, anyway."

"How's everybody?" Jimmy said on the way back to the house.

Mikey gave him a rundown on who all was at the house as they made their way up the path.

Inside, Alice brushed the snow off Finn and hung up Sam's coat.

Mikey said, "How are things with you, man?"

Jimmy said, "I'm good, you guys. I'm really good." He wore slim-fitting jeans, a cream button-down, and a dark wool jacket, which he removed. He ran a hand through very glossy dark locks.

Alice looked him over and said, "*Damn*, Jimmy. I wouldn't've thought it possible, but you've managed to get even more handsome. What's your secret? Maybelline?"

Jimmy said, "You're catching me right after a six-day cleanse."

"What's that mean?"

"Six days on juice. I do it every year after the holidays."

"Just juice?" Alice said. "Good God. Does gravy count?"

Alice and Mikey followed Jimmy through the kitchen, where he rummaged through the refrigerator and prepared a plate of cold leftovers for himself, then to the liquor cabinet, where he picked out a bottle of Côtes du Rhône. He poured a glass for each of them. They went into the main room, where Jimmy started to eat his leftovers at the coffee table.

Alice sniffed the air and looked at Mikey. "Is that me or you?" she said. "Because it's obviously not Jimmy. Rich people don't sweat."

She sniffed her own armpit, then leaned over to sniff Mikey's. "It's you," she confirmed. "Very . . . athletic."

"Thank you for that."

Jimmy swallowed the food that was in his mouth and wiped his lips. "Guys," he said, "how are we doing with this Sally stuff? Everybody doing okay?"

Mikey nodded.

Alice briefly filled Jimmy in on the conversations they'd had earlier with Lynn and Sam, and then she told him about her own romantic relationship with Sally.

Jimmy said, "Oh, I knew all about that." He turned to face Mikey. "You didn't know about that?"

Mikey shook his head. "You did? How?"

"Sally told me," Jimmy said.

Alice said, "*Really?* She told me she didn't want anyone to know . . . I had no idea the two of you talked."

"Yeah," Jimmy said. "She came to me about it because . . . well, because she knew . . . She thought I would understand." Jimmy set down the silverware on his plate and leaned back into the couch.

"Look, I don't want this to be a big thing. I was sort of hoping to avoid doing it in front of everybody in any sort of *lookie-at-me* way, but—" His blue eyes darted up toward the ceiling.

Alice cut in, "You're gay."

Jimmy let out a big laugh. "I should've known . . . Nothing gets by Alice Clancy!"

Mikey said, "You'll have to excuse her. In case you've forgotten, she—"

"Knows everything about everybody?" Jimmy finished the thought.

Mikey said, "Oh. Oh?" He stared at Jimmy, who laughed again.

"Yeah, I'm gay," Jimmy said. "I'm *out* out in LA."

Alice said, "I was partly joking, Jimmy, but, jeez. I mean . . . I'm happy for you!"

Jimmy said, "You guys remember my parents. Catholic as they come. It's part of the reason I moved out west. There were other reasons, but I knew I wasn't ready to come out to my parents, and I also didn't want to keep pretending in everyday life. Modifying my voice, my body language. Faking interest in girls. I wanted to start a new life where everyone knew. So, at least this way, I only have to pretend once or twice a year when we do family trips."

Alice said, "Your parents still don't know?"

Jimmy shook his head. "We haven't had the talk."

Mikey said, "I hope you were never scared of *our* reaction . . ."

Jimmy said, "The only reason I didn't come out sooner to you guys was because, Mikey, I know you're still local, and I didn't want you to be in a position where you'd have to lie to my parents or other mutual friends. I didn't want anyone else to have to tell lies to keep my secret. It's always seemed easier to just keep these lives fully separate," Jimmy explained.

Alice said, "I'm sorry you've had to keep this from your folks.

That's heavy. I mean my parents weren't *thrilled* when I started dating women, but they've always been live-and-let-live. No secrets."

Jimmy said, "I always thought that maybe when I met the right guy, when I was actually ready to settle down, think about getting married . . . maybe that's when I'll be ready for them to know."

Mikey said, "So, when did *you* know?" His calves were hard from their trek through the snow, and he massaged them with his thumbs.

"I always knew," Jimmy said. "But around thirteen, fourteen is when I *knew* knew. Even once I knew, though, I tried to reverse it. Tried to make my voice deeper, my laugh, you know, less of a *giggle*. Tried to use my hands differently. Sat on them so they wouldn't flip around the way they wanted to flip around."

Alice said, "And Sally knew, too? You told her?"

Jimmy nodded. "Sally and I confided in one another about a lot of things. Her mother, for example."

"What about her mother?"

Jimmy was quiet for a bit. "Corinne . . . had a lot of troubles," he said. "Full-blown alcoholic, for starters. That was obvious. Started every single day with a glass of vodka before she could even get out of bed. Shaking like a leaf, Sally said, if she went more than an hour without a sip of something." Jimmy gripped his bottom lip with his teeth, then continued. "And Corinne had men in and out of their house *constantly*. Sally was exposed to it all. And way too early. Thin walls."

Mikey said, "I always sort of got that impression, but never knew for sure."

Jimmy said, "The reason Sally first confided in me was because she slept in my basement sometimes."

Alice said, "She didn't feel safe in her own home?"

Jimmy nodded. "We were just two houses down from Sally, you

guys remember. And we had that storm window that led into the basement—tiny thing, no grown person ever would've been able to crawl in. But when Sally was ten or eleven, she asked me if she could sneak over and sleep in our basement sometimes, when things got noisy at her own house. Noisy, and also . . . *God* . . . this still haunts me. But there were times when Corinne would be passed out cold, and the men would go wandering through the house . . ." Jimmy paused and rubbed his eye sockets hard before looking directly at them both, his bright eyes watery.

"Oh, no," Mikey breathed, aching, a deep, deep cramp of sorrow in his chest.

Jimmy was nodding slowly. "So . . ." He sighed but eventually continued. "I made it part of my nightly routine to unlock and prop that basement window open so Sally could have a safe and quiet place to sleep when her mother had a man over. My parents never knew."

"Did she sleep over often?" Alice asked.

Jimmy nodded. "Sometimes, if I happened to be up anyway, I'd go down to the basement in the middle of the night. If Sally was there and if she was awake, we'd talk. That was when we told each other our *hard* secrets. The ones Sally and I only shared with each other."

"Like who her mother really was," Alice said. "What Sally was exposed to in their own home."

Jimmy nodded. "And eventually, when I learned what it meant to be gay, and realized that I was, and worked up the courage to say that word aloud . . . Sally was the one I trusted with that hard secret."

Alice said, "And Sally trusted you with our secret—hers and mine I mean—that she thought she might be gay, too."

Jimmy nodded.

Mikey said, "Did Sally ever tell you why she cut us all off?"

Jimmy shook his head sadly. "She didn't give me any more warning than she gave either of you. And she never sought me out personally later to explain. It was just . . . it must have been a terrible, terrible place she was in."

Mikey said, "Alone."

"Alone," Jimmy repeated. His eyes skittered back and forth between Mikey and Alice. "Look, it kills me to say this, but it was my fault that she left us."

Alice said, "No, Jimmy, there's no—"

Jimmy held up a hand, silencing her. "I mean it," he said. "The thing is, these secrets . . . it was too much. Sally needed help. I'm not even talking professionally. I just mean . . . she needed more than I could offer her. I wasn't equipped to talk her through everything she was feeling. In my mind, I think, I equated my own problems— discovering that I was gay and coming to grips with that—with what she was going through, but the reality is, I didn't have a clue how to talk to Sally, how to help her. If I had encouraged her to reach out to you guys, or to an adult, to *anyone*, her burden might have been less. I didn't, though, because I was too wrapped up in my own self, and I was too afraid."

Mikey said, "Afraid of what?"

"I was afraid that if Sally's secrets came out, mine would, too." Jimmy swallowed and gripped his nose, then released it. "Things might have turned out so different. She might not have . . . broken."

Alice said, "You didn't break her, Jimmy."

Jimmy said, "I didn't fix her either, and I was *really* the only one who had the chance."

The three of them sat in a dark silence for a bit, and then Alice rose to use the restroom.

After she had left the room, Jimmy leaned close to Mikey and said, "There's something else I really need to tell you, Mikey. Just you." Jimmy's voice was thick and strained with nerves.

Mikey felt a deeply unsettling little tremor of adrenaline spike through him. He said, "What is it?"

The muscles of Jimmy's lips were trembling. "It's about . . ." But before he could continue, he was interrupted by a creak that suddenly rose from the stairway across the room.

Lynn was in red flannel pajamas and making her way down the stairs. Issa followed, in sweatpants and a UPenn T-shirt. Sam followed closely behind, rubbing his sleepy eyes as he lumbered down the stairs in navy pajamas with white piping.

Jimmy leaned toward Mikey and whispered, "We'll talk sometime when it's just the two of us." He gave Mikey's shoulder a squeeze.

Lynn cried, "Jimmy!" when she saw him, and she ran to him. Sam said, "Jimbo!" and his whole posture immediately woke as he saw his old friend. Jimmy embraced both of them, and Sam erupted in happy laughter, holding Jimmy close. Alice returned.

Lynn introduced Jimmy to Issa. Then she said, "Jimmy, I had no idea you were here! I just dragged Sam out of bed and was coming down to tell everyone the news."

Jimmy said, "What's the news?"

Lynn smiled broadly and said, "He said yes!"

"What now?"

Lynn pushed curls from her face and said, "I woke Issa up and asked him to marry me."

Alice shook her fists and said, "Yo-ho-ho!"

They all exchanged hugs and happy words, then Jimmy corralled the group into the kitchen, where he located ingredients for a nonalcoholic fizzy red drink, which he served from a punch bowl, and Alice popped a bottle of champagne.

Jimmy turned on the stereo and found a station that was playing a sultry ballad. He turned the volume up and grabbed Alice by the waist and spun her around the kitchen, dipping her, nearly dropping her, singing lyrics to her with great emotion.

"*It had to be youuuuu*," Jimmy sang. "*Just say yes, please doooooo.*"

Sam cut in as Jimmy's partner, and the two men laughed and sung and spun one another clumsily through the room.

Alice asked Lynn if they had set a date, and Lynn told her to cool her jets.

Issa and Sam took dinner leftovers from the refrigerator, removed the foil, made themselves plates, and microwaved them.

Sam asked Jimmy about life in LA and gazed at him curiously when Jimmy told anecdotes that included details the rest of them simply could not fathom: tacos with raw fish in them, surf competitions held right outside his back window, wheatgrass, Bikram yoga—the room set to 104 degrees, with forty percent humidity, Jimmy explained.

"Why would you want to do that?" Alice said, blinking at Jimmy incredulously. "Why would anyone, ever, want to do that?"

Mikey and Lynn went to the main room, where they stood next to each other at that massive wall of windows, looking out across the great snowy expanse.

The snow was blue and gray and white and silver and pink and gold. It spun up in little frosty cones that danced over the landscape. Mikey could still see his and Alice's and Jimmy's footprints in the path leading down to the beach.

"What's it like to find love?" Mikey said to Lynn.

"Hm." Lynn was quiet for a bit. Then she said, "It's like finding the ground."

"The ground?" Mikey didn't understand.

Lynn hooked her arm through his elbow.

"You'll come to my wedding, won't you?" she said.

Suddenly, Alice was behind them, then between them, putting both Mikey and Lynn in a gentle headlock on either side of her.

"Of course," Mikey said. "You'll need someone to keep Alice in line."

Alice said, "Wouldn't a wedding be boring and terrible without me?"

Lynn laughed.

Alice sang, "*Can't hold me back, can't hold me back, get a heart attack, can't hold me back!*" Then she skipped across the room to Finn, who lay in front of the fire. She roused him and said, "Watch me!" She performed a wild and clumsy dance before him, and Finn's tongue sagged long out of his mouth.

Lynn and Mikey watched Alice for a bit, then Lynn leaned close to Mikey and said, "There's something Alice isn't telling you."

Mikey turned to face Lynn. "Oh?"

Lynn nodded.

"I didn't think there was anything Alice didn't tell anybody," Mikey said. "Hm." He wondered if it had anything to do with whatever Jimmy had to tell him, too.

Sam sidled up next to Mikey once Lynn had gone to join Issa elsewhere in the room.

"Mikey . . ." Sam spoke softly. "Your face earlier, when we talked. I know you think . . . You think I'm a bad man?" Sam spoke these words earnestly, a direct question with no trace of self-pity.

Mikey shook his head. "No," he said.

Sam said, "I know you don't think I'm a *good* man. You couldn't."

Mikey thought of Lynn's words from earlier. *That's what friends are for, isn't it? To tell you you're good even if you're bad?* He couldn't decide if he agreed with this. There were a lot of things he couldn't feel sure about. He couldn't speak for Sally on how much that moment with Sam had affected her, the scope of the impact. It might have changed everything; it might have changed very little. Mikey gazed at Sam's pink face, which timorously awaited a response. He couldn't quite bring himself to say, "You're good," or "We're good," or even "It's okay."

Instead, he placed his hand on Sam's round, warm shoulder and said the truest thing he could think of: "You are my dear friend."

Sam gripped Mikey's hand and said, "You are *my* dear friend."

Mikey wondered if having a dear friend, and being a dear friend, might be almost as good as being a good man.

He gazed across the room, where Alice sat on the floor next to Finn, who was curled tail to chin on the knotted umber rug in front of the fireplace. Alice was holding Finn's paw in her hand and staring into the fire, where the coals had gone blue-gray and the flames rippled low.

Jimmy cracked open a bottle of Lagavulin several minutes later and poured a half inch for himself, then one for Alice and Mikey, too.

Alice said, "What're you trying to do here, Jimmy? Force-feed me your fancy-pants drinks until I black out? Get me to howl at the moon and shit myself? That the plan?"

Jimmy laughed.

Sam said, "Hey, speaking of blacking out, do you guys remember Blackout?"

"Of course," Mikey said.

Sam said, "My cousin Marcus is the one that taught me Blackout, then I taught you guys. Remember? Anyhow, Marcus is principal at some rich-kid school in Pittsburgh. Calls me up the other day to tell me they had to make a rule prohibiting it. Too many fatalities. None at their school, but a handful in the area. Crazy, right? Penalties worse than getting caught with drugs."

Issa said, "Blackout?"

"The Fainting Game," Lynn explained. "Choking Game. Purple Haze. Fuzz. Really? None of these?"

Issa lifted his hands.

"You make yourself pass out," Alice explained. "You get this crazy high, sleep for a minute, have like a lifetime of dreams."

Issa said, "Oh. Erotic asphyxiation. Sure."

"Well," Jimmy laughed. "We weren't doing the erotic part. And we did it to ourselves—we didn't choke each other out or anything. But yes."

"How did you do it to yourself?"

Sam said, "You crouch on the floor, breathe super heavy, like giving-birth breathing, then sit up, hold your breath, and go stiff in all your muscles. Then you pass out. Wanna make sure you've got a pillow where you're gonna land."

Issa said, "Show me."

"Yes!" Alice cried. "Show us, Sam!"

Jimmy clapped his hands. "Show us, show us, show us!"

Sam grabbed a throw pillow from the couch and went to the center of the room, where he lowered himself to his knees, which crackled like twigs as they bent beneath his weight. He had rolled up his sleeves exposing meaty forearms, thick wrists.

"Put the pillow behind you," Alice said. "Remember?"

Lynn said, "Make sure you're tilted backward when you go tight, so you fall straight onto it. Remember?"

Jimmy said, "What are you hoping to dream about?"

"None of your business," said Sam.

Alice said, "You don't have high blood pressure, do you?"

Mikey said, "Don't die."

Sam breathed heavily in and out, wheezing with the effort, stopping once to cough into his fist, counting silently through his lips, and the others watched.

Then Sam straightened up and leaned slightly backward, his full weight on his ankles, cheeks tomato-red, and he went tight, the muscles in his thick neck bulging.

A loud, high-pitched trumpety fart squealed out from Sam, and he collapsed, not limp backward onto the pillow, but clumsily to the side, laughing now, holding his big belly, laughing so hard he gasped. Alice leapt up from the couch to straddle Sam and pin him down, and she tickled him under his arms as she had done many times when they were children. Sam laughed silently, tears eventually appearing in the corner of his eyes.

Lynn was laughing as she said, "Alice, leave him alone! He can't breathe!"

Alice crawled off Sam. "Can you breathe?"

Mikey sipped the expensive scotch Jimmy had poured for him. Alice sat back down on the couch. "By the way, Sam," she said, "isn't it about time you fessed up to taking my picture that night I spent alone at The Gunner House?"

Everyone looked at her.

Mikey said, "When was that?"

Sam said, "What now?"

Jimmy said, "I remember. Sam put her up to it because she said she didn't believe in ghosts."

Alice nodded. "I spent the night there. Must've been, what, twelve years old? Thirteen? You guys don't remember?"

"Vaguely," Mikey said.

"I had my camera with me that night," Alice explained. "The disposable kind. Spent the night in the house and didn't think anything of it until I went to get my film developed a month or two later. It had a picture of me, from that night. Someone snuck in and took a picture of me sleeping."

Mikey felt a chill race through him from tailbone to fingertip.

Lynn said, "Really?"

Jimmy said, "You didn't tell us!"

Sam propped himself up on his elbows and said, "It wasn't me!"

Mikey said, "Why didn't you tell us?"

"I was freaked out," Alice said. "But I didn't want you guys to be scared of the place because I didn't want us to stop hanging out there. Besides"—she turned to Sam—"I eventually just convinced myself it was you. You were the one who wanted me to believe there was a ghost, and I figured it was your way of trying to scare the bejeebus out of me, so I was *especially* determined to put on a brave face."

Sam said again, "I seriously swear it wasn't me."

Lynn said, "Maybe it was the ghost."

Jimmy said, "It must've been the ghost."

Alice said, "Ghost-schmost."

Mikey said, "Maybe it was Sally."

They all turned to look at him.

Lynn said softly, "Maybe it was."

Jimmy said, "If it wasn't any of us, it had to be either the ghost . . ."

"Or Sally," Lynn said.

Alice frowned. "Why, though?"

Mikey said, "Maybe Sally wanted us to believe in ghosts."

They shared a quiet and chilly silence for a few moments. Mikey found himself suddenly grateful for Alice's solid presence next to him.

Eventually, Alice rose from her seat on the couch in order to lie down next to Sam on the ground. "You wanna Indian-wrestle?" she said.

The two of them scooted around so that they were lined up at their hips, head to toe. With effort, both raised their inside leg while Alice counted, "Three, two, one—*go!*" They hooked their legs together at the knee, and Sam won almost immediately, flipping Alice over into a lopsided back-somersault. Mikey, Lynn, Jimmy, and Issa applauded.

Alice rose, fixed her braid, did a bow, massaged her knee.

Jimmy turned up the music in the other room, which was now featuring an energetic jazz trio, and Issa sat at the piano, improvising a rich harmony along with the recording.

Mikey leaned toward Alice and said, "What are you not telling me?"

"What?"

"Lynn said there's something you're not telling me."

"Oh." Alice smiled. *"That."* She threw her dark braid over her shoulder. "I'm not telling you."

Jimmy returned and took a seat between Alice and Sam. Alice sipped her Lagavulin and pulled her legs up onto the couch and rested her head in Jimmy's lap.

Mikey felt himself being pulled into a balmy haze of nostalgia.

Alice said, "Tell us a story, Jimmy."

"About what?"

"Life," Alice said.

Jimmy was quiet for a moment and ran a hand through his glossy dark hair. "Once upon a time, there were six best friends," he said. "They were all different, but they fit together very nicely. One of them loved numbers and solutions. One of them loved music, and she wished the world was more beautiful. One of them was a fearless leader who wanted to protect the others. One of them always wanted to make the others laugh. One of them was kind, and he taught the others how to be good to one another. The last one was . . . a mystery. The six of them needed one another. They belonged together." Jimmy was quiet for a bit. Then he said, "The end."

Alice scowled up at him. "That's not a story! And I don't like being typecast."

"Yeah," Lynn said. "That's not a story. What happens to them?"

"You have to tell us, Jimmy," Alice said. "What happens next?"

Lynn said, "A story has to have an ending."

Jimmy said, "I already said the ending."

"What was it?"

"They belonged together."

Lynn said, "But that's only a beginning!"

"Yeah!" Alice said. "And . . . what does it mean to *belong* together? What does it actually mean?" Alice's voice rose in pitch and wavered with emotion. "Tell us something *real*, Jimmy."

It was quiet for a bit.

Alice said, "Somebody, anybody, say something real."

It was quiet for a long time, except for the soft music Issa played, the crackle of the dying embers of the fireplace, and the distant lament of the wind whipping over the frozen lake, singing low then soaring high, a curious melody.

Mikey said, "I can hardly remember her voice."

# CHAPTER 22

The fire hissed in the corner. The air had a softness to it, and the snowy landscape before them looked swollen and resplendent. Time felt flabby, dubious, and unnatural.

Alice finally said again, imploringly, "A real story, someone?"

Jimmy said, "How about a real scary story?"

"Ooooo." Alice shivered dramatically and poked at Sam and Mikey on either side of her. "Yes, please!"

Jimmy got up to throw another log on the fire. It sparked and crunched over the coals. He used a wrought-iron poker to adjust the placement of the log and said, "How scary on a scale from one to ten?"

Sam said, "Eleven!"

Jimmy laughed and returned to the couch.

Lynn said, "I want scary enough to keep me up all night!"

"Okay," Jimmy said. He swirled his fingers together. "Okay. Let me think for one more minute . . ." He paused. "Okay," he said. He looked around the circle, making sure to meet the eyes of everyone there. "There was a place," he said. "We've all been there. A place that had a darkness to it. Being at the place made people want to do bad things."

Sam said, "Stop! I'm already too scared!"

Alice laughed. "No, go on!"

Mikey said, "More!"

Jimmy said, "The feeling a person got when they were at this place . . . It gave you . . . I can't even find the right words. It made you feel near to evil. It made you want to do bad."

Sam said, "Like what?"

"Evil. It made you feel dark, dark in your heart. Death in your heart. There's no way to explain it, but everyone who ever went there shared this wicked feeling about it. The thoughts they had when they were there . . . A blackness in the soul."

Alice whispered, "Where was it?"

"I can't tell you," Jimmy said.

Mikey said, "But you said we've all been there?"

Jimmy nodded.

Sam said, "Together?"

Jimmy said, "Yes."

Alice sucked in her bottom lip. "Was it The Gunner House?"

Jimmy shook his head. "Nope."

Lynn said, "Really? But where else have we all been together?"

Mikey said, "You're one-hundred-percent sure we've all been there? Together?"

Jimmy nodded.

Alice said, "Continue."

"One day," Jimmy said, "I was at this place. I was having this terrible feeling, this darkness, when a couple, they looked like they were in their forties or so, walked by. They had a camera. He was taking pictures of her. I asked if they'd like me to take a picture of the two of them together, with the water behind them."

The fire popped once, very loudly, and Mikey jumped.

Lynn giggled nervously.

Mikey said, "So this place was on the lake?"

Jimmy nodded. "And they said *sure*. The man put his arm around the woman. They both smiled. I took their picture."

Alice said, "Then what happened?"

"I handed the camera back to the man," Jimmy said. He hesitated again.

The wind outside howled. Mikey felt as if his skin were about to jump out of itself. Faintly, a train's wheezy horn sounded, *Whooo-whoooooooo?* Jimmy put a finger in the air.

"I could hear a train that day, too," he said. He softly imitated the whistle. "*Whoooo-whooooooooo?* It sounded just like that one sounds right now."

Alice's eyes were enormous, brows arched with anticipation, practically at her hairline. "And?"

Jimmy said, "And I watched as the two of them walked directly inland, to a wooded area about a quarter of a mile away. I was still at the water's edge but could see them the whole way. Hand in hand they walked. They looked so happy and loving with one another that I was starting to doubt the darkness of the place. I was starting to think that maybe my feelings were wrong—that it was just in my head."

The train sounded again. *Whooo-hhooooooooo?*

Jimmy said, "And I could hear the train."

Sam whispered, "Then what happened, Jimmy?"

"I watched as the couple approached the train tracks. Still holding hands. They stood at the train track's edge. *Whoooo-whoooooooooo?* Moments later, the train was approaching, barreling down, and a split second before it passed them, the woman shoved the man onto the tracks and the train ran him over. The woman was gone by the time the whole train had passed."

A very weighty silence crashed into Mikey's ears, and his entire body prickled with goose bumps.

Lynn said, "Wait, is *this* the place you were talking about? Right here? It happened on those train tracks just up the road?"

She buried her face theatrically in her elbow.

Mikey said, "This is the place that makes people want to do bad?"

Sam said, "Is this where it happened?"

Jimmy nodded.

Alice cried out, "That's not fair!" She wildly scratched at herself and shook out her hair. "That's not fair, Jimmy. Too scary! We're supposed to *sleep* here tonight. Too much!"

"Yes, too scary," Mikey agreed.

Jimmy laughed. "You guys asked for eleven out of ten!"

"Wait," Sam said. "But that didn't really happen, right? You just made that up."

Jimmy was still laughing. "No, no, no."

Lynn said, "What if . . ." She paused and looked around the circle. "What if that kind of place *does* exist? What if Sally was there?"

Sam said, "Do you mean when she decided to commit suicide?"

Lynn nodded. "What if she just found herself at a place where, like you said, Jimmy, there was just a terrible darkness that made her want to do bad?"

Jimmy said, "You mean maybe not an *actual* place but a state of mind. Beyond her control."

Mikey's thoughts returned to Jimmy's words earlier, when he had said Sally must have been in a terrible place.

Mikey said, "Alone."

Alice looked directly at Mikey and said, "Have you been over the Skyway since Sally's suicide?"

Mikey was quiet for a moment. He shook his head. "I take the long way around."

"Is it because you don't want to think of her in that place?"

Mikey said, "I don't want to think about what she was thinking about when she was there."

It felt too close to him somehow. Sally, even now that she was gone, felt too close. He couldn't explain it. And he was fearful that if he found himself up on that soaring overpass, if he pictured a slim, pale body dropping straight like a nail to the river a hundred feet below, if he even began to imagine the sort of darkness that could overtake a person, that could take them to a place that was so far away and so alone . . . When Mikey pictured this scene, sometimes he wasn't sure if it was Sally in it, or himself. Mikey felt as if now that Sally had taken her own life, he understood her better than he ever had before.

# CHAPTER 23

Somehow, it was two o'clock in the morning.

Issa and Lynn were the only ones who made it up to bed; Mikey, Jimmy, Alice, and Sam slept on the couches of the main room, holding one another. Arms and legs crossed all over each other, someone's shoulder for a pillow, someone's heavy sleeping arm a comfortable weight across the chest, someone's slow and peaceful breathing, a slight rattle at its peak.

Then, somehow, it was seven o'clock in the morning.

They were woken by the bright sun skimming over the snow, when it sailed into the room and onto their faces.

Alice watched Mikey as he located his glasses, which were perched on Jimmy's knee, and he rubbed his eyes and yawned before putting them on. Mikey's tongue felt as thick and dry as a stone. A dream was still knocking around inside of him, but he couldn't quite grasp the details.

Alice said to Mikey, "You look god-awful."

Mikey said, "And yet I feel even worse."

Alice accused Sam of snoring like a hog and the entire group of passing gas.

Mikey rose to stretch out his stiff back, and his muscles screamed.

Jimmy had brought breakfast supplies with him the night before, and he toasted up some bagels: blueberry, whole wheat, asiago cheese, rye. He laid out an assortment of butter and jam and cream cheese: scallion, strawberry, honey-walnut, garlic and chives. He brewed coffee. He set out a pitcher of orange juice and a basket of bananas.

They ate together.

Alice complained about a hangover, and Jimmy offered Advil. Chris said she had enjoyed a marvelous deep sleep and asked what she had missed. Lynn said that she and Issa had talked it over and planned to marry in their hometown in Pennsylvania in about a month, mid-February, if that would suit everyone. Sam said he hoped Justine would join him for the occasion.

Alice and Chris were the first to depart, heading back to Lackawanna to visit Alice's parents before leaving town. Alice carried Finn, who she had swaddled in a wool blanket like a large child, over her shoulders, and she panted under his weight and waved good-bye to the group with Finn's paw.

Lynn and Issa went next, promising they would send details about their wedding in the next few days.

Mikey, Jimmy, and Sam cleaned up around the house for several hours.

When it came time for Sam to leave, he required their help to push his rear-wheel-drive Nissan up and out of the driveway.

Once Sam had gone, Jimmy brushed snow from his knees, looked at his watch, and said to Mikey, "You wanna grab lunch and chat at McDowd's? I haven't had their fish sandwich in about a decade, and my mom's not expecting me till dinner."


McDowd's was the greasy pub located a few miles up the lake, where as teens they liked to go for sandwiches and fries after school and on weekends, as soon as Alice got her driver's license and could take them.

Mikey followed Jimmy, who had rented a four-wheel-drive black Suburban for the day. They passed Jackie's Flower Shop, Yaya's Donuts, and the Dollar General. They passed the 7-Eleven where Mikey bought cereal and milk when he wasn't up for a trip to the grocery store.

At the restaurant, Jimmy chose a table that overlooked the frozen lake. The dining room decor had not changed over the years: walls covered in fiberglass fish mounted on lacquered wood, a row of trucker caps nailed to the wall where it met the ceiling, red and green plaid curtains, bright felt NFL mini-pendants, photos of Buffalo Bills players with autographs in Sharpie, an old-fashioned cash register that *ka-chonk*ed noisily as the drawer opened and closed and rattled with change, '50s music playing through old Marshall speakers mounted high on the wall.

Jimmy and Mikey ordered fish sandwiches and Labatt Blues from the server, who looked as if she were about fourteen years old. She had green stripes in her hair and a diamond stud in her nostril, which looked to be infected.

Jimmy ran his finger along the windowsill to his right, collecting a bit of dust, then blew it back into the air. He had pockets under his eyes, the light bruises of insufficient sleep.

The server returned with their beers. They *cheers*-ed, and both drank.

Jimmy cleared his throat and said, "Listen. I mentioned it yesterday before we got interrupted, and there's something . . . been eating me practically alive, Mikey. I've almost called you up to tell you a hundred different times over the years but never could quite get myself there . . ." Jimmy paused and swallowed. "There is something I need to tell you." Jimmy's voice was suddenly thin and unsteady, all breath and no muscle.

Mikey looked at him.

Jimmy's eyes were a hundred different shades of blue with the sun directly on them. He ran his palm over his lips and black beard. "Something Sally knew about you," Jimmy said.

"That I didn't know?"

Jimmy nodded. "Sally swore me to secrecy, and I held it in confidence," Jimmy explained, "out of respect. It was not my information to share. But now that she's gone . . ."

"What is it?" Mikey said, a strange and fearful pulse zooming through him.

Jimmy sipped his beer once, twice, more, until half his beer was gone and his eyes were watery. He looked directly at Mikey. "Your father is not your father."

Mikey frowned. "What? Who is he?"

"He was just a neighbor."

"*What?*" Mikey said. "Whose neighbor? What are you talking about?"

Jimmy said, "John Callahan, the man who raised you, is not your father."

"Then *who is*? I don't understand. Is this about my mother? What do you know?"

Mikey felt a thick and powerful desperation, like mud moving through his organs.

Jimmy said, "Sally's father fled to Canada while Corinne was still pregnant with Sally, to get out of paying child support. When Sally was a baby, Corinne became pregnant again. The father of that *second* baby, a son, is unknown. See, Corinne . . . couldn't even narrow it down."

Mikey stared at Jimmy, this knowledge not yet seeping into him but skittering along the surface of his consciousness.

"You were the second child," Jimmy explained, his voice soft and round with sympathy. "Corinne is your mother. They don't know who your biological father is, but it's not John."

"Oh, God," Mikey said. "Oh, God." He felt as if he had been crushed by a wave and was gasping for life. Breathing in pure salt that hurt him and choked him. "How did I end up . . . Why did I end up . . . My dad . . ."

"At the time John was already living in the house where you grew up. You were living up the street with Corinne and Sally. When you were very small, two years old, you somehow made your way out of Corinne's home and up the street a short way one afternoon. John looked out on his front lawn, and all the sudden, there was a kid there. No parent in sight. He went to you."

Mikey stared at Jimmy with his mouth open, a dry hole.

Jimmy continued, "John had good enough knowledge of the neighborhood to figure you had come from Corinne's home. He didn't know her personally but knew her reputation, and knew she had little ones in the house. He went to return you to her. And when he got to her house . . . Well, apparently whatever he saw in her house that day . . . apparently he couldn't find it in himself to leave you there."

Jimmy's speech was too rapid and precise. Mikey couldn't latch on. These words sounded as if they had been thrown into a blender. They came out senseless and unpalatable.

"So . . ." Mikey said. "Slow down. Corinne just let the neighbor *take me*? To live with him and *raise as his own*? And why would he . . . Did Sally . . . I don't understand."

Jimmy's eyes searched over Mikey's face, his own expression mirroring Mikey's despair. "I'm sorry," Jimmy said, a sharp, painful break in his throat.

Mikey said, "Tell me."

Jimmy took a moment to collect his emotions in order to continue the story. "Some arrangement was made," he said. "I imagine it might've involved threats from Child Services, might've involved money . . . They reached some agreement, and it was decided that you would remain under his roof and be raised as his own."

"But why . . . Wait, Sally knew that we were half-siblings? When? *How?*"

"Sally didn't find this out until she was about sixteen. She didn't have any early memories of you; she would have only been about three years old at the time when you left their home. She discovered all of this out just shortly before she cut herself off from us."

Messy emotions were bashing up against one another inside Mikey. "How?"

"She overheard a conversation between Corinne and John. Every now and then Corinne would call John up and cry to him about wanting you back in her home. John always managed to talk her down, but Sally overheard Corinne in the middle of one of these conversations. When Corinne got off the phone, Sally confronted her and Corinne confirmed it. Of course, Corinne painted herself in the best possible light—nothing about leaving you to wander the streets as a toddler. Nothing about whatever John saw in their home that made him change his mind about leaving you there."

"So how did *Sally* know that part of the story?"

"Sally confronted John next. She went to him that evening, when you weren't home, and told him what she had overheard and what Corinne had told her. John confirmed everything and told his part of the story willingly, except for what it was that he saw that very first day that made him change his mind about leaving you there. He said that that was better left forgotten. And he implored Sally not to tell you any of this. He knew he had no legal right to act as your guardian."

Mikey's thoughts turned to Sam's recollection the previous night, of Sally leaving Mikey's home in an emotional state over an interaction for which Mikey was not present. "So," Mikey said, "why did . . . whatever my dad saw in Corinne's home, why did he save me from it but leave Sally?"

"He told Sally he wanted her to come with him, too. Sally was very small, of course, but old enough to understand the question, and old enough to answer it."

"And she didn't want to go with him?"

Jimmy shook his head.

"Corinne?"

"Apparently, Corinne was too far gone to register much of what was happening at the time."

Mikey said, "But Sally wouldn't leave her mother?"

"That's right," Jimmy said.

"Sally wouldn't leave her mother," Mikey repeated, considering this. "And Sally just kept all of this inside? Well, except for sharing it with you, of course."

Jimmy nodded. "She swore me to secrecy. John was adamant that none of this come to light. He thought that was the best thing for you." Jimmy twisted a napkin into a rope, then wove it through his fingers.

"My dad . . ." Mikey swallowed and felt a hot shivering rise of emotion. Not toward his biological father but toward John Callahan, the man who had found Mikey on his front lawn.

Then Mikey closed his eyes and pictured Sally's face. *Of course, how could it have been more obvious?* The arc of her eyebrows identical to Mikey's, the straight, narrow nose, the placement of the freckles. Everything corroborated this. Corinne, too. Her appearance had been ravaged by addiction, but Mikey could still recognize the likeness even in what remained of her.

Mikey stuffed a napkin into his eye sockets and released a heavy exhale.

Sally, his first friend.

Mikey drank two-thirds of his beer very quickly and stared out over the frozen lake, which shimmered like a sea of diamonds. The smell of grease and fish was overwhelming as the server passed with food for another table. He felt like he understood nothing.

Jimmy said, "You okay?"

Mikey didn't know what he was.

Sunlight surged in through the window of the diner. Warm on Mikey's hands. Reflecting off his silverware.

Mikey understood, from a logical standpoint, why John had not wanted him to know, why he had felt it best to protect Mikey from this information. But why Sally? Why wouldn't she want this bond to be known? Why wouldn't she want him to understand? Why did she want both of them to go through life alone?

As though having followed Mikey's thoughts, Jimmy said, "By the time Sally told me all of this, her mind was made up."

"But," Mikey said, "*why*?"

Sally still fit into the storm window of Jimmy's basement even when she was sixteen years old, although it required a sharp bend at the waist and a collapse of the shoulders, which were the widest part of her. It was late March, just a week or so after Sally's sixteenth birthday. It had been many months since she had paid Jimmy a midnight visit, because her mother spent more and more nights away from home these days, allowing Sally to sleep peacefully in her own bedroom. Sally let herself into Jimmy's basement and settled herself on the couch where she had spent so many nights before. She didn't expect that Jimmy would come find her there, but she hoped he would. And eventually he did.

Jimmy woke in the night to a bright beam of moonlight on his face, as luminous as white silk. It tugged him gently out of sleep, and he rose to use the bathroom. Before returning to his room, Jimmy was struck by the familiar sensation that someone was awake elsewhere in the house. Sally was his first guess, even though she hadn't spent a night in Jimmy's basement in months. It was a very particular feeling that accompanied Sally's presence, a heavy sort of precariousness. Jimmy peered out the hall window and could not tell from two floors up if the grass between his and Sally's home had been recently trampled or if the basement storm window was propped open, but his intuition whispered that it was Sally, so he went to the basement.

Sally was on the couch where she always slept, but she was not asleep. Instead, she sat upright, hands folded over her lap, wearing a large gray T-shirt and ankle-length yellow pajama pants with a pink flowered design, and she was staring across the room at the dartboard, its green surface peppered with tiny holes. When Jimmy entered, she turned toward him, and her face was white and long. Jimmy suddenly felt cold. He went to the couch and sat next to her.

Sally said, "Do you remember anything that happened when you were three?"

"Years old?"

Sally nodded.

Jimmy thought. "My earliest memory, I think, is around school starting. Vaguely. Not much before, really. Not anything before, maybe."

Sally was quiet for a bit. She said, "Anything that we have no memory of, it's like it never even happened. Right? It doesn't matter. It's like it doesn't even exist."

"I wouldn't say that."

Sally said, "Think about it, though. If you don't remember something, it might as well have never happened. It wouldn't make any difference to you."

Jimmy and Sally had never had this sort of conversation. Usually, Sally's concerns were immediate and straightforward, her afflictions easy to trace.

Jimmy said, "I don't understand."

"Can you promise not to tell something if I tell you?"

"Of course." Jimmy and Sally had shared many, many hard secrets between them before, but they had never sworn one another to secrecy; it was unspoken that the trust between them would never be broken. It hurt Jimmy a little bit that she felt the need to ask. "I promise," he said.

Sally said, "Mikey is my brother."

Jimmy stared at her. "He's *who*? How?"

Sally explained to Jimmy how she had come upon this knowledge. She explained that John had begged her not to tell Mikey, fearing that Mikey would feel betrayed and deceived by John, and abandoned by Corinne and his biological father. John told Sally that he didn't want Mikey to feel alone.

Sally told Jimmy, "I told John I don't want that either."

Jimmy said, "But Mikey's not alone. He has his dad, even if he's not his dad. He has us. And if he knew . . . he could have a sister, too."

Sally was quiet for a bit.

Jimmy felt desperation brimming within himself. He said, "But what you were just saying . . . If Mikey never knows, if this just dies in your heart . . . It's like you were saying, right? It's like it never existed, and it doesn't matter. But that *can't* be what you want. Is that what you want?"

Sally's brow was furrowed, her thin, sharp jaw working. "I promised John."

Jimmy's throat was becoming tight and hard. A memory reached him from many years earlier, the time Mikey had given him his best baseball card because Jimmy's parents were fighting and Jimmy was sad. He thought of Mikey's constancy, his goodness, and the solemn heavy sorrow that Mikey always seemed to carry but of which he never spoke.

Jimmy tried to reason with Sally. "I think Mikey should know, even if John doesn't think so. I think it would be better for him. And I think it would be better for you, too." Jimmy hesitated, knowing how this next part would sound, coming from someone whose own parents didn't know he was gay. He said, "I don't think it's good for a heart to get so full of such big secrets."

Sally was quiet for a long while. Eventually, Jimmy lifted his eyes to study her face, and her hard expression contradicted the light gloss of tears now trailing down both cheeks.

She said, "You promised, Jimmy."

Jimmy said, "I know."

"I'm serious," she said. "You promised."

"I know."

Jimmy peeled at the foil label on his beer with his fingernail. He said to Mikey, "Sally wasn't one to reverse herself or to break a promise. She'd rather die with something hidden in her heart."

Mikey said, "Or die *because* something was hidden in her heart."

Jimmy's hands went to his own face, and he uttered a soft but aching and sustained sob. "Can you forgive me, Mikey?" he murmured through his fingers, which were damp with tears. "Can you forgive her? And John? We all . . ." Jimmy wiped his eyes with the back of his wrists and looked directly at Mikey. "You deserved to know," he said.

Mikey didn't hesitate before reaching across the table to reassure his friend. "Of course," he said, gripping Jimmy's forearm warmly. "Forgive? It's so easy. Of course."

Jimmy nodded and sniffed. "But you deserved to know."

"And now I know," Mikey said.

It was quiet for a bit.

Jimmy sipped his beer, then released a heavy sigh. "The one thing I wish . . . Whoever Sally was by the end, whatever all she kept hidden in her heart and however much those things tortured her, I hope she knew that she was loved. It hurts when you can't tell a person that. When they're too far away to hear it, or it's just too late."

Mikey had a sudden and uncomfortable flashback to his conversation with Alice on the beach the previous night. The alcohol and pot had muddied the conversation in his memory, but he had hurt her, refusing to acknowledge that he loved her, or was loved by her. He was too far away to hear it.

Jimmy said, "Did you ever have any sort of inkling about any of this?"

Mikey shook his head. "But something . . . Well, it's never been easy, me and my dad."

The server appeared with their fish sandwiches, served on greasy paper in little red plastic baskets with Cajun fries on the side.

Mikey ordered a second beer. A fierce sadness and longing was climbing through him. He wished he knew what he felt.

The two of them talked of other things as they ate: Jimmy's recent travels and recent investments, his apprehension about seeing his own parents later that day. He described the guilt he felt over not telling them the truth about his sexuality weighed against his fear of their judgment, their disappointment.

Jimmy said, "I still want to be *me* to my parents, I still want to be *their son Jimmy*, not *their gay son Jimmy*. But how much of *me* is being gay? I'm afraid of throwing the whole ratio out of whack if I tell them. I don't want *who I am* to be overshadowed by the fact that I'm gay." Jimmy paused and sighed again. "Anyhow. I won't know how they're going to react until I let them react."

Mikey said, "Sometimes life feels like one big guessing game, doesn't it? I don't know what I mean by that." He felt unspeakably weary.

Jimmy drank lots of beer very quickly, his turquoise eyes distant and watery. "I know exactly what you mean by that," he said.

Eventually, Mikey finished his beer, and Jimmy waved down the server for the bill.

Mikey and Jimmy parted ways outside of McDowd's. The wind had picked back up, and it skimmed across the frozen lake, bringing with it a painful chill. The sun loomed over them like a weight. Mikey shrank his neck so that the collar of his coat reached his nose. He hugged Jimmy tightly.

Jimmy said, "Guess we'll be seeing each other in Pennsylvania for the wedding next month."

Mikey nodded. "Take care, brother. I hope you have a nice time with your folks."

Jimmy nodded, and Mikey watched as a certain melancholy passed through Jimmy's bright eyes at the mention of his parents.

Jimmy said, "I know they love me. I'm not sure what I'm so scared of."

Mikey took a right out of the parking lot at McDowd's instead of a left, which would have taken him home. He took Route 11 six miles north, then got onto Route 68, out toward Eden.

He had never been to his father's workplace and wasn't even sure he'd be able to find it.

# CHAPTER 24

The Galway Brothers Meat Processing Plant was not hard to find; it was the biggest business in Eden. The building itself was practically a mile long, set just off the main street through town, beyond the only stoplight. Smoke rose from the plant in dark columns from many black chimneys of varying height. The sign at the main entryway featured a square brown paper parcel tied with string as the logo, alongside the name of the company. Mikey followed signs to the visitor parking, then made his way across the salted lot to the front entrance.

Inside, the place smelled of bleach, and the lighting was a piercing, sterile white-blue. Mikey approached the front desk, where a heavyset middle-aged woman wearing a bright green silk top sat before a massive computer.

She looked at Mikey over her reading glasses, then lowered them from her face so they dangled against her large breasts on a string. Her lips were glossy pink, and her teeth were yellow. She wore a very thick and opaque application of foundation, an uncomfortable look akin to someone wearing way too many layers of clothing in a hot room.

Mikey said, "My father works here."

"What department?"

"Department?"

"Department."

"Oh . . ." Mikey thought for a moment. "Probably slaughter. Is that a department?"

"I'm gonna need to see some ID," the woman said.

Mikey reached for his wallet.

"Gotta make sure you're not a YouTuber," the woman said.

"How's that?"

"Oh, these kids sneak in here with their hidden cameras, going after some footage for their animal rights videos and whatnot. That's why security's the way it is," she explained, running her thick tongue over her lips.

"Sure," Mikey handed her his ID.

"What's your dad's name?" she said.

"John Callahan."

She typed this into her computer. "He expecting you?"

Mikey shook his head.

The woman said, "Lemme call on back. Go on and have a seat." She nodded toward several brown vinyl chairs in the lobby, next to a small table. Mikey picked up a *Field & Stream* magazine from the table and paged through it.

The woman spoke into the phone, "Says he's here to see John Callahan. You wanna send him up? I see . . . Right, I'll let him know."

She hung up the phone and looked at Mikey.

He set the magazine back on the table and said, "If it's any trouble, I'll just come another time." Suddenly, he felt squeamish and shy, uncertain of himself and how he would explain his visit.

"No, hon," she said. "He's just in the middle of something. His colleague's on his way up, though."

Mikey stood up and made a subtle move for the door. "It's all right. I don't want to interrupt anyone."

The woman waved a floppy hand at him, and her bracelets tinkled against one another. "Just sit tight."

A few minutes later, a man approximately his father's age appeared around the corner of the lobby. He wore a white hard hat, rubber gloves, a large rubber apron over work boots, and a grimy-looking white uniform decorated with blood splatters, just like Mikey's father wore. He had a gray beard, a bulbous red nose, friendly eyes that shrank to coin slots when he smiled.

"I'm Don," he said. "I'd shake your hand, but the gloves."

Mikey said, "You work with my dad?"

Don nodded. "Forty-two years. You believe that? We started within a month of each other, right after finishing high school, been working side by side ever since."

"Really!" Mikey didn't want to offend the man by making it any more obvious that his father had never mentioned this colleague of forty-two years.

Don said, "Why don't you come on back to our workroom, have a coffee?"

Mikey said, "If he's busy . . ."

"Nah." Don was already making his way back down the hallway from which he had come. "He's probably about to finish up and take lunch."

Mikey followed.

It began to smell less like bleach and more of something pungent and weird and raw and unpleasant. Mikey breathed through his lips.

"We're goin' *allllll* the way back," Don said. "Nobody wants to be close to the guts and gore." He laughed. He glanced briefly at Mikey. "It's good to meet you after hearin' all about you from your pop over the years."

"Really?" Mikey was legitimately surprised by this. He could not fathom one single thing that his father might have said about him.

Don said, "Says you're quite the cook. Brought me one of them croy-sants you baked a couple months back."

Mikey blinked. His father had barely acknowledged the croissants. Machines whirred behind doors as they continued to make their way down the hallway. Mikey peeked in through the windows. Machines churning pink meat. Conveyor belts where tubes spat pink meat into little tins. Women in hairnets writing on clipboards. Printers shooting out colorful labels. Huge stacks of mail. Empty boardrooms.

Finally, they reached the far end of the hallway.

Don walked Mikey into a small workroom with a single Culligan's water cooler, a Mr. Coffee, and two long rectangular tables, where half a dozen men were seated, eating sandwiches from Saran Wrap or soup from steaming Tupperware containers. Uniforms stained with blood. The slaughter crew. Only half of them looked up from their lunch when Don and Mikey entered the room.

Don said, "Got John's kid here."

The smell was making Mikey nauseous. He adjusted his glasses.

A red-haired guy with an Australian accent raised his can of Coca-Cola and said, "Cheers."

A guy with no eyebrows said, "We been wantin' to meet you," he said. "So's we could say thanks."

Others in the room nodded.

Mikey said, "What for?"

The Australian said, "Holidays."

Mikey didn't understand. "Holidays?"

The guy without eyebrows clarified: "How your pop always works the holidays. So's we can be with our families."

All the men in the room nodded.

The Australian said, "Your pop says you've always been real understanding about it. Easygoing."

Mikey said, "Oh." He felt something sort of broken and confusing.

"Anyhow," Don said, "let's see how much work your pop's got left." He walked Mikey through the door on the far side of the workroom, which took them to a dark, smaller room with a single window opening on a massive chamber filled with animal carcasses that hung from hooks and rods and chains.

Mikey stared into the room. Massive. There had to be two hundred dead animals hung up in there. Blood everywhere. He felt his stomach lurch. He couldn't believe the sheer volume of the operation.

Don nodded toward a locker just to Mikey's right. "Grab an apron and a hat in there. Mask, too, if you're worried about the smell."

Mikey stared at him.

Don said, "I'll walk ya through. Find your pop. Not every day a boy gets to see his old man hard at work."

Mikey was almost certain he'd vomit upon entering that room, but he didn't want to appear weak or judgmental or squeamish. He opened the locker and pulled out a bleached apron that covered his clothing from his collarbone to his knees. He tied it around his back and put on a white hard hat. He pulled a mask from a box and put it over his face so that only his eyes were uncovered, and fit his glasses over the mask. He put on a pair of rubber gloves.

Don clapped him on the back and led him through a door into the main chamber.

It was very, very cold.

Mikey continued to breathe through his mouth, sucking in the fabric of the mask.

They walked briskly past rows and rows and rows of animal carcasses, some very recent kills, Mikey guessed, many still dripping blood into a wide tilted canal on the floor beneath them. Men in various stations were actively and methodically butchering animals. Very few wore masks. Cleaning the animals. De-hairing them. Removing heads. Stripping meat from bone. Hooves sawed off. Kidneys in bowls. Blood spray on the floor and counters. Great mounds of yellowy fat globules. Don and Mikey walked through unnoticed; the butchers did not interrupt their work to acknowledge them.

They walked the full length of this chamber; then Don led Mikey into another room, this one smaller but with a similarly high ceiling. Above the noisy whirring of machinery, Mikey could hear the distant bray of cattle. On the far side of the room, he could see small columns of daylight, snow, the outdoors. Mikey's eyes fixed on his father at the far end of this room.

His father stood in full uniform with several other men along the far wall, which was a mass of metal boxes and gates. One of the men held a two-foot-long black apparatus. A wide conveyor right in front of these gates stretched the length of the room, leading through a six-by-six-foot opening in the wall, protected with plastic flaps, that went back toward the large carcass chamber from which they had just come. This room, Mikey understood, was where the animals died.

Don leaned toward Mikey and said, "Don't wanna get any closer till they're finished. High voltage and all."

Mikey watched as an animal entered the area, a tight space behind the conveyor. He could tell that it was a cow, and from behind the gate, he could see only the top of its bristly brown back. It did not appear to be resisting or in any sort of panic. The man with the black apparatus nodded toward the other men. Then he approached the animal and reached the apparatus over the metal gate with a swift, practiced movement, and administered a shock that caused his own shoulder to jerk a bit with the jolt. Immediately after, this man jumped out of the way as the gate to the conveyor was lifted with large hinges, and the animal fell forward onto the conveyor. Here, Mikey could see the cow in its entirety: a nice rust-caramel color, hooves still wet with dirty snow, floppy ears, a numbered yellow tag through one, black eyes wide and glassy.

Mikey watched as his father moved closer to stand over the animal as its legs kicked violently for a few seconds. His father lowered himself so his own face was near the animal's head, and he removed his rubber gloves from his thick arms and stroked the animal's face gently with his bare hand as it kicked.

Don explained, "Thing loses consciousness right away . . . it's not in any pain. Legs kickin' is just a reflex. It'll get slaughtered in the other room. That's when it'll actually die, but it won't feel a thing between here and there."

Mikey nodded. Then he watched as his father knelt fully to the ground before the animal's head and gently touched it near its eye.

Don said, "That's how you make sure it's actually out. No corneal reflex. Otherwise you need to stun it again."

Mikey nodded.

Don said, "Most guys say that's the worst part. Nobody wants to be near the face, lookin' straight into the eyes of somethin' while it's dyin'."

Mikey watched as his father stroked the animal's cheek again, still with his bare hand, as gentle and kind as if it were a newborn child. He saw his father's lips move as his fingers continued to softly graze over the broad cheek of the animal.

Even after the other men involved with the stunning had moved to another part of the line and were chatting with one another, wiping their brows and laughing over some crack, Mikey's father was still bowed low before the animal. Still touching its face, until finally the conveyor belt groaned into action and started to move and the animal was slowly dragged away from this site and into the slaughtering chamber.

Mikey watched as his father put his palms on the ground to steady himself while rising to his feet, wincing noticeably with the effort. Mikey felt something hot and sad pressing on his insides.

"I keep tellin' your pop it's no wonder his knees are so bad," Don said, "gettin' down on the ground like that for every single one."

# CHAPTER 25

**D**on called out across the room. "John-John!"

Mikey's father looked their way, and did not register immediate surprise; Mikey realized his own identity was still hidden behind his mask, his glasses shadowed by the hat. His father walked slowly in their direction, removing his own hard hat to wipe his brow into his elbow.

When he drew near, Don clapped a hand over Mikey's back and said, "Your boy here to see you."

John's posture suddenly stiffened; his eyebrows lifted as he met Mikey's eyes.

Mikey gave him a nod. He felt shaky and ill, his voice on the verge of breaking out in high and desperate pitches.

His father wiped his face into his elbow again and said to Don, "I'll meet you back in the workroom. I've got a few more before my break."

Don said to Mikey, "Good to meet ya, son," before heading back for the long walk through the slaughter chamber.

Mikey's father gazed at Mikey. He wore an expression of mild irritation. "What's this all about?"

Mikey said, "I was thinking—"

His father gestured toward his own lips. "Can't hear ya behind the mask," he said.

Mikey lowered the mask so that it crinkled across his chin and his mouth was exposed. The smell was hot and rancid, and he coughed.

His father laughed. He offered his hard hat, upside down, to Mikey. "If you're gonna yak, do it in here."

Mikey didn't take the hat.

"Why'd you come here?" his father said. He had hair and blood on his apron and gloves. Flecks of sawdust on his rough face. Behind him, a garage door groaned, metal on metal, as it rose a few feet off the ground, and Mikey heard the distant bray of cattle once again. In addition to the smell of death, this fresh air brought with it the aroma of animal shit and cigarette smoke and snow. He could see hooves through the sliver beneath the door. Men in rubber boots slogging through shit and mud and snow, whistling as they herded the cattle.

"I didn't know this is what it's like," Mikey said.

"My job?"

Mikey nodded. "You never talk about it."

"What am I gonna say?"

Mikey was quiet for a bit.

"You've got my number, ya know," his father said. "No need to come trampin' around my workplace to find me."

"Sure," Mikey said. He couldn't explain, of course, the source of his sudden and desperate need to be in John's presence, the compulsion to come here as sharp and painful as a blade at his back.

"Anyhow." His father ran a thick knuckle under his nostrils and said, "I only packed one sandwich."

"I'm not gonna stay for lunch," Mikey said, "But why don't you come to my place for dinner sometime this week?"

Mikey's father had never once been to his home in the twelve years Mikey had lived there.

A strange sound slid out of his father. "Huh."

"Why don't you come over?" Mikey said. "Why won't you ever come over?" The first was a question, and the second, Mikey realized as it came out of his mouth, was an accusation.

"I'm allergic," his father said.

Mikey laughed. "To me?"

"Cats."

"Oh. Really?"

His father nodded.

Mikey said, "Oh." He looked at John Callahan's wrinkled old face—so obvious now that they shared no physical resemblance whatsoever. John Callahan's rough skin, rough bones, rough thick nose, chapped purple lips, deep creases at the corners. John Callahan had 20-20 vision, even at age sixty-six. John Callahan, with the bad knees, who knelt to the ground for each animal. Touched them with his bare hand. Mikey felt something lifting up off of him. Some dark weight that had been camped out on his chest for as long as he could remember.

From across the room, a gate was cranking and shifting, an animal was entering, black hair visible between bars. A stocky mustachioed man waved at Mikey's father, and the man with the black stunning apparatus glanced over to make sure he knew it was almost time, to make sure he was on his way. "Another one comin', John-John!" the stocky man hollered across the room.

Mikey's father nodded and waved back, indicating that he'd be right there.

He turned briefly back toward Mikey as he put his hard hat back on. "We'll figure something out," he said.

•

As he made his way up the endless hallway to the lobby of the plant where he had entered, Mikey recalled Lynn's words about love—*It's like finding the ground*—and he was struck by a memory from childhood, when he had attended the Erie County Fair with his friends.

It was Alice's parents who had taken them, but the children were old enough to split off and be on their own. Alice quickly decided, for the group, that they would start the day on the giant spinning swing ride. The ride terrified Mikey, who hated heights and had a weak stomach, but he didn't want to miss out, or ruin the fun. He got into the last available seat, behind the others, strapped in with a leather buckle between his legs, a bar over his groin. Jerky circus music blasted out through speakers mounted at the base of the center post, which was bright and ornate, covered with scores of gaudy fake jewels in every color.

The giant disc rose into the air and began to spin. Faster and faster, the seats swooping out far and wide. Happy shrieks, hands in the air. Mikey clutched the chains at his side and closed his eyes. Stomach churning, lungs swollen with silent terror, brain rattling within his skull, a terrible time.

Finally, finally, the ride reached its end, the spinning disc slowed, the swings gently drew inward, the wheel lowered. Everyone's hair blown back, laughter, relief. Mikey felt no relief. He was slick and cold with sweat. He felt certain he was going to either faint or vomit in public, and he wasn't sure which would be worse. It would be terrible. He would not recover. Everyone would witness his shame.

The seats lowered farther, and Mikey stretched out his little feet, desperate for the solid ground, but still they did not reach. He was not going to make it. Mikey felt hot vomit brimming up through his esophagus. It was going to happen right now. He would try to contain it in his lap. Oh, everyone would see.

And just when the vomit burned at the back of his throat and he had lost all hope, Mikey felt something perfect—the ground rising up to meet his feet. His stomach settled instantaneously. His heart rate slowed, his body went calm. Logically, of course, Mikey knew that the ground couldn't move; this could not actually be the way it happened, and yet . . . that *was* how it had happened—he was certain of it. The ground rose, the earth swelled up and found him.

# CHAPTER 26

**P**oor Friday was famished by the time Mikey made it home that afternoon. Mikey poured him dry food, which Friday devoured, and a dish of whole milk, a rare treat, and he ran his hand over Friday's spine.

Mikey plugged in his charger to power up his phone, which had died several hours earlier when he was at lunch with Jimmy. He unpacked his toothbrush and the flannel pajamas he hadn't worn since he had fallen asleep fully clothed in the arms of his friends. He took off his shoes. He opened his refrigerator and pulled out a Labatt Blue, an overripe clementine, and a little baggie of Black Forest ham. He went to his living room, sat in the La-Z-Boy, reclined it. Friday came bounding into the room and onto Mikey's lap, where he settled himself and purred. Mikey peeled the clementine and ate it several slices at a time. He popped open the beer.

He turned on the TV to *Jeopardy!* and watched for a few moments before realizing that something was wrong. He squinted at the screen. He listened to Alex Trebek read the question aloud, and a contestant buzzed in with the correct answer. Mikey took his glasses off and cleaned the right lens with the bottom hem of his shirt. He rubbed his right eye with the heel of his hand. He looked back at the TV, where another question was being displayed on the blue screen.

This time it was undeniable: a cloud had appeared. Misty and gray and amorphous, it occupied a third of the TV screen. A new blind spot.

Mikey turned the TV off.

He ran his hand over Friday's warm little skull and closed his eyes. The sound of Friday's purring was practically deafening. Mikey's hearing and other senses had grown noticeably, remarkably sharper in the past few years, as he had practiced traversing his home and accomplishing simple tasks in darkness. He would call the doctor tomorrow; then he would talk to human resources at his work.

What would be the strangest part? he wondered. Would it be the dreams? He'd heard you continued to dream with sight if you went blind as an adult. Would it be the fact that he wouldn't see himself age, would never know how well or how poorly his face weathered time? How strange, Mikey thought, that after longing for invisibility since he was a child, as it turned out, he would not become invisible to the world, but the world would become invisible to him. It was time. For what, exactly? Time to just resume life, he supposed. It was happening. He could hear electricity in the walls. He could feel blood swirling around his own veins, and booming through his heart.

# CHAPTER 27

One week before Lynn's wedding, Mikey received a phone call from Alice while he was preparing dinner. Friday did figure eights around Mikey's legs as he stirred risotto. Mikey had tape over his right eye and was feeling very pleased with himself, having prepared the entire meal thus far without peeking. He had lifted the tape only briefly to locate his phone in the other room when it began to vibrate, so he wouldn't miss the call.

"Alice!" he said happily, returning to the stove and continuing to stir. "What's up?"

"It's been a day," she said.

"What happened?"

"Finn's got worms or something. Can't keep anything down."

Before Mikey could respond to this, Alice added, "And Chris and I broke up."

"I'm sorry to hear," Mikey said.

"Finn's on meds now, so hopefully that'll get sorted out. But he's an old dog. It's only a matter of time. And Chris . . . I told her I'd made the final decision to move back to Lackawanna. She's got no interest in moving, of course. We decided it was best to end things, clean and quick."

"You didn't want to try long-distance?" Mikey said.

"Oh, *God*, no," Alice snorted. "Me? Never. I need constant attention. Anyhow, she took it just fine. She's young, Mikey. We weren't any good for each other, anyway."

"Can we talk about her voice, then?"

Alice laughed like gunshot. "Mean!" she cried.

"I'm just trying to make you feel better," Mikey said. "You're doing all right, though?"

"It's the right thing. My pop's in real bad shape, and they need me. Anyhow, it's all gonna happen pretty quick. I'm planning on moving in a couple weeks. Early March. I'll work up through Lynn's wedding next weekend, go to that, then spend the next two weeks packing. Already got someone who wants to buy the marina here, offered me a fair deal."

"That right?"

Mikey propped the phone against his cheek with his shoulder and reached for the bottle of Pinot Grigio with his right hand. He could tell the risotto had thickened a bit too much, so he dumped in a splash of wine and continued to stir.

Alice continued, "And I've got my eye on some real estate up in Lewiston. Place to live and a place to open another marina when I've got the time. I'm thinking I'll be there for a while, Mikey. Put down some roots."

"I didn't realize it would happen so soon!" Mikey said. "I'll want to help you move in, so let me know as soon as you've set the date."

"Anyway," Alice said distractedly, "Lynn spilled the beans, but there is something I wasn't telling you last weekend."

"Oh?" Mikey had forgotten about this interaction entirely.

"Lynn and I had talked before that weekend—I called her up to get her take on it. I was gonna talk to you about it that weekend, when we were together, but damned if I didn't have too much to drink and mucked it up, then got shy."

"You? Shy?"

"I know."

Alice got quiet for a moment.

Mikey said, "What's up?"

"I've been thinking about this for quite some time now, so I don't want you thinking this is just one of my harebrained cockamamie ideas. It doesn't have anything to do with my breakup, or the fact that my dog's on his last leg. Okay? This is something that's been cookin' in my head for a *long* time. Okay? Anyway, I think I am a person who wants to have a child."

"What?" Mikey momentarily stopped stirring his risotto.

"I know," Alice said. "It's so unlike me! But . . ." Alice fell silent again.

Mikey said, "You'll be a wonderful mother, Alice. You just said it a weird way, caught me off-guard. *A person who wants to have a child.* Anyway, are you planning to adopt, or . . ."

Alice said, "I'd like to carry my own child. At least try. That's what I wanted to talk to you about. Now . . ." Alice's voice fell off again for a moment, and when she started speaking, it was rushed, shaky with nerves. "Now, I wouldn't ever ask for any financial help, but . . ." Alice's voice had shrunk to something small and scared, something Mikey barely recognized, coming from her.

Mikey pulled the tape from his right eye. He went to the kitchen table, found his glasses and put them on, then returned to the stove.

"You're my favorite person in the world, Mikey," Alice said.

Mikey blinked. He reached for the bottle of Pinot Grigio and took a big swig, straight from the bottle. It was immensely refreshing, even at room temperature.

"Are you asking me to help you have a kid?" he said. "To donate my sperm to you?"

"Yes," Alice said, and Mikey could hear her relief that he had spoken the actual words, that he had understood and said the actual thing aloud so that she wouldn't have to.

"Now," Alice said, speaking very quickly again, her nerves spilling through, "I don't want you to think I was actually trying to make it happen last weekend. When we were down by the beach, I got carried away in the moment. Drunk and silly. Reckless. I wouldn't have gone through with that. But I'd been thinking on *this* for a while. Like I said, listen, I wouldn't expect anything from you. It could end at the . . . donation. Hah! And we don't even have to do it the old-fashioned way, Mikey. We could do it, you know, with a tube . . . I've done my research. Anyway, I'm going to be moving down there next month, so we can talk about it more in person . . . You're going to be seeing a lot more of me, pal."

Mikey had stopped stirring again.

Alice cut forcefully into the silence. "The point is, when I first started to have thoughts about a baby, and then once I started thinking about *when* and *how* and *who*, you were the first person that came to mind. You're very . . . companionable."

"Companionable?"

"*Or*," Alice said, "we don't ever have to talk about it again. If you already know the answer is no, you don't even have to give me a reason. I'll leave it be. We're going to see each other at the wedding next weekend, and I don't want it to be weird. We don't have to talk about it then, or ever again."

"Alice," Mikey said, and he stared into his risotto, unable to distinguish the individual grains of rice even now, with his glasses on. "I'm going blind."

Alice was quiet for a few beats. "You mean your eyesight is getting worse, or you're going to be blind?"

"I'm going to be blind," Mikey said. "I was in to see my doctor last week. It's happening. I might have a year of sight left, tops. I don't know for sure if it's hereditary . . . That's not why I brought it up. I'd have to ask my doctor. It's just that I have a lot on my mind."

Alice made a soft noise that was indecipherable. Then she said, "Are you scared?"

"Not really," Mikey said. "I've had a lot of time to consider the possibility and prepare. I walk around the house with tape over my eye all the time. I can get myself dressed. Even make decent meals."

Alice said, "Sheezus, Mikey." She sniffed. "What are you going to do?"

"Work for a few more months, then go on disability. Listen to a lot of music. Get a dog if Friday will tolerate it. Go on walks. Find some work that I can do. Accept pity visits from you and the others. Wait for the Rapture. It won't be the worst thing in the world."

"Why is this happening?"

Mikey said, "Early-onset macular degeneration. Rare but not unheard-of. Exact cause typically unknown, although my doc reassured me it's not because I looked at the sun when I was a kid. Or because I masturbated too much."

Alice laughed. "What?"

"Isn't that what the Catholics say?" Mikey said. "If you masturbate too much, you'll eventually go blind or lose all your senses or something?"

"Oh," Alice said. "If that was true, I'd be blind and deaf and dumb and dead."

Mikey laughed. "Listen, though. There's something else that's been on my mind, too," he said. "Jimmy told me last week. My dad isn't my dad."

"What? Who is he?"

"Just a neighbor. Nobody knows who my biological father is. But my *mother*, I now know, is Corinne. Sally and I were half-siblings."

Alice was silent, so Mikey continued. "John came onto the picture because he didn't think Corinne was . . . suitable."

Alice breathed a low and drawn-out "*Wow.*" Then she said, "You and Sally look *so much* alike. How did we never know? Sally knew?"

"Yes," Mikey said. "She's the one that told Jimmy. It's . . . not entirely clear why she didn't tell me."

"Why wouldn't she want you to know? I don't get it," Alice said. "I *hate* not getting things. I don't know if there's anything I hate more."

Mikey said, "So, why did you divorce The Saint?"

"God!" Alice shrieked. "You're like a dog with a bone!"

"I hate not getting things, too!"

Alice sighed. "I'd rather not talk about it. But now wait, I wasn't done asking . . . So your father—"

"I don't feel like getting into it more right now," Mikey said. "And my risotto's about to disintegrate. We can talk more at Lynn's wedding, after the grown-ups have gone to bed. Are you getting them a gift?"

"You don't think our presence is enough of a gift?"

"I don't think that's how it works."

"I disagree," Alice said. "We bring the party. That's our gift. See, Mikey, the party is never not where we aren't."

"What?"

"Think about that one for a bit," Alice said. "But are you going to miss my face?"

"What?"

"When you're blind."

"Oh. No. No, definitely not," Mikey said. "It's the one upside, actually."

Alice cried, "You're mean! Oh, my God, you are *actually* the meanest man!" She was silent for a moment, then she said, "Finn's pukin'. I gotta go."

# CHAPTER 28

Mikey was the first of his friends to arrive at Lynn and Issa's home, where the wedding was being held. It was snowing lightly. Lynn had said to watch for a church; it was the nearest building to their home, and their driveway was a quarter mile beyond it. The church was a tiny thing, nestled within eastern white pines and blue spruce trees. Its white siding was peeling off in large strips. Green shutters. It looked like a birdhouse. The sign out front read COMMUNITY PRESBYTERIAN. A yellowed roadside swinger offered the date of an upcoming spaghetti meal: FAMILY STYLE, ALL WELCOME, BRING YOUR OWN PLATES & FORKS.

Just up the road, a bundle of red balloons tied to a mailbox marked the driveway to Lynn and Issa's house. The air smelled of woodsmoke and wind.

As Mikey was getting out of his car, a white BMW SUV pulled into the next spot. Jimmy hopped out of the driver's seat and gave Mikey a hug. He had shaved his black beard, and his hair was tied back in a neat ponytail.

"Meet my squeeze," Jimmy said, nodding toward the passenger door.

A tall, heavyset man with a wild red beard came around the

front of the BMW and stood before them. He wore a little green plaid cap.

Jimmy said, "Mikey, Audwin. Audwin, Mikey."

Mikey shook the man's hand.

Audwin said in a deep voice and with a strong German accent, "Please to meet you."

Jimmy stood smiling up at his date. "Audwin lives in Hamburg. We've been emailing for years now, just finally met in person for the first time, when, this past Thursday?"

Audwin nodded.

Jimmy explained, "We both flew into New York. We'd settled in advance that if it didn't click, we'd go our separate ways after one dinner, but . . ." Jimmy smiled sheepishly.

Mikey said, "It clicked?"

Jimmy turned to Audwin. "Would you agree?"

Audwin said, "I don't know what this *click* means."

Jimmy laughed. "We've just spent the past few days buzzing around the city. Had some great meals. Checked out the museums. After the wedding, we're going to buzz up to Montreal, hit the slopes."

Audwin had a kind, pleasant face. He wore loose khaki pants and off-brand tennis shoes.

Jimmy said, "And, *yes*, we met online, God help us. We both had inferential statistics listed on our profile as a top interest."

"That's a math thing?" Mikey said.

Jimmy nodded. "This was years ago. We got to chatting online about conjoint analyses, kept in touch over time, and recently just decided it was high time we meet."

Audwin said, "I finally convinced Jimmy I wasn't planning to chop him up and have him for supper."

Jimmy said, "And when Lynn heard, she was so excited she insisted I bring him to the wedding."

Audwin straightened the little plaid hat on his head. "I did not pack right for a wedding. I could not know. This is why I am wearing these dumb shoes."

Mikey laughed. "Are you guys staying at the place Lynn recommended tonight?"

Jimmy shook his head. "We're gonna try and get a few hours' drive in tonight, make it to Montreal by midday tomorrow. You?"

Mikey nodded. "Got a room at the Budget Inn."

Audwin led the way into the house.

The sidewalk had been shoveled and salted. Jimmy slowed his pace and threw an arm around Mikey's shoulders. He said, "I finally had the talk with my parents last month, when I was home. That same evening after you and I had lunch."

"You came out to them?"

Jimmy nodded. His glossy hair, slicked back from his face, was shiny as black gold.

Mikey said, "It went okay?"

Jimmy nodded again. "It wasn't the easiest thing I've done. But . . ."

Mikey gripped Jimmy's gloved hand over his shoulder. "Glad for you."

Jimmy said, "How are things with you? Your dad?"

Mikey said, "He came over for dinner a few weeks ago, first time he's ever set foot in my house."

"How was that?"

"Like you said. It wasn't the easiest thing. But . . ."

•

Mikey had vacuumed the entire house and locked Friday in his bedroom before his father's visit. His father arrived ten minutes early, wearing nicer clothing than Mikey had ever seen on him— clean khakis, a blue button-down shirt, brown dress shoes with mismatched laces. He brought with him a green tissue-paper cone full of spray-painted carnations, which Mikey found so strange and touching he nearly wept. When his father handed it to him, he said, "Forgot the liquor stores would be closed today, otherwise I'da brought you that. Didn't wanna show up empty-handed. This is what the Internet told me to bring in a pinch."

Mikey had prepared pan-seared scallops with garlic and butter and thyme, a rich bean salad with ham hocks and sweet onion, grilled peach slices and thickened cream. They ate at the kitchen table. Mikey's father ate every bite and asked for seconds.

At one point, his father poked a scallop with his knife and said, "Don't know how you know how to put it all together, cook it right. This fancy stuff. Me . . . I got simple tastes." He paused, then added, "Not that I don't like what you make. Fancy stuff. I just wouldn't know where to start."

Mikey thought back to their cabinets and refrigerator from when he was a kid. Cereal, white bread, cold cuts, apples, Chips Ahoy!

His father continued, softer, as though to himself, "Guess you shouldn't take it personal when your boy outgrows the things you can offer him."

Mikey stared at him. "You took it personal?"

His father didn't answer.

They sipped whiskey after the meal, and Mikey told his father that he was going blind. That he probably had a year, or less, before his vision would be completely gone.

His father was quiet for a bit. Then he said, "I'm not your biological father, you know."

"I know." Mikey paused, then said, "I know about Corinne, too."

"I figured." His father set down his whiskey. He stared into the glass, the whiskey caramel-colored, melted ice swirling like oil. "Figured you found out somewhere along the line. Figured that's when things went sorta . . . south between you and me. Didn't know for sure, though, since you never said nothin' about it. Anyhow. I did what I thought was best at the time, but even so, I surely wasn't prepared to raise a kid," he said. "Never planned on it. A kid, I mean. Didn't think it was in the cards for me. Anyhow, I know it wasn't easy for you. Without a mother, I mean." He paused. "I surely wasn't prepared," he said again.

Mikey lifted his whiskey and shook the glass gently to disperse the ice. "What did you see in Corinne's house that day?" he said. "What made you change your mind about leaving me there?"

His father went very still, his expression dark and slack and faraway, as if he had been slapped but lacked the will to retaliate. Finally, he said, "There are some things that don't bear repeating."

Mikey sipped his whiskey. "There was a suitcase you kept in your closet. I found it poking around one day when I was really little. It had a familiar . . . It gave me a funny feeling. And it also didn't fit right in our house, didn't look like something you'd ever buy."

His father lifted his whiskey to his lips and drank from it twice, the second more of a gulp than a sip. Ice cracked between his teeth. He said, "The first night you stayed at my place, I had you sleeping in my bed, and I slept on the couch, but you moved around a lot in your sleep, kept falling out of that big bed. So the next day, I was gonna go out and buy a crib for you on my own, but then I thought you'd probably be most comfortable in whatever you were used to anyway. So I went down to Corinne's place first thing the next morning to see if she wouldn't mind lending us your crib until you outgrew it. When I got to her house, Corinne was off in another room, but Sally was there in the main room. I asked if she could she show me where your crib was. She looked at me sorta funny. I said, *Where does your little brother sleep?* And she pointed at this suitcase, sitting right at the base of the TV in the main room. I thought she must've misunderstood the question. I said, *Where does he sleep? Like, at night?* She pointed back at the suitcase again." Mikey's father's voice was thinner now, broken and indistinct. "So I took it home with me," he said. "Didn't know what else to do. Back at my place, you crawled into the thing. Curled up and settled yourself in there. Pulled the top up over your head. Like you'd spent every night, every day, of your little life learning how to . . . disappear." He paused and rubbed his index finger under his nostrils, which flared for air.

Mikey felt something soft and dangerous and defenseless opening inside himself, so powerful it shook. What could he say to this man? He began to cry a little bit, and his father passed him a napkin and looked away.

It was quiet for a while. The wind had picked up outside, and it moaned against the house.

Mikey's dad eventually said, "How're you plannin' on gettin' around when you can't see?"

"I'll manage," Mikey said.

"Still got your bed made up if you need it."

"What's that?"

"Once you moved out," his dad said, "I kept that little twin bed in your room made up in case you ever wanted to come back home."

•

Mikey nursed the memory of that evening quietly inside himself as he and Jimmy made their way up the snowy path to the house. Weeks later, the thought of that conversation with his father still actually *moved* things inside him. It hurt. It hurt, and it was good to feel.

Inside the house, Lynn and Issa greeted Jimmy and Mikey and Audwin at the door.

"Lynn, you're radiant!" Jimmy said.

She wore a deep burgundy silk caftan over loose-fitting cream silk pants and ballet flats. Issa wore a black suit with a burgundy silk tie, and he introduced the three of them to his mother, sister, uncle, and several cousins.

Lynn walked them in to the kitchen and pointed out the many different hors d'oeuvres options and the prosecco in the refrigerator.

Then Lynn pointed out their officiant, an elderly woman in a neat little navy suit, who was drinking coffee and looking at photographs attached to Lynn and Issa's refrigerator.

"Her name is Lee," Lynn said. "She's a former atheist, former nun, former secular Buddhist."

"So what is she now?"

"She's the only interfaith officiant in town. She does all the atheists and the gays and the couples who already live together," Lynn explained.

Back in the main room, Mikey chatted with Lynn's mother, who asked about Mikey's father. She introduced him to her own sister, Lynn's aunt, who was eating cheese cubes off a toothpick. Lynn's aunt had a little sourpuss face with colorless lips and tiny eyeballs, and she was displaying some uncomfortable cleavage.

"Mikey Callahan, one of Lynn's best childhood friends," Lynn's mother explained.

"Sure," said Lynn's aunt, looking Mikey over from head to toe. She reached out to poke his cheek. "Cute!" she said. "Cute, cute, cute."

Lynn's mother said to Mikey, "Is this your first time in Jim Thorpe?"

Mikey nodded.

She said, "Now, listen, in the next town over, it's *not* a long drive and it is so worth it . . . The Mason Jar Museum. You *cannot* miss this while you're in the area. The tour? *Ahhhh!*" She shook her fists emphatically. "Telling you, they know everything there is to know about the Mason jar. It just blows my mind that Lynn never wanted to try and get work there."

Mikey smiled.

Lynn and Issa's home was decorated beautifully with twinkling white lights along all the walls, dozens and dozens of mismatched white and burgundy candles, flames bright, quivering in synchrony as people passed through the rooms. A gleaming piano. Two entire walls of books, waist-high stacks of sheet music. They had fashioned a beautiful arbor of fresh and fragrant evergreen branches wrapped around split wooden planks that still had their bark. Long burgundy ribbons held the evergreen in place.

Sam and Justine arrived. Justine was petite and bright-cheeked. She wore her long curly blond hair in a half-ponytail, and her wide smile gleamed with silver braces. Sam wore the same brown suit he had worn to Sally's service, badly wrinkled from the long drive.

"So nice to meet you," Mikey said.

Mikey and Sam embraced.

Justine said, "How about this snow?"

Mikey said, "Did you run into much on the way?"

"Mountains in Virginia," Sam said. "Stuck behind a plow for an hour." He nodded out into the open room. "That Lynn's mom?"

Mikey nodded. "She's going to recommend that you make time for the Mason Jar Museum in the next town over. You just wait."

Sam laughed. "Sounds like a thrill."

Mikey turned to Justine. "Remind me where you're from originally?"

"Minnesota. Just outside Saint Paul."

"So you grew up in this kind of snow. You ever miss it?"

Justine nodded. "I keep trying to twist Sam's arm, get us back north a ways. See now, I like Buffalo, too, where y'all are from. I wouldn't mind living there either."

"So what's keeping you down south?"

"He's got good work," Justine said. "We like our church. Maybe someday, though . . ."

Mikey turned to Sam. "Alice is moving back to the area, ya know."

"Is she?"

Mikey nodded. "I'll be seeing a lot more of her."

Sam said, "Lucky you!" and wiggled his eyebrows. Then he laughed. "Alice is great. I just don't know that I'd want her for a next-door neighbor." He nodded down the hallway, toward the front door. "Speak of the devil."

Alice was kneeling to untie her work boots at the front door. She wore black pants and a loose-fitting dark green sweater over her broad shoulders. There was snow in her hair.

"She looks upset," Mikey observed when he saw Alice's face, but Sam did not hear him because he was already walking Justine up the hall for introductions.

Mikey went to the kitchen and ate a crostino with prosciutto and fennel slaw. He waited until Alice had said hello to Sam and Jimmy, been introduced to Justine and Audwin, then been greeted by Lynn and Issa before he approached her. He offered a hug, and Alice was stiff. She accepted the hug but did not reciprocate.

Mikey said, "What's up?"

"I'll tell you later," Alice said.

Mikey leaned closer to her. "Alice, are you okay?"

She offered a tight-lipped "Mm-hm," and her black eyes darted across the room. "I'll tell you after the ceremony." She nodded in the direction of the kitchen. "I don't imagine there's any booze at this party?"

"There's prosecco in the fridge," Mikey said. "You want a glass?"

"How about five?" Alice said. "By the way, I lost ten pounds, thanks for noticing." She pulled a toothpick from her pocket and began to suck on it voraciously. "I'm trying this new fad diet. Read about it online. It's called eat less food."

"Oh . . ." Mikey said, leaning in to examine the side of her face. "Oh, I'm afraid you're not going to like this."

"What?" Alice said.

"You're not going to like this one bit."

Mikey gripped a three-quarters-of-an-inch-long black hair from just beneath Alice's jawbone and pulled it out. It curled in his fingertips. He held it up for her to examine.

"Good God," she said, and batted it out of his hands.

Mikey opened a bottle of prosecco and filled a flute for each of them, and one for Lynn's aunt, who suddenly appeared at his side.

Alice looked directly at the woman's cleavage and sang, "All righty, then."

Mikey asked Alice if she was staying in town that night.

She rotated the toothpick over her lips and nodded. "Budget Inn Lynn recommended. You?"

Mikey nodded. "Same place. Sounds like everybody else is taking off tonight—Jimmy heading north, Sam back south, has to work a half-day tomorrow. Lynn and Issa have a five a.m. flight out of Philly, honeymooning in Scotland."

Alice said, "I guess it's just you and me for the night then, pal. We can eat Bugles and watch *Law & Order* and play doctor."

Lynn's aunt, who had been listening to the conversation, stared at Alice.

From the main room, Mikey could hear Lynn's voice as she assembled the group.

They made their way back to that room, and Alice and Mikey stood next to Jimmy, Audwin, Sam, and Justine.

Lynn and Issa were up at the arbor, and people were gathering before them. Lynn was counting heads.

"Nineteen, twenty, twenty-one, twenty-two," she said. "That's everybody."

The crowd grew quiet as Lynn and Issa stepped beneath the arbor. They held hands. Lynn introduced Lee as their officiant. The petite, gray-haired woman did not hold notes or a microphone as she took center stage.

"Lynn's only request was that I keep it brief," Lee said.


"Love," Lee announced, "is not a mystery. It is not poetry, it is not pure, it is not sacred. Nothing humans do is."

The room, already quiet, was now completely silent.

"Love," Lee continued, "is simply the time you spend loving. There are no other rules. That's it."

•

Alice was still sucking noisily on her toothpick. She rolled it to the side of her lips and whispered down the row to Sam and Justine, the only married couple among them, "Is that true?"

Justine was nodding in agreement. "I think so. Hon, don't you think?"

Sam said, "It helps if you like the same TV shows, too."

Alice whispered, "Also, I imagine, you hope they don't end up having some weird fetish. Toe-sucking. Or bread-crushing."

Mikey made a face at her. "The hell?"

Jimmy giggled.

Alice's whisper grew louder. "It's a real thing! Guys pay women in high heels to crush loaves of bread in front of them. I swear!"

Mikey said, "*Sh.*"

Lee led Lynn and Issa through their vows, then they exchanged their wedding bands, placing them not on each other's fingers but on long chains over each other's necks. When Lee pronounced them husband and wife, a cheer rose up from the small group, and one of Issa's cousins, who was seated at the piano, began to play Thelonious Monk's "Ruby, My Dear."

Issa took Lynn by the waist and kissed her, and they slow-danced while the others cheered and then joined the dance. Sam held Justine's head against his chest and kissed it.

Alice took Mikey by the elbow and led him to the kitchen, where she grabbed a crostino with smoked salmon and capers, then walked him to the front door, where she knelt to put her boots back on.

"Follow me," she whispered forcefully, her mouth still full of crostino, breath smelling of fish. "We gotta talk outside, just in case I spring a leak."

Mikey said, "Excuse me?"

"In case I *cry*," she said.

"You don't cry," Mikey said.

"Exactly."

Mikey put his own shoes back on and followed Alice outside. A bit of fresh snow had accumulated in the last hour. Already, at only five o'clock, the sun was gone. The sky was navy to the east and rose-colored to the west, with stars beginning to wink overhead. They stood on the porch. Alice sighed heavily and stared out over the snowy landscape. A blackbird strutted across the telephone line before them. She reached into her pocket, withdrew a little tab of Nicorette from a foil packet, and crunched into it.

Mikey glanced at Alice's face, and he knew immediately. "*Finn*," he said.

Alice nodded. "Yesterday," she said, in a voice so thick with pain.

Mikey embraced her. His neck on hers, he felt her swallow hard many times in a row.

He said, "Do you want to talk?"

Alice shook her head. "I want you to stand here with me for five minutes and not talk, then I'll be ready to go have fun."

Mikey gazed at her.

Alice tapped her left wrist with her right index finger. "Five minutes," she said. "Starting now. Don't talk. Just tell me when it's time, and I'll be ready."

Issa's cousin was at the piano and playing "North of the Sunset" when they reentered the house. Alice took a few calming breaths and blew her nose into a cocktail napkin she'd pulled from her pocket. Then she bobbed her head along with the whimsical tune as she removed her boots. She threw her hair out of her face in handfuls.

As they made their way back toward the group, Alice whispered to Mikey, "I just had the best idea for the most messed-up trick to get back at Jimmy."

"Get back at Jimmy? For what?"

"For that evil story he told us at his lake house! Scared the crap out of me. I think about it every time I see a couple getting their picture taken. Every time I hear a train."

"What do you have in mind?"

"I'm not telling you because you'll forbid it."

Mikey filled a plate for himself with barbecued chicken and curried cauliflower, and he refilled his glass with prosecco. He watched Alice out of the corner of his eye as she engaged in conversation with Lynn's aunt.

The two of them parted, and Alice made her way across the room where, Mikey could see, she had a good view of Jimmy.

Mikey made eye contact with Alice. Her expression was giddy with anticipation. She tipped her chin toward Jimmy, indicating that Mikey should listen in. Mikey posted himself up against the wall several feet away from Jimmy and Audwin, and he sipped his prosecco.

Lynn's aunt casually approached Jimmy and Audwin. She introduced herself to the two of them, and Jimmy introduced himself as a close childhood friend of Lynn's.

"Another one!" Lynn's aunt said.

Jimmy nodded.

Lynn's aunt said, "So now I've met you, and Alice, and Sam, and Mikey, and the blond."

Jimmy cocked his head at her perplexedly.

Mikey felt a pumping, mischievous laugh in his chest, a perverse thrill as he realized what Alice was up to.

Lynn's aunt looked at Jimmy, her face owlish and quizzical. She said, "The thin blond. Another childhood friend? Introduced herself to me outside before the ceremony, then she just sort of disappeared."

Jimmy's face displayed a stunned horror for only a split second before his eyes rolled dramatically and his posture relaxed. "*Alice*," he growled, looking for her in the room. He turned briefly to Lynn's aunt. "She's good," he said. "And you're good. Almost had me."

Alice bounded over from the far side of the room and practically tackled Jimmy.

"Almost had you!" she said.

Jimmy said, "You and your twisted, nihilistic little games."

They laughed and laughed as Mikey explained the trick to Audwin, whose eyes glimmered with admiration as he clucked his tongue at Alice and said, "This woman seems very hip."


They ate and drank and toasted and danced and laughed for hours, the whole room loose and dizzy with happiness.

Eventually, it was completely dark outside, the food was gone, and the bride and groom were weary.

They all said their farewells to Lynn and Issa and one another, and made plans for a reunion in June or July. Sam suggested that everyone come to Georgia, but said they had only one spare bedroom at their home. Jimmy said he'd look into a week-long rental in their area that would accommodate all of them.

Outside, there were several inches of fresh snow, packed hard on the streets, which had not been plowed. The sky was starry and clear.

# CHAPTER 29

Mikey followed Alice to the Budget Inn ten minutes away, where they both checked into their rooms. Alice gave Mikey the second key to her room and invited him to come over as soon as he was settled in. She said she was going to order a pizza and asked if Mikey had a preference on toppings.

Alice was sitting upright in the queen bed when Mikey entered her room a bit later. A bottle of whiskey was on the bedside table, and she was sipping out of a little plastic cup. The pizza had arrived and was on the middle of the bed. Alice plucked a steaming pepperoni off it.

The TV was on, an old episode of *Law & Order* playing at low volume.

Alice patted the pillow next to her.

Mikey poured himself a whiskey, using the plastic cup sitting next to the single-serve coffee machine, and took a seat next to her on the bed. The springs of the cheap bed bounced and crunched beneath him.

Alice said, "I beg of you, please do not pass gas in my bed."

She reached for a piece of pizza and pulled it onto a paper plate, a string of hot cheese trailing behind it. She twisted this around her finger until it broke.

It was quiet for a few minutes as they ate pizza and watched TV.

Eventually, Alice said, "Just so you know, I'm not going to make you talk about what you don't want to talk about. Unless *you* want to talk about it."

Mikey helped himself to a second slice of pizza. "You mean the phone call. A baby."

Alice nodded. She looked utterly miserable. "Please just don't," she said. "I know what you're going to say. Don't speak. Shut up. Leave me alone." She tossed her black hair over her shoulders.

Mikey looked at her.

"Sorry," she said. "I'm being mean because I'm feeling vulnerable. And I know what you're going to say."

"Do you?"

She pointed at the actor on-screen. "I read that that guy kicks his dog in real life."

"Really?" Mikey said.

"No, I'm just trying to change the subject."

Mikey adjusted his glasses over the bridge of his nose. "I talked to my eye doctor," he said.

Alice turned to face him.

Mikey said, "It's over a ninety percent chance it's hereditary. Can't be sure without any information on my biological father, but there's a very high likelihood that my children would suffer early-onset macular degeneration. Go blind at a young age."

Alice nodded. "I understand," she said.

"I don't want to pass this on to someone." Mikey sipped his whiskey. "You know, I'd never given much thought to having kids before you brought it up. When the doc told me this . . . it upset me more than I thought it would."

"The idea of not having kids?" Alice said.

Mikey shook his head. "Not that." He chewed on a piece of ice and swallowed. "The idea of not being able to give you what you want."

Alice said, "Oh." She tapped a crust of pizza over her knee.

Mikey was quiet for a bit. Then he said, "Would you consider doing it any other way?"

Alice took a bite of pizza and chewed slowly. She looked directly at Mikey, pushing black hair from her eyes. "I won't do this if it's not with you. And I'm not saying that to make you feel bad." She paused, gulped down the last of her whiskey, poured herself another, and handed the bottle to Mikey. "I know I'm pushy, but I couldn't push you into something this big. I wouldn't. I won't. I respect your decision, it's over, and it's okay." Alice looked back toward the TV.

Mikey shifted on the bed. "Maybe I'd reconsider if—"

Alice cut him off with a hand in the air. "Mikey? It's over. And it's okay."

Mikey caught her hand out of the air, laced his fingers through hers, and held it tightly. A few seconds later she pulled away and said, "Your hand is hot and wet, and I don't like it."

It was quiet for a long while.

Eventually, Alice closed the empty pizza box and tossed it toward the foot of the bed. She said, "The Saint and I divorced because he tried to force me to have a kid with him. So I'm not about to do that to you."

Mikey turned to face her. "He wanted kids and you didn't?" he said. "Was that it?"

"Not exactly. I just wasn't sure one way or the other. Hadn't even given it much thought. Then, all of a sudden, I was pregnant. I missed my period, bought a test, and took it on my own. Got the ol' double line."

"Huh?"

"Means it's positive."

"Did you tell him right away?"

Alice sighed. "No. I wanted to think things through privately first. I called up the nearest women's health center to talk through my options. I was only six weeks along. I didn't make an appointment, but I got all the info and decided to sit on it for a bit."

"So what happened?"

"That same night, Jason saw the number for the women's health center in my phone."

"Who?" It occurred to Mikey that he had never even known The Saint's real name. "Oh, oh, oh."

"Apparently he snooped on my phone all the time," Alice said, "paranoid that I was cheating. I wasn't. I was careful with the pregnancy test itself to hide all the evidence, the receipt, all that, but I didn't think to erase the outgoing call in my phone. He saw the number on my phone that same night and figured out what was going on."

"He was upset?"

Alice nodded. "Furious that I would even *consider* not keeping it without consulting him first. I tried to explain that I hadn't made the decision yet, I'd only wanted to weigh my options on my own first, but that didn't matter. He threatened to put me on lockdown. Take my phone and the keys to my car and my credit cards, so I couldn't do anything without him. He threatened to basically hold me hostage for nine months. Threatened to sue me. Told me I was legally required to get his consent. I'd done my research; I knew I wasn't. He told me I was possessed, I was evil. He threatened to bomb the clinic. All sorts of craziness."

"Had he ever lost his head like that before? Did he scare you?"

Alice shook her head. "Not even close. Nothing like it. But,

Mikey, as soon as I learned that I was pregnant with his child, something inside of me just knew it wasn't right. Why else wouldn't my first phone call be to him? Something inside of me just *knew* it was not the life that I wanted."

Alice tucked her hair behind her ears. She uncrossed and recrossed her long legs over the bed, and picked at a little stain on the comforter beneath her.

"So then what happened?"

"I ran out of the house and never went back. Left all my clothes, my computer, my books . . . everything I owned. Ran out the door and drove to my brother's house a couple hours away. Never looked back."

"*Sheezus.* And . . . the pregnancy?"

"I miscarried a few days later. They say stress can bring it on."

"And how did you feel?"

"Mostly relieved."

"I'd imagine."

"He tried to get in touch with me through everyone we knew right after I left: my parents, brothers, mutual friends . . . He told everybody I had run away with his baby, and he begged them to stop me from ending the pregnancy. He even said he didn't even care if he never saw me again; we could separate, and he would happily raise that baby on his own. Can you believe that? My brother finally told him I'd miscarried, and then my brother helped me with the paperwork, got the divorce legalized without my ever having to sit in the same room with him. Years later, Jason looked me up on Facebook. Said he'd come to peace with me, even though I had hurt him worse than anyone ever had and probably ever would. I sent him some curt little response. He still reaches out from time to time. And every time I hear from him, he reminds me that he's still praying for me." Alice snorted. "Although he's never specified what exactly he's praying *for* for me. Salvation or the seven plagues. I just hope whoever's listening to his prayers gets where I was coming from."

Mikey said, "Why did you never want to tell me any of this? Were you worried what I would think?"

Alice was quiet for a bit. "Do you remember back at the lake house last month when somebody brought up the worst thing you've ever done? Or the worst thing someone has ever done to you? I can't remember the context. I bet you if someone asked The Saint what the worst thing anyone has ever done to him was, his answer would be that I called to find out the price of ending a pregnancy before telling him I was pregnant. What I'm saying is that, in his mind, what I did to him will probably always be *the worst*."

"You're probably right."

"But for *me*," Alice went on, "questioning whether I wanted to keep it and then ultimately deciding to leave him was probably the *best* thing I've ever done."

"So?"

"That sucks!" Alice said, throwing her hands into the air. "Shouldn't my answer to the question *What's the worst thing you've ever done?* be the thing that hurt someone else the most?"

"No way," Mikey shook his head. "This is just the reality when you have reasons for doing something that could never be understood by someone else."

"It wasn't until years after we separated that I could actually appreciate the loss from his perspective. I didn't share his feelings about the pregnancy, but I couldn't discount them entirely either. Frankly, I'm amazed by the depth of emotion he had toward that tiny little sac of cells. See, I don't think this was entirely about controlling me; that had never been part of his nature before. I think this was *actually* about the baby. He cared that deeply. Wanted that badly to protect it, felt that was his duty. He . . . dare I say . . . already *loved* it? Is that possible? I don't actually know the answer to that." Alice paused and sipped her whiskey.

Mikey said, "I don't either."

"My point is that I can laugh at The Saint. I can resent him. Despise him, even. But I can't quite find it in me to diminish his pain, or find any humor in it. I don't want to be someone's worst thing. That hurts me."

"I'm surprised you're bothered by a thing like that."

"Mikey, you know I like to consider myself a loose cannon but ultimately harmless."

"Nobody is harmless," Mikey said. "Sorry."

Alice sniffed and rubbed each nostril.

It was quiet for a few moments.

Eventually, Alice said, "Sally cutting herself off was one of the worst things that happened to all of us. Maybe *the* worst. But maybe it was the best thing for her. Like you said. We could never understand her reasons." Alice reached for her cup of whiskey and finished it in a single swallow. "Like you said," she remarked. "Nobody is harmless."

Mikey said, "How do we live with that?"

"What's the alternative to living with something that hurts?" Alice said. "Jump off a bridge?" She hesitated. "I don't mean that as a joke. How does anybody live with anything? You just . . . march on, I guess, even when your heart's not in it."

Alice was quiet for a little while. Then she lifted her own sleeve, rolled it back, and pointed at a large patch of inflamed red skin running all up her forearm to the inside of her elbow, some small areas gleaming with pus, some spots of dried black blood. "Poison oak," she said matter-of-factly. "From bushwhacking behind the marina. New owner's gonna put in a two-car garage. It's driving me nuts, and if I scratch, it only gets worse. Disgusting. Are you disgusted?"

Mikey said, "I'm impressed."

"Impressed?" Alice rolled her sleeve back down. "A *scar* is something to be impressed by, Mikey. A *rash* is just vulgar."

She patted her forearm, pulled a pillow onto Mikey's lap and rested her head there. She turned up the volume of the TV, as though she was done talking.

An hour passed.

Mikey watched a full episode of *Law & Order* as Alice rested. Benson was right about the perp again. When would those other cops ever learn? Benson's instincts were never wrong!

Mikey gazed down at Alice's face, moving his head around to bring her fully into focus as best as he could. Broad, pale cheeks, small C-shaped indents at the corners of her mouth, lips parted, uncommonly peaceful, although even in sleep her eyebrows arched high, as if she were waiting for a punch line. Mikey felt deeply sad. He looked around the hotel room. A single rogue slat on the gray drawstring shutters, and beyond that, the black outdoors, dusted with stars that were low and shy. A bone-colored ashtray sitting on the bedstand, hilariously, next to a small laminated card that read NO SMOKING. A sizable purple stain on the carpet. Cheap red wine—had to be. A shabby little desk, no accompanying chair, with a thick blue Ethernet cord snaked across it. He looked back at Alice's face—*Debussy's Arabesque No. 1 for piano*—then he had to look away.

Eventually, Alice stirred. She sat upright in the bed, rubbed her eyes, yawned, pushed black hair from her face, and squinted over at the digital clock on the cable box. It was nearly midnight.

She said, "I suppose I oughta send you back to your room for the night. I don't sleep well with anyone else in the bed, anyway. And you'd probably sweat up the sheets. But first I'm going to tell you about dying."

Mikey gazed at her, and she stared straight ahead at the TV.

Then she said, "You remember Jake, my dog when we were kids?"

"Of course."

"Good dog," Alice said. "I was in my freshman year of college. Jake was old as dirt by that time. Blind and deaf. Couldn't keep food down, he was skin and bones. My parents said that it was time, they were gonna put him down, and I begged them to wait until I was home for Christmas so I could say good-bye."

"Did they?"

Alice nodded. "They kept him around until I got home, the week before Christmas. But that same night, after I'd seen Jake, middle of the night and while I was in bed, he crawled down to the basement, God knows how, his hipbones were probably practically dust at that point. He hadn't done stairs in ages, but he made his way down there and into the far corner, way back behind the water heater, far as he could get from the people in the house, curled himself up and died. It took us forever to find him the next day."

"They say that's how animals often do, right? They prefer to be alone."

Alice nodded. "It's a wild instinct; they've got it in their blood. See, chemicals given off by a dead body can be toxic to the ones left behind. Nature knows it's better for the pack if the dying one makes their way off quiet in the night. Anyhow. That was Jake. Now, *Finn* . . . Finn was a *bad* dog," she said. "Growled at little kids. Pooped and peed all over my house. Like it was his job. Tore up every piece of furniture in the place, destroyed every pair of shoes

I owned, never did learn to sit or stay. He ate a bird. He barked incessantly. He was so stupid. You know I loved him, Mikey, that dog was the love of my life, but my God, he was a *bad dog*. And then all of a sudden, before I knew it, Finn was an *old* dog. Poor thing, his insides were just stalling out. Inoperable. Last week, a couple nights in a row, Finn got up from his bed in my room in the middle of the night, where he *always* slept, and made his way out of my bedroom and over to the front door, like he had someplace to go. I knew what was happening, what he was trying to do. I knew it was time. But I didn't want him to be alone in his final moments, like Jake, even if that's what nature was telling him to do."

Alice swallowed and closed her eyes before continuing. "Yesterday, before the vet put the needle in Finn, I held him there, hugged him and rocked him over the table. I hadn't planned out what I would say or do or how it would go because I just couldn't bear to think of it before the time came . . . But . . . when the time came, I held his tired gray face in my hands and I said, *You are the perfect dog. You are perfect. You can rest now. You were always the perfect dog."*

Alice stopped speaking and Mikey didn't know if this was the whole story, but she seemed to be done telling it. She cried a little bit, and he held her.

# CHAPTER 30

Several weeks later, Mikey was picking up gloves, a trowel, and a five-gallon bucket from the Bed Bath & Beyond in Tonawanda. Alice, who now lived in the area, was planning to take him worm-picking as soon as the ground thawed. She had instructed him on what materials to bring for himself. She had told him to get a mask if he thought the smell of earthworms would bother him—she knew he had a weak stomach—but Mikey said he thought he'd manage.

It was gray outside, very cold and very windy. Early March. Mikey wasn't technically supposed to be driving anymore, with the recent changes to his eyesight, but he made exceptions for himself and avoided highways.

The wind swirled around Mikey and hollered in his ears.

While he loaded these materials into the backseat of his car, his eye fell on the vehicle parked next to his. An old teal Chevy Chevette with rusted-out wheel wells, one of its back windows punched out and replaced with tarp that was sloppily duct-taped to the outside of the door.

Mikey gazed at the shopping cart parked at the back end of the Chevette. The cart was positively stuffed full and overflowing with fake flowers. Massive plastic tiger lilies, silk peach roses, polyester peonies, way-too-blue baby roses on green strings, lightweight plastic pots with fake soil units.

Mikey stared at the flowers, then at the woman who was now unloading them into the trunk of the Chevette.

The woman wore a puffy black coat over gray sweatpants and little pink sneakers. Her yellowy-gray hair was very thin, parted in the center and pulled into a low ponytail. Her skin looked both incredibly shiny and incredibly dull, and she had a little burr of a face. Everything about her had a gray hue, including her pale, creamy eyes. Her posture was bent and humpbacked, and it took Mikey only a moment to recognize the woman as Corinne.

Mikey stared at Corinne, unwilling to allow the word *mother* to enter his mind, as she continued to unload the fake flowers into her trunk, moving painstakingly but with purpose. Corinne was focused on the task at hand, untangling a length of rosebuds on a string before gently placing them in the trunk.

Mikey tried to picture Corinne unloading all these plastic plants into the home she had shared with Sally on Ingram, just several houses up from his father's. That sad little gray house, its siding faded and splintering off, roof tiles practically shredded, the lawn an absolute disaster of overgrown ryegrass and bull thistle.

Mikey tried to picture Corinne carrying these fake flowers into that home, using them to replace the wilted flowers she would have received around the time of Sally's death. He wondered if Corinne had already disposed of those dead flowers and the vases full of foul and cloudy water. He wondered if, in this collection of plastic flowers, Corinne had gotten an exact replica for every single one she had received at the time of Sally's death, and would arrange them the exact same way in her home. He wondered if she intended to spend the rest of her life in a static and unchanging version of grief, these flowers collecting dust but never dying. Never even fading.

Mikey didn't have a clue what Sally and Corinne's life together had been. How much there might have been between them. Love or other stuff. He had not a clue how they lived. His thoughts flickered briefly to his own biological father. Not a clue about this man either. Not a clue how his own life might have been different had Sally's biological father stuck around to be a father to her, or if Mikey's biological father had stuck around to be a father to him. Not a clue how things would have been different if he hadn't wandered out of Corinne's house and up the street that sunny afternoon. Or if he had ended up on a different front lawn.

There were things that Mikey's heart simply didn't have the energy to even try to imagine.

Corinne had finally loaded all of her plastic flowers into the trunk and was struggling to reach the door to close it, the strain of stretching out her bent back causing her to grimace.

Mikey said, "You need a hand?"

Corinne stepped back, giving Mikey room to help her with the door. She did not seem to recognize him. Mikey gripped the door and slammed it into place. He patted the bumper of the Chevette. Before getting into her car, Corinne gazed briefly at Mikey with a face that was utterly stricken. So much pain Mikey had to look away.

Mikey watched, a frosty wind biting at his face, as the teal Chevette pulled out of the parking lot. He wondered if Corinne had been over the Skyway since, or if, like him, she still took the long way around. He watched as her car, far away now, inched slowly north, from one gray land to another.

# CHAPTER 31

I t was nearly a month later before the ground had fully thawed. Alice picked Mikey up at two o'clock in the morning on the first Sunday of April. She told him she'd need his help, so he'd better not sleep through his alarm. He wore an old Carharrt work jacket belonging to his father, jeans, boots, and gloves. She drove them thirty miles east, to the woodlands near Corfu.

Alice wore a headlamp and carried a shovel. Mikey had a five-gallon bucket hanging from his elbow, a trowel, and a knit cap in the bucket.

The world crunched beneath their feet.

Mikey's vision was deteriorating very quickly now, with a noticeable change almost every day. It was especially poor in the dark, so Alice held his hand as they made their way up a narrow trail, and she watched for obstacles in his path. The only sounds aside from their own footsteps were of faraway night birds, and leaves muttering against one another when the wind stirred.

At one point, Mikey said, "You sure this is safe for us to be out here, middle of nowhere, middle of the night like this? You sure we're not gonna stumble onto some wacko's private property?"

Alice said, "Safe?"

"Have you seen the movie *Deliverance*?"

Alice snorted. "Mikey, you really need to get with the times."

Alice used a GPS to pinpoint the exact location that had been recommended to her by a fellow local fisherman, who she had met while scouting out locations for her marina.

Mikey had accompanied Alice on a number of these trips, up and down the Outer Harbor, by the Erie Basin, near the Times Beach Nature Preserve. Although he couldn't see well enough to offer much of an opinion on the location and structure of the buildings she was considering, Alice liked to get his take on the "sentiment" of the place. The first time she had asked Mikey what he made of the sentiment of a certain location, he'd misheard the question. He sniffed the air and answered, "Dead fish. Cigarettes. Boat gas. They all smell the same."

"Not the *scent*, you dummy," Alice said. "The *sentiment*."

"What do you mean?"

"How does it *feel* to you?"

"The air? Damp. Cool. Fresh. Fishy."

"What does your heart feel?"

"My heart? Aside from the obvious, I rarely know what my heart feels."

"What's the obvious?"

"Just that it's still working."

Once the GPS indicated that they had reached the proper spot, Alice told Mikey to sit tight while she dug in with the shovel. The ground gave easily beneath the blade of the shovel and made gentle *fwoomp* noises as she lifted out shovelfuls of wet soil, until she hit limestone and a loud clash sounded. She continued to dig around it, grunting with the effort, then she paused to assess. Mikey could hear her fingers combing through soil.

The night air smelled of evergreen and overturned earth and iron.

"They weren't lyin'," Alice said.

"Lots of worms?"

"Yuh."

Mikey said, "What do you want me to do?"

"Hold the bucket for me," Alice said.

Mikey stood next to her and held the bucket while Alice rooted around on her hands and knees, and soon she started depositing worms into the bucket with little plops.

"Good, good, good," Alice murmured. "Fatties."

The air was very cold on Mikey's face. Faraway, an eastern screech owl bawled into the night. Mikey's sense of smell had continued to intensify with the loss of his sight, and he wished now that he had taken Alice's advice and brought a mask. The ripe, raw scent of earthworms being pulled from the ground was making him a bit sick to his stomach. He could feel movement in the bucket. He nosed under the collar of his shirt, breathing in the scent of laundry detergent. Some small animal rustled in a nearby bush, then bounded swiftly away. He could hear it moving for a long time.

The screech owl sounded again, and Mikey's thoughts turned to a conversation he'd had with Sally when they were children. She had told him about the strange and unpredictable migration of various solitary animals she had learned about in her science class, including the snowy owl. Mikey didn't know what *migrate* meant, so Sally explained, "It's a long journey that an animal takes."

Mikey said, "To find food?"

"Sometimes," Sally said. "But sometimes they go for reasons the scientists don't understand. Sometimes . . . well . . . it's like sometimes nature just puts something in their heart that makes them need to go, and so they go."

Eventually, the bucket Mikey held began to grow heavy.

He said, "Why am I holding this thing, anyway?"

"Huh?" Alice stopped her work, and he could tell vaguely from the flash of her headlamp that she had turned to face him.

"Why am I holding this bucket?" Mikey set it down on the ground next to his legs. "There's nothing for me to do," he said. "I can't drive, can't dig, can't follow a GPS, can't see the worms to pick 'em. And there's no reason for me to be holding this bucket. Why am I here? Why did you make me come? I'm not helping you."

They had walked a good twenty minutes from where Alice had parked in order to reach this particular spot, and Mikey could tell from the sounds and from the texture of the air here that it was very thickly wooded. Spongy and pungent. He could hear no evidence of human civilization; no cars, no voices, no white hum of electricity. The air felt old and cold and alive and haunted.

"I'm not helping you," he said again.

"Yes, you are," Alice said.

It was quiet for a while; then Alice returned to her work, humming as she tossed more worms into the bucket, which now rested on the ground. *Plop, plop, plop.*

Far away, the screech owl sounded. A scream in the darkness. Mikey wondered if the thing was waiting for an answer or just howling to howl.

Mikey said, "You are my best friend."

# CHAPTER 32

John Callahan was admitted to St. Mary's Hospital on a Tuesday afternoon in May after experiencing pain in his chest. He was released within hours when his EKG returned completely normal, but the doctor advised that he retire or find other work that involved less heavy lifting. John did not want to stop working altogether, so Mikey offered to help him look for job postings on Craigslist. By the time he accepted Mikey's help, John had already been hard at work on his own résumé, using a sloppy and outdated template that, inexplicably, he had paid some website $2.99 to download.

The two of them sat together at Mikey's kitchen table one evening, and Mikey listened as his father read aloud the entire contents of his résumé: the date that he graduated high school followed by a single paragraph describing his duties at the meat plant.

Mikey helped his father respond to ads online for cashier positions at the Home Depot, Tops, and Walmart.

His father seemed quickly exhausted by this, so they decided to call it quits and drink a beer together. It was a mild spring evening, and they took plastic chairs out onto the porch. Up the street, a push-mower buzzed back and forth across a small lawn, children chafed the sidewalk with skateboards and rollerblades, and the air smelled as green as could be.

Mikey's father said, "Hell of a sunset." He glanced over at Mikey. "You seein' any of that?"

Mikey squinted out across his lawn, over the darkness of the tree line to the west. "Little bit of pink," he said, "little bit of blue. That's about all I can make out. Colors are all thin and faded to me now. Like the whole world was washed in too-hot."

His father was quiet for a bit, then he said, "There's pink, and there's also purple, and blue, and yellow, a strip of gold, some more pink, almost like tiger stripes, against purple . . . and also . . . orange."

Mikey was struck by the peculiar idea that he and his father were trying to become friends.

His father said, "You had a thing about skies, didn't you? You remember that solar eclipse when you were a kid?"

Mikey nodded. "Happened when I was in school."

"You were *all* charged up about it," his father said. "I'd never seen you so excited for something. They must've really got you worked up about it in your science classes. You made me promise that morning that I'd go out on my lunch break, so I'd see it, too."

Mikey said, "Did you?"

"No," his father said. "I forgot all about it, worked straight through the afternoon."

They sat in silence for a while longer. As Mikey sipped his beer, he was suddenly rewarded with a clear and distinct memory of the solar eclipse. He let the memory sail into him, and he grabbed at every detail.

The students had spent weeks preparing for the eclipse with their science teachers. They learned how, in ancient cultures, a solar eclipse was attributed to the supernatural and thought to be a bad omen, but these days, of course, they knew better. They learned that the diameter of the sun was approximately four hundred times that of the moon. They learned the definition of *corona*, *umbra*, and *annulus*. They learned about the dangers of exposure to sun even at this great distance. The teachers explained that they must protect their eyeballs while viewing the eclipse, so that they wouldn't burn their retinas off. Anyone who didn't use their pinhole viewing box could go blind, the teachers said. So each student had been given their own cardboard box, uniformly sized and without a bottom seam. Each box had the name of the student Sharpied big and black along the side.

On the afternoon of the solar eclipse, the children were arranged outside by grade, which meant Mikey was separated from his friends, who were all one grade above him. The principal was giving instructions over a megaphone.

It was late fall, and a dry wind spun through the schoolyard.

Now they were told to put their box over their head.

Mikey shivered inside his box. He had reminded his father about the eclipse that morning, and his father said he would try to take his lunch break at that time so he could be watching it, too, at the same time.

A strange, holy silence settled over the schoolyard.

Mikey couldn't help himself. He lifted his box back up over his head and set it at his feet. He did this carefully and silently, making sure he did not brush against the students on either side of him. He then gazed across the schoolyard, a massive labyrinth of brown boxes held at different heights but identical upward-tilted angles. All those brown boxes with all those names written across them, all those little heads inside watching and waiting for the beautiful thing to happen.

There were his five friends, all next to one another, several rows away. He knew them by their shoes and pant legs and postures, without even reading the names on their boxes. Alice was either dancing or stamping her feet impatiently. Everyone else was still. Sally's words from several weeks earlier returned to Mikey's mind. *It might be the most beautiful thing we'll ever see in our whole lives,* she had said of the eclipse.

It was a clear, cold November sky above the schoolyard, with just a few thin smeary clouds, like hurried white brushstrokes, and Mikey stared right up into the brilliant amber sun as the moon moved into place. It was not like Mikey to break the rules, but now that the beautiful thing was happening, he could hardly bear not to feel it on his whole face.

What a universe. There was so much to see! So much to feel!

And yet, if there was one thing Mikey knew of feelings . . . There was always that *other* feeling, crouched and waiting nearby in the shadows, even at a moment like this, even when he was on the brink of the most beautiful thing he would ever see in his life. It was the low tide. The sacred, empty void after the birds had taken flight. The tangled thing that tugged on Mikey, kept him sewn up inside himself, made happiness hard. Mikey didn't yet have words for this feeling, but already at this young age, he understood that it would never leave him entirely—nature had put it in his heart, and there it would always remain, even when he thought he was in the clear, even when he thought he had left it behind.

Mikey had asked his father about this feeling once, years earlier, when he was *very* small and before he had learned that it was foolish to talk plainly about feelings. Mikey had said, "I have a bad, sad feeling in me sometimes." His father said, "Me, too." And knowing that his father shared this had been such a great comfort to Mikey that over time he began to cherish that shadowy feeling, which proved to be as sure as the tides, as persistent and reliable as a dear friend, as real and as much a part of his universe as the sun.

# CHAPTER 33

Jimmy had rented a house on Lake Oconee, an hour from Sam and Justine's home, for the second week of June. Aside from Mikey and Alice, it would be the first that any of them had seen one another since Lynn's wedding, although they had stayed in close touch via email over the intervening months.

Justine was now twelve weeks pregnant, and they were ecstatic. They planned to wait to find out the gender, but both suspected a boy. Sam's company was opening a second branch near Cleveland in the fall, and they planned to move back to the Midwest to be closer to both families. They would miss their church, Sam said, but weren't too crazy about the new pastor anyway.

In September, Lynn and Issa would depart for Addis Ababa, where they would spend one year teaching music at the grade school Issa had attended as a boy. When they returned to the states, they planned to move to Buffalo in order to be closer to Lynn's mother. Issa planned to record his first album. Lynn had spoken to the current head of the AA chapter in Buffalo and conveyed her interest in a position with them upon her return.

Audwin had moved to LA in April and met Jimmy's parents on their most recent visit out west. Jimmy said that his father went through an entire fifth of sambuca in two days and didn't say a whole lot, but his mother absolutely adored Audwin. She couldn't stop touching his red beard. The two of them could do a bang-up impression of each other's accents. She taught Audwin the tarantella dance, which originated in Puglia, and he taught her his grandmother's recipe for apple zwieback torte and marzipan nougat.

Jimmy said that he and Audwin planned to spend summers at the lake house in Buffalo in the future—Audwin simply couldn't stand the heat of an LA summer. Jimmy said that they were in love.

Alice now lived ten miles from Mikey, in Allentown, and had purchased storefront property for her marina, just off the northern shore of the Times Beach Nature Preserve. It was still several months away from opening, but she was slowly getting the place set up.

She visited Mikey several times a week and called him every day. Often more than once a day, and often with no apparent agenda. She would put him on speakerphone while folding her laundry or cooking a meal, or call him just to sing along to whatever song was playing on her radio while she drove.

Shortly after moving, Alice had learned that Buffalo Philharmonic rehearsals on Tuesdays and Fridays were open to the public, so on these days, she would drop Mikey off at the auditorium and leave him there to listen to the entire rehearsal while she ran errands downtown. Mikey couldn't believe that in all his years in Buffalo he had never known about these rehearsals. He had never once attended a Philharmonic concert, couldn't justify the cost to go alone, and it had never even occurred to him that there might be another way. Alice had no interest in sitting there with Mikey for a full two-hour rehearsal, but she also never complained about taking him, and she would always ask all about it on the way home. She loved to hear about when one of the musicians had been singled out for playing out of tune or missing a cue.

Back in May, Mikey had fallen in his own home, and he had to call Alice to take him to the doctor, where a cast was put on his broken wrist. Mikey was so disgusted with himself. Humiliated. Alice had stayed at the hospital with him the whole time and listed herself as his emergency contact when the receptionist asked.

Several days later, when Mikey was at her house, Alice had tried to outright deny the construction taking place on her front porch until he pressed her on it and she confessed that she was having the stairs converted to a ramp.

"I'm blind, not helpless," Mikey said. "I was just being clumsy."

"I know," Alice said. "But I don't want you to fall and break your neck at my house then sue me."

Mikey laughed.

It was quiet for a bit.

"Don't lie to me," Mikey said. "I'm serious. Not about the ramp out front or anything else. It's not fair, because I just have to take your word since I can't see things for myself anymore."

Alice gently took his hand and patted it, then she forcibly dipped his fingers into a dish of something sticky and too warm.

Mikey pulled his hand back into his chest and shook out his fingers. "What the hell was that?"

Alice was laughing. "I'm making marmalade," she said. "Lick your fingers if you don't trust me."

"I sure don't," Mikey said. He sniffed then licked his fingers.

Alice said, "But in the spirit of full disclosure, there is something I need to tell you."

"Oh?"

"The other night when I took you home from the hospital, you dozed off in the car, and I took the Skyway."

Mikey was quiet for a bit.

Alice said, "I'm sick of taking Niagara Street. It adds fifteen minutes to the drive every time I want to take you anywhere. And anyway, Mikey, it's just time you got over it. Not Sally. I mean, I don't know if a person ever gets over something like that. But it's time you got over your fear of that place. Because now you've been there. You were right at that edge, and you never even knew it. We just passed right on by."

# CHAPTER 34

Alice and Mikey had purchased seats next to each other on the flight to Atlanta, where Jimmy, Audwin, Lynn, and Issa would meet up with them at the airport, and the six of them would rent a car and drive together to Lake Oconee.

Alice had promised to be at Mikey's home at six o'clock in the morning to pick him up and drive him to Buffalo Niagara Airport. It was now a quarter after, and Mikey was nervous about missing the flight.

Friday was weaving between Mikey's legs and his suitcase, and Mikey knelt to touch Friday's warm face. Mikey's father had offered to stop over several times throughout the week to feed Friday and clean out his litter box. In recent months, Mikey's father had started coming to Mikey's home on Sundays instead of Mikey going to his, since it was no longer safe for Mikey to drive, and his father now had plenty of time on his hands; he was working twenty hours a week at the AutoZone. John had also discovered that if he took a Claritin an hour before coming to Mikey's home, his allergies weren't so bad at all.

Mikey reached for his cell phone and dialed Alice.

She answered after a single ring.

"Jiminy-Christmas, you Antsy-Pants!" she said. "I'll be there in five minutes. I stopped to get McDonald's breakfast. You're *wel*come."

The two of them got breakfast from McDonald's together at least once a week. Alice always ordered three hash browns, a Coke, and a steak bagel for herself. The first time she had gotten this, Mikey watched as she ate the steak bagel. *That actually steak?* he had said. *Or just a burger on a bagel?* Alice had scowled at him. *It's steak, or they wouldn't say so.*

"I got your usual biscuit and coffee, light and sweet like you like. You're welcome," Alice said again. "Anyhow, are you gonna need my help with your luggage?"

"No, I only have one suitcase. I'm just worried about missing the flight," Mikey said. "I've heard early morning security line's a beast, especially on the weekend."

"We can use your special blind-person Go-to-the-Front-of-the-Line-Free card if we need to."

"You know I hate doing that."

Alice said, "Chill."

She hung up the phone.

In the past month, Alice had helped order and install voice software for Mikey's home, extra railings, separate drawers for sharp kitchen items versus dull ones. She created an organization system for the refrigerator and his dresser, socks knotted together as pairs and arranged by color. She set up an alarm system that would contact her directly, immediately, on her cell phone if Mikey's carbon monoxide detector went off. Mikey needed her every bit as much now as he had when he was eight years old. Oh well.

•

And now she was out front his house, tooting her horn impatiently. Mikey leaned over to give Friday a final nuzzle on the top of his head, and Friday leaned up into Mikey's hand with his little skull and damp nose.

Mikey opened his front door, single suitcase in hand.

The smell of the warm spring air was luscious. Magnificent. Soil and sprouts. Mikey could pick out the different aromas of individual blooms: dogwoods, hyacinths, bluebells, lilacs, lunarias. He could picture his forsythia in full bloom, exuberant and banana-yellow. Gustav Holst's Jupiter suite.

Mikey felt buoyant. Dizzy with euphoria. He was going to see his friends! He sniffed the air in, long and hard, greedily.

"We are *late*! Hurry *up*! What the hell are you doing?" Alice hollered at Mikey from her Jeep, tooting her horn to animate him.

Mikey stepped off his porch and started to make his way up the short paved path to the sidewalk, the little wheels of his suitcase scraping noisily behind him.

"I was just waiting," Mikey called back to Alice.

"What for?" Alice said. "Come on, ya slowpoke!" She tapped her Jeep's horn again, a cheery little rhythm. God, she was annoying!

"Waiting for you to tell me what to do," he called back.

Mikey felt a glorious warmth spread over his cheeks. This was how his doctor had said it would happen: visual perception of light would be one of the last things to go. But Mikey didn't have to see the light to know the sun was on his face.

That word *love* . . . it was scary and outlandish to him. But what was life if not a long series of scary and outlandish things you did and said and asked of your heart, so you could carry the wild and unreasonable hope that someday someone would hold your face and say, *You are perfect. You can rest now. You were always perfect to me.* Not because you were even remotely close to perfect, or brave, or strong, or even very good, but because you had been very dear friends for a very long time.

# ACKNOWLEDGMENTS

Thank you, Michelle Tessler, Jessica Gotz, Jack Shoemaker, Megan Fishmann, Nicole Caputo, Wah-Ming Chang, Jenn Kovitz, Sarah Baline, Jenny Alton, Dustin Kurtz, Olenka Burgess, Kelli Trapnell, Miyako Singer, Julie Buntin. And my love and immense gratitude, as always, to my friends and family, who make life a joy.

# READING GROUP GUIDE

1. Many readers have mentioned that reading about The Gunners brought back memories of their own childhood friendships. Was this true for you? How have your friendships changed with time? In what ways does this book complicate nostalgia?

2. Think about the sense of danger in The Gunners' lives—from Mikey's illness to Lynn's injury to Jimmy's secret. How might this connect to the group's interest in games like Blackout? How might this also connect to the previously mentioned theme of "finding the ground"?

3. There are many references to animals throughout the novel—Sally shares facts about animal behavior and migration, Alice tells stories about her dog, Mikey discovers key details about his father's work in the slaughterhouse, etc. What do these references tell you about the characters? What is Kauffman saying about friendship, love, and the nature of caring for others?

4. We learn about Mikey's vision loss in the first chapter, and about Sally's suicide in the second chapter. How did know-

ing the futures of these characters early on influence how you get to know them as the story progresses? How or why are certain pieces of information revealed or hidden throughout the book? How does this influence how you read the book?

5. Talk about how Mikey's gender and socioeconomic status influence his experience of macular degeneration.

6. As a teenager, Alice discovers a photo of herself taken while sleeping at The Gunner House alone on a dare, and she remembers Sally asking, "What if ghosts think *they're* the real ones, and *we're* the dead ones?" Why do you think Kauffman included this scene in the book? Alice later compares Sally to a ghost, saying, "I had this sense that she was going to pass through me, like a ghost, then go on to somewhere unknown." Think about this in light of the novel's epigraph from Michael Ondaatje's *Divisadero*.

7. Near the end of the novel, Lynn tells Mikey that love is "like finding the ground," which later causes Mikey to remember an experience of "the ground rising up to meet his feet." How could this connect to Sally and Mikey hunting for earthworms together? What about Mikey's dad "gettin' down on the ground" for his work, or Sally's death and the Skyway?

8. How does Jimmy's revelation about Mikey's family change Mikey's relationship with his father? What changes for Mikey when he visits his father at the meat processing plant?

9. Near the end of the book, Mikey wonders "if having a dear friend, and being a dear friend, might be almost as good as being a good man." Do you think that being a good person and being a good friend are the same thing? What is the relationship between these two distinctions?